P9-CCO-770

"GET IN THERE!
MOVE IT!" WORF YELLED.

The Klingon pushed two more people through the hatch and got a whiff of sheer sweat, terror and anxiety. He wasn't looking forward to going inside —until he heard the noise.

The noise was the sound of hundreds of tree trunks snapping at once, a mountain of debris clattering along at 400 kilometers per hour. It was a dull, horrifying roar, and Worf found himself tossing the colonists through the tiny hatch.

Worf could barely hear his own words as the roar filled his senses and the ground vibrated with impending doom. The Klingon never moved faster or more efficiently as he leapt through the hatch and spun the wheel shut behind him. He braced himself on the wheel, daring the terrible, oncoming force to rip the hatch from his grasp. . . .

Look for STAR TREK Fiction from Pocket Books

Star Trek: The Original Series

Star Trek: The Next Generation

STAR TREK®
THE NEXT GENERATION™

'23

WAR DRUMS

JOHN VORNHOLT

POCKET BOOKS

New York   London   Toronto   Sydney   Tokyo   Singapore

An *Original* Publication of POCKET BOOKS

POCKET BOOKS, a division of Simon & Schuster Inc.
1230 Avenue of the Americas, New York, NY 10020

This book is published by Pocket Books, a division of
Simon & Schuster Inc., under exclusive license from
Paramount Pictures.

ISBN: 0-671-79236-9

First Pocket Books printing October 1992

10 9 8 7 6 5 4 3 2 1

POCKET and colophon are registered trademarks of
Simon & Schuster Inc.

Printed in the U.S.A.

For my buddies
Barbara Beck and Steve Robertson

Where drums beat, laws are silent.

—Ancient Earth proverb

Foreword

I had decided to break with tradition and write an entirely upbeat foreword to this book, praising the cast of the Next Generation. But just as I was finishing the final chapters, the Los Angeles riots broke out all around me. My family and I live in Los Angeles proper, and we watched our city turn into a war zone. For days, we were choked by smoke-filled skies, and many stores we frequented were destroyed or looted, especially in the Hollywood and Korean areas. There is plenty of blame to go around for this tragedy. All of us who habitually turn our backs on bigotry, poverty, and despair in our cities are at fault.

I take no pleasure from the fact that this book is made more topical by these events. I was all too aware while writing it that people are a long way from perfect. It would be nice if our government invested in cities and all of our people for a change, but change has got to start with each of us. There is cause for hope if we can just remember that there is no enemy; there is no Other. There are only people like you and me who want to live in peace and dignity.

John Vornholt

Chapter One

A CACOPHONY OF bird calls abruptly stilled as three women and three men entered a heavily wooded glade carrying baskets, buckets, blankets, and assorted hand tools. All six wore simple brown outfits of coarse hand-sewn material and heavy boots, befitting settlers in a pristine world. Their voices were subdued, as if in respect for the cathedral-like setting of towering black trees, each about a meter in diameter. The few words that could be heard distinctly were comments about the fine weather, tales about the antics of children, and the sort of small talk any group of neighbors might make.

In the center of the glade two of the women began to brush away the ankle-deep accumulation of leaves, twigs, and branches that had lain undisturbed on the forest floor since the last heavy rain. Then they carefully laid a blanket on the clearing and began to unpack their picnic baskets. Meanwhile, the other four broke into two groups—two men and a man and a woman. They carried the buckets and tools to the trees and began to inspect the sturdy trunks. Soon the peace of the forest was broken by hammering as the two teams began to pound sap-catching spigots deep into the trunks of the trees. As the women on the blanket unpacked deviled eggs and sandwiches the other four settlers hung buckets on the spigots and speculated on the quality of the sap they would be harvesting.

Suddenly the idyllic peace was rent by an unearthly screech. A naked figure came leaping out of the trees, landing in the midst of the food. It was hairy, but not hairy enough to be an ape, and there were distinct ridges on the creature's forehead.

One of the women scrambled to escape, but the other reached into the bottom of her picnic basket and pulled out a hand phaser. The creature was evidently prepared for this maneuver and attacked her viciously, knocking her down with one sweeping blow, then pummeling her until she was unconscious. Then the Klingon—that's plainly what it was—began to scoop up every picnic basket, utensil, and morsel of food in sight.

The other humans reacted with alarm, but before they could come to the woman's aid other naked Klingons swarmed out of the woods, screeching and leaping on the humans like a pack of wild dogs. The attack degenerated into a bloody battle that made Captain Picard squirm uncomfortably in his cushioned chair, but he never diverted his eyes from the viewscreen. He had seen Klingons behave violently before, but never like this. Klingons were warriors who relished a fight, but they relished the ritual, weaponry, and rules of battle just as much. The scrawny, unkempt Klingons in this visual log were little more than animals—snarling, feral creatures who bit and slashed rather than stood and fought.

The object of their attack was plainly the picnic baskets and supplies, because the first Klingon made off with them as quickly as possible. His comrades were evidently there to make good his escape, because as soon as he was gone they tried to disperse. Three of the humans lay on the ground, not moving, and all were badly bloodied; but one strapping human was not content to let the Klingons escape. He staggered into the woods after them, pulling out a phaser weapon and shooting indiscriminately. One of the Klingons, too small to be anything but a youth, was caught squarely in the back by the glowing beam. He spun and slumped to the ground.

Now the scene shifted—the first obvious edit in the visual log—and the bedraggled Klingon prisoner was led, limping and bruised, into a walled compound. Someone had tied a rag around his waist so that he wasn't completely naked anymore. The welts and bruises on his face could not have been caused by any sort of fall or phaser wound. The boy looked as if he fully expected to die, but his battered face remained proud and defiant. With that expression, thought Picard, he looked like a Klingon, not a beast in the woods.

"End visual," said a deep voice.

The screen blinked off, and the lights came up slightly in the observation lounge of the starship *Enterprise*. The large bearded man who had fired the phaser and captured the Klingon youth stood before them. Every seat at the oval table was taken by one of Captain Picard's most trusted subordinates—First Officer Will Riker, Commander Data, Doctor Beverly Crusher, Commander Geordi La Forge, Counselor Deanna Troi, Ensign Ro Laren, Chief O'Brien—but every eye wandered in the direction of the burly security officer who sat at the far end of the table, Lieutenant Worf. The Klingon sat slumped in his seat, still glowering at the blank screen, his breath coming in guttural bursts.

One by one they turned away from Worf, all except for the man standing at the front of the room. Raul Oscaras glared hatefully at the big Klingon.

"Lieutenant Worf," he growled, "do you still deny that we are being attacked by Klingons?"

Worf sat up, his teeth clenched. "No, I do not. It is also evident that you have beaten your captive, in blatant disregard of Starfleet regulations."

"In the year that we have been on Selva," countered Oscaras, "we have been attacked by this roving gang of Klingons forty-two times. We have suffered eleven dead and sixty-nine wounded. Our children cannot leave the compound and play in the beautiful forest that covers our planet—for fear of being killed. Our scientists cannot study the wildlife of Selva, and our healers cannot look for herbs. When we came to Selva we didn't have a single phaser weapon. Now the replicator is working overtime to make them, and only armed parties dare to venture forth. And you think we should coddle these savages?"

Before Worf could respond the captain held up a hand to defuse the situation. "It won't do any good to quarrel among ourselves," he declared. "Mister Oscaras—"

"President Oscaras," the man corrected him.

"President Oscaras," Picard continued, "we sympathize with your plight. New Reykjavik is a Federation colony, and Starfleet sent us here to resolve this problem. Whatever you may think of Klingons at the moment, I can assure you *those* are not typical Klingons. I have spent considerable time among Klingons, and I've never seen them act like that. They're warriors, yes, but they have strict codes of behavior and a great deal of pride. They do not behave like wild animals."

His jaw clenched, Oscaras gazed out the observation window at the stunning expanse of stars. "I wish you could hear their drums," he murmured. "They play them for hours on end, all night, while our children cry and no one sleeps. We've tried to hunt them down, but they're part of the forest. They sleep in the trees or burrow in the ground. Despite what you say, Captain, they *are* animals, and you must help us hunt them down."

"I don't understand this," said Riker, leaning forward impatiently. "The Federation only sponsors colonies on uninhabited planets. Were the Klingons there when you arrived, or did they come later?"

The big man scowled. "We scouted Selva for three years, along with other planets. There was no evidence of sentient beings, past or present. You can check the studies. But now that we realize how the Klingons blend into the forest—and how they live like animals —we know they were hiding from us.

"For the first few months," he continued, "there were no outward signs, just a few things missing every now and then. There are nonsentient animals on the planet, and we assumed chucks or sloths took the food. Then they became bolder, and the attacks started. Always hit-and-run. They never tried to make contact or anything. They just started attacking and stealing what they wanted."

Picard nodded grimly, "Then our first order of business is to find out where they came from." He turned to Worf. "Lieutenant, I suggest you contact the Klingon High Command and find out how there came to be Klingons on Selva."

Worf stirred, as if awakening from a private reverie. "Yes, sir," he said, standing. "With your permission, I will undertake that investigation immediately."

"Make it so," replied Picard.

Worf, with obvious relief, left the observation

lounge. No sooner had the door shut behind him then Raul Oscaras leaned across the conference table.

"Captain Picard," he said, "if I may speak frankly, I don't believe your Klingon can be trusted in this matter."

Tight-lipped, Jean-Luc Picard glared at his guest. "First of all, President Oscaras, he is not *my* Klingon. He's Starfleet's Klingon and a valuable member of this crew. I can assure you he's no happier about these developments than you are. Secondly, if we establish the fact that the Klingons arrived on Selva *before* the settlers, then *you* have violated the Prime Directive by establishing an open settlement on an inhabited planet."

"We didn't know!" protested Oscaras.

Data cocked his head and observed, "Ignorance is no excuse for the violation of law."

"God help me!" moaned Oscaras. "Out of all the ships in the fleet, why did they send *you?*" His angry gaze moved from Data to Ensign Ro, who self-consciously touched the bony ridge between her eyes. "Half the crew isn't human!"

"No," replied Ensign Ro, "but we make do."

Will Riker smiled slightly before his expression turned serious. "President Oscaras," he warned, "I wouldn't continue with this line of thought. Every day the Federation encompasses more species who aren't human, some who aren't even humanoid. Your settlement may be one hundred percent human, but your planet obviously isn't."

The burly man sighed and lowered his head. "I apologize," he muttered. "When you've been the victim of guerrilla warfare for months on end you get a little . . . irrational. You've got to help us find some sort of solution."

Captain Picard nodded and got up from the table.

"We will," he promised. "Right now it's night on your part of the planet, and you probably want to return to your people. Let us conduct our research, and a party will beam down in the morning."

Oscaras bowed, "Thank you, Captain."

"Chief O'Brien is our transporter operator. He'll make sure you get home all right."

"Right this way," said O'Brien, motioning to the door.

"One thing," asked Deanna Troi, "is the captured Klingon available to talk with?"

"Yes," replied Oscaras. "But he won't talk. We've tried both the universal translator and sign language."

"Perhaps we'll have better luck," the Betazoid remarked.

After O'Brien had led their angry visitor out of the lounge the captain turned to his assembled crew. "I would welcome suggestions," he said.

Data replied, "I would like to assist Lieutenant Worf, if I may."

"Absolutely," said Picard. "Check Starfleet records, too, in case there was a distress signal or other sign of missing Klingons in this sector."

Geordi volunteered, "I'm going to run a complete scan of that planet. Maybe there are other things they don't know about."

"Ensign Ro will assist you," said the captain. He shook his head troubledly. "Beverly, what were your impressions of that . . . incident?"

The red-haired doctor frowned, "One thing bothers me. To get that video log, they must've set up an observation post outside the compound. Then to show up in that exact place with a picnic lunch? Did you see how thin and undernourished those Klingons are? It was almost like they were inviting an attack."

"They knew we were coming," said Deanna Troi.

"They wanted to have proof. I sense that President Oscaras is an extremely clever man. He may have used these attacks to solidify his control over the colony."

"Yes," said Picard. "And they took their time notifying Starfleet. Number One, you and I will go on the away team. Who else?"

Riker glanced around the room and answered, "Counselor Troi, Doctor Crusher, and Data. Normally I would say Worf, but—"

"But," agreed Picard, "until we find out how many others think like President Oscaras, we had better spare Lieutenant Worf. Ensign Ro, I would like you to accompany us."

The slim Bajoran nodded curtly. "Thank you, sir."

"Very well," said Picard, "the away team will assemble in ten hours in transporter room three."

"Get some sleep, everybody," said Doctor Crusher. "We may need our wits down there."

Worf grunted impatiently, not hiding his irritation with the archivist who had put him on pause, as signified by the jagged Klingon insignia on the viewscreen of his weapons console. He had to admit Klingons were not the best or most conscientious record keepers, and those who chose that unpopular profession often became arrogant beyond belief. This gangly librarian was so surly he could put the meanest Klingon assassin to shame.

The screen blipped on, and the archivist slid back into his seat and said snidely, "The information you want is classified. We cannot release this information to the Federation. You must apply through security channels or receive authorization from the council."

"I only want information on a few refugees," Worf muttered. "It was ten years ago, when there was a series of Romulan attacks on the Kapor'At colonies."

"All of those colonies were deserted, and the Kapor'At abandoned," the archivist interjected.

"Yes, I know," groaned Worf, trying to suppress his anger. "That information is in the Federation histories. But what happened to the refugees from those attacks? Could they have gone to the Plyrana system? It's directly between Kapor'At and the home planets."

With boredom the clerk intoned, "There was a negotiated settlement with the Romulans, and one of the agreements was that the records be classified."

Worf growled, "But everyone knows about it! It's in the Federation histories. There must have been some accounting of the refugees and the missing."

"There is," agreed the clerk, "but it's classified."

As Worf was about to detonate with anger Data stepped to his side and cocked his head at the screen. "Good day," said Data.

"Who are you?" asked the Klingon archivist.

"Lieutenant Commander Data," answered the android. "Are you aware that article 749.3 of the Klingon/Federation Alliance states that the Klingon Empire and the Federation will freely exchange *any and all* information pertaining to the rescue and safety of stranded refugees? We are attempting to rescue Klingons made homeless by armed hostility with the Romulans, and this supersedes any security designation."

"Are you sure about that?" the Klingon asked doubtfully.

"You claim to be an archivist," said Data, "look it up."

"The information you want is ten years old," muttered the Klingon. "How can you be trying to rescue them now?"

"How can you be trying to prevent them from being rescued?" asked Data.

The clerk scowled. "Open your data channel—I am transmitting the records now. I would appreciate your keeping it confidential." The screen went blank.

Worf hurriedly punched in the command to receive a subspace transmission, noted verification, then settled back on his heels. He glanced at Data and nodded. "Thank you. You knew exactly what to say to him."

"I understand the way bureaucrats think," said the android. "Like myself, they are most comfortable with set rules and regulations."

"Unlike you," replied Worf, "they don't want to think for themselves."

"Thank you," said Data, "I will take that as a compliment. What do you expect to find?"

"I've reviewed the visual log twice, stopping it at several points, and I estimate the oldest of those Klingons to be about fifteen in terran years. I saw no adults. The way they behave, as the captain tried to explain, is atypical."

"Unless they were raised without the benefit of Klingon heritage," added Data, "to channel their aggressive tendencies."

"Exactly," agreed Worf. "When there's a war it's customary for Klingons to send the youngest children away while everyone else remains to fight. To the death, if need be. Therefore, I began by looking for hostilities involving Klingon colonies in a time period of about ten years ago. The Kapor'At solar system was settled by Klingons, even though the Romulans claim it, as they do everything. Conflict was inevitable, and the Romulans initiated a series of raids that eventually led to the Klingons abandoning the solar system. Federation records mention the conflict and the settlement, but there are no details about escape vessels and refugees. Kapor'At lies only forty-two light-years from here, and it is possible that an escape vessel might have reached Selva."

Data nodded and glanced at Worf's console. "The transmission is complete," he observed. "Would you like me to review the records? I could do it in five percent of the time it would take you."

"Very well," agreed Worf. "I shall try to sleep before the away team goes tomorrow."

Data turned to a console behind Worf and punched up the freshly received information. "You are not going on the away team," he remarked.

"I'm not?" asked Worf with surprise.

"The captain wanted to determine the depth of anti–Klingon sentiment before subjecting you to it," said Data, scrolling through dense screens of information nearly as fast as the computer could display them.

"Perhaps I should thank him," muttered Worf. He glanced around the bridge but saw only replacement crew members, all of whom were concentrating on maintaining the orbit around Selva. "Once humans have made up their minds to hate Klingons, there isn't much that can be done."

"The reverse is true as well," answered the android. "Despite seventy years of peace, conditioned antipathy is a strong emotion. Here, I believe I have isolated the information you seek."

Data stepped back and allowed Worf to peer at his screen. "At the height of the attacks," the Klingon read aloud, "the Der'Nath colony put forty-eight young children on a freighter bound for Kling. But they never reached it. No wreckage was ever recovered, and the freighter was presumed destroyed by the Romulans."

"I believe your theory is correct," said Data. "If the freighter was only crippled by the Romulans, it might have reached this solar system."

"It was *chunDab* class," added Worf, "which means it could have entered the atmosphere of Selva. The children ranged in age from infants to six, which matches the ages of the Klingons in that visual. The pilot would have looked for the first available land, which means it is logical they landed near the coastline."

"If they were proven to be the survivors of the freighter," asked Data, "what would be official Klingon policy in this matter?"

Worf frowned. "That's difficult to say. The way this entire incident has been hushed up and the records classified, I would guess that the council must be ashamed of the way they capitulated to the Romulans. Perhaps the Romulans bought them off or made some sort of secret deal for Kapor'At. As you know, Romulans and certain Klingon factions have been known to bargain in secret, and this occurred during a very unstable time for the empire."

Data concluded, "You are saying they may not wish to have the survivors found and everyone reminded of what happened at Kapor'At."

Worf nodded thoughtfully. "I think we should wake the captain."

Captain Picard sat on the side of his bed with a beige robe wrapped around his wiry body. He listened intently as information, theories, and conclusions about the mysterious Klingon youths were related to him by Worf and Data. He strode to the computer console in his quarters and read the formerly classified records himself.

"We can operate under the assumption that these are the missing children," he agreed, "but unless we find the wreckage of that freighter or we identify the children through their medical records, it's just a theory."

12

"Captain," said Worf, "it's imperative that we talk to their captive. He is the key."

"Oscaras doesn't know it yet," said Picard, "but we're going to try to have the boy released in our custody. For his own safety, if nothing else."

"I know I'm not a member of tomorrow's away team," remarked Worf, "but sooner or later someone will have to go down to that planet and locate those youths. I am the logical choice."

"I agree," said Picard, "but we have to see how much cooperation we can get from the colonists. Data, according to regulations, what rights do the Klingons have?"

The android cocked his head and replied, "Klingons are allies of the Federation, so they have the same rights as Federation citizens. Since their residency on Selva predates that of the colonists, they cannot be removed from the planet without their consent, according to regulation 3144.5, subparagraph eight. Under normal circumstances, the colonists would need their permission to be there."

Picard sighed and rubbed his eyes. "I think we'll forgo legal considerations until we get the parties to stop trying to kill each other. Reasoning with Oscaras and the settlers will be hard enough, but how do we talk to teenagers who have grown up alone in the woods?"

"Captain," said Data, "the three of us speak Klingon, so we can communicate with them if they retain a memory of their native language. If we equip them with comm badges containing the universal translator, they will be able to understand any member of the crew or colony."

"We can't delay this mission," insisted Worf. "There were males and females on that ship, and they are reaching an age when they'll have children of their own."

"Codifying their behavior and society," Data added. "In our favor, the Prime Directive does not apply to our allies, and all Klingons are our allies, whether they know it or not."

Picard jutted his chin and vowed, "We have to find them and help them all we can. Lieutenant Worf, would you please inform the Klingon High Council about our suspicions. We have to give them the opportunity to make a recommendation."

"Yes, sir," nodded Worf.

"And Data," the captain added, "when we meet their captive, memorize his coordinates—so we can borrow him if need be."

At the master systems display in main engineering Ensign Ro peered at various colorful graphs and graduated computer representations. She viewed awesome mountains, oceans, canyons, and other geological formations from impossible points, such as underneath a volcano. The computer compiled the enormous amounts of data, but there would be time to study it all later, she decided. For now, Ro just wanted to get impressions, to see if anything stood out from the ongoing scan of the planet. Commander Geordi La Forge prowled the other side of the master display, and they found themselves drawn simultaneously to a computer simulation of earthquake fault lines and tectonic plates.

"It's a very young planet," observed Ro thoughtfully. "No wonder it doesn't have any sentient life of its own. It's still evolving."

"Yeah"—Geordi frowned—"those tectonic plates aren't exactly fitting together like a jigsaw puzzle. What do you think of the place they picked to settle?"

"Plenty of water," the Bajoran answered. "They're on the stablest continent. And they're close enough to the ocean—about twenty kilometers—to benefit

14

from warm currents, but far enough away to avoid the brunt of storms. After you automatically eliminate the forty percent of the planet that's covered by glaciers, there isn't much stable land left. I wouldn't want to build a skyscraper down there, but I'd say they did all right. My people are living in places that are far worse."

"I would be willing to bet that ocean is uninhabitable," said Geordi. "The salt and mineral compounds are substantial—it's like the Dead Sea on Earth. All those springs and underwater volcanos must keep it pretty warm, though."

"Like a big spa," answered Ro. For a second there was a smile on her normally dour face. "I would like to see it."

"I would, too," said Geordi. "The whole planet is the reverse of Earth: the water is hot and uninhabitable, and most of the land is cold and has glaciers. I'd say they definitely picked the best spot."

"Except that there were Klingons already living there."

Geordi sighed. "I'm not sure what the captain can do to solve that problem. But I'll keep monitoring the planet while you're down there to see if I can pick up any patterns. At least I can tell you what the weather will be like."

"This could be a difficult mission," Ro observed, more to herself than to Geordi. "I'd better say good night."

The chief engineer smiled, and she could imagine the warmth in his hidden eyes. "Take care of yourself down there, Ensign," he added.

The Bajoran managed a smile and said, "Did you notice that I was the token bumpy-head on the away team?"

"Well"—Geordi shrugged—"they have to understand that no race is alone in this universe. I think the captain made a good choice in taking you for other reasons. You're likely to have compassion for both sides, or for anyone who is trying to make a go of it in a new world."

"Sometimes I wish the Bajora were like those Klingons," Ro said thoughtfully. "If we had been more aggressive and fought like animals, maybe we wouldn't have been kicked from planet to planet. But it's too late—we're civilized."

"It happens to the best of us," said Geordi. "Just be careful."

"I will, Commander. Good night."

Ensign Ro took the long way back to her cabin on deck eight, meaning she meandered down countless corridors, through empty labs and recreation halls, shunning the closest turbolifts for more distant conveyances. Finally she found herself on deck ten, as she knew she would, and she made her way to the ship's ultimate recreation lounge, Ten-Forward. The tasteful and subdued cafe was home base for her best friend on the *Enterprise,* the mysterious bartender Guinan.

At this late hour Ten-Fore was more subdued than normal, and only the endless array of stars glittering through the observation windows gave it any life. From the port side of the ship the rust-colored curve of the planet Selva was visible below, most of it bathed in the darkness of night. Ro stood at the window for several moments, gazing at the planet, before she was aware of an outlandishly dressed presence standing beside her.

"Scuttlebutt has it you're going down there in a few hours," said Guinan.

"Yes," answered Ro. "I should be sleeping, but I can't."

"Why not?" asked Guinan. "Simple assignment— just conquer bigotry and fear."

"Right," sighed the Bajoran, crossing her arms in front of her.

"Especially fear of the Other."

"The Other?"

"The different," said Guinan, "the unusual. The one who won't play by the same rules you do. You've been the Other all your life, and now you've got to teach people not to fear it."

"I doubt I'll have that much time. I don't think the captain intends to leave me down there," Ro said.

Guinan agreed. "I doubt if the captain knows *what* he intends to do, but I have a feeling this is no normal assignment for you. I have a feeling that you are desperately needed down there."

"I'm just along for tokenism," Ro countered. "A bumpy-head to show the settlers we can live in peace. Counselor Troi, Doctor Crusher, Captain Picard— they're the ones who will make the difference."

"*Everyone* makes a difference," Guinan responded. "Lead by example. Shall I bring you some tea that will help you sleep?"

"No," said the Bajoran. "There's no reason I should be nervous. I'm sure I'll be taken off this mission in no time. I'll come back tomorrow and tell you what it's like down there."

"Perhaps." Guinan smiled enigmatically. "Whenever you come back, please stop by and tell me about it. I'm very interested."

"Good night," said Ro.

"Peaceful dreams," replied the bartender.

Chapter Two

IN SPARKLING COLUMNS of dancing molecules, the away team of three women, two men, and an android materialized in the central square of the village of New Reykjavik on the planet of Selva. One by one Captain Picard, Commander Riker, Lieutenant Commander Data, Ensign Ro, Doctor Crusher, and Counselor Troi stepped forward and surveyed the tiny village, home to barely over two hundred souls.

After having read about the settlers and their ideals of self-sufficiency and simplicity, Deanna Troi expected to see a quaint hamlet with, perhaps, sod houses and mud-packed roofs. Instead she saw a fortress. The houses and public buildings were ugly and built of corrugated galvanized metal. The walls of the compound towered at least fifteen meters into the air and were also constructed of fortified metal sheeting; they were topped with barbed wire and jagged metal stakes.

Turrets that were little more than stilt houses guarded each corner of the fort and the lone vaultlike gate. The square had three black trees in it, but they looked forsaken and lonely compared to the riotous profusion of plant life that towered over the gleaming walls and undulated into the distance. The trees in the square and those close to the walls had been drastically pruned so that no one could hide in them and leap into the compound from their branches.

A child of about six or seven stood looking curiously at them. "Have you come to kill the drummers?" she asked.

Will Riker knelt down to meet the child eye-to-eye. "We haven't come to kill anyone," he answered. "We've come to make peace. Isn't that better?"

"No." She shook her head firmly. "My daddy says there won't be any peace until they're dead."

Before this disturbing conversation could continue they were surrounded by adult colonists and children of various ages. All of them sported the same nondescript but practical brown clothing, and they all wore a wary expression that said "We don't trust strangers." They looked uncomfortably like prisoners to Deanna Troi, especially with the barbed wire and walls surrounding them.

The counselor noticed several of the colonists staring at Ensign Ro, as if they trusted her least of all. But the slim Bajoran seemed oblivious to their scrutiny as she studied the readings on her tricorder.

President Oscaras came striding out of the crowd. "Welcome!" he bellowed. "Had we known when you were coming, we would have arranged a formal welcoming party."

"We don't wish to interrupt your daily routine," Picard said, forcing a smile.

Oscaras shook his head with frustration and declared, "That's our problem. We have no daily routine, because we can't go out of the compound! We had intended to subsist solely off the wealth of this planet—you could live off the sap contained in those trees—but the savages have made it impossible. The replicator we have was only supposed to tide us over until we got crops planted and harvested, but now we depend upon it for everything—from the clothes on our backs to the food we eat. As I told you on your ship, we never intended to manufacture phasers, but that is what the replicator is doing now."

"Do you have a transporter?" asked Data.

"No," answered Oscaras. "That is one concession I refuse to make. At least we will get exercise by carrying our goods and walking."

Beverly Crusher knelt down to examine the little girl who had spoken to Riker. Smiling warmly, she maneuvered her medical tricorder from the girl's dirty face to her skinny legs. "I'm a doctor," she assured her. "I just want to make sure you are feeling all right. How do you like living here?"

"I want to go home," the girl answered honestly. "Back to Iceland."

A red-haired woman who looked like a grown-up version of the child cupped her shoulders and spoke to her disapprovingly, "This is home for you, Senna. You know that. You shouldn't complain."

"But she *asked* me," the girl protested.

"Actually," said a young man in the crowd, "there are a lot of us who would like to go home."

His announcement was met with a mixture of boos and muttered approvals.

"Enough of that talk!" snarled Oscaras. Under his stern gaze the murmurs died down. "The crew of the *Enterprise* hasn't come here to listen to our complaints or take us back to Earth. They've come here to make this planet habitable by ridding us of those vermin who plague us!"

That statement was followed by cheers. Picard glanced uncomfortably at his crew, then cleared his throat. He kept harrumphing until the cheers faded.

"I hate to inform you," he began, "but the Klingons have as much right to be on this planet as you do. There's good indication that they're refugees from a war and survivors of a crash. If so, they've been here nine years longer than you have. What we will endeavor to do is to reach them and persuade them to live in peace with you."

There was hooting and mocking laughter from some, while others stood dumbfounded, staring at the strangers as if they had two heads. Deanna sensed a bewildering array of emotions, from despair and acceptance to rage and disbelief. Clearly, this was not the happiest colony in the Federation, and she tried to have compassion for the stress they had been under from the constant threat of attack. She tried to imagine their joy in first arriving on this pristine planet, only to be replaced by fear and bigotry after the attacks started.

"You could sooner talk to the trees," scoffed one man.

A woman turned her anger on Oscaras. "You told us they would help. They're siding with *them*—the savages!"

The president scowled. "I said I would call the Federation for help, nothing more. They don't know what we're up against. They even have a Klingon on their vessel, although they had the decency not to bring him. I say let them go into the forest and search for the Klingons! They will soon learn there is no way to deal with these beasts."

This solution was clearly not popular with anyone, and loud arguments commenced. Some of the colonists began to wander away from the impromptu town meeting, their faces reflecting disgust and resignation. Deanna felt driven to do or say something that would lighten the somber mood of their arrival on Selva.

The Betazoid pointed to the stockade that surrounded them. "We want to help you tear down those walls," she declared. "Isn't that what you want? To be able to wander freely on this world you've chosen for yourselves? More deaths and hatred won't achieve it."

"Can't you capture them?" asked the red-haired mother of the six-year-old. "Take them back to their own people. That would be all right with us."

Several colonists seized upon this idea and voiced their approval. Picard held up his hands to quiet them.

"We are contacting the Klingon High Council to inform them of this situation," he explained. "But there's very little we can tell them—we have to find the Klingons and learn more about them first. I must warn you that capturing the Klingons and expelling them from this planet against their will is a last resort."

"Give us better weapons and scanners!" shouted a burly man. "We'll finish them off without you."

Judging by the cries of approval, this was the most popular suggestion yet, thought Deanna. Oscaras shook his head at his visitors as if these sentiments, grotesque as they were, couldn't be helped.

"There is Marta," he said, pointing to a pretty blond woman. "She lost her husband in the first attack. And Joseph—his wife was on a science team that was studying the chucks, which is our name for the predominant mammal on the planet. She was killed for the food in her pack. Ask Lucius to show you the souvenir he got from his encounter with the drummers—a scar that runs from his neck to his navel. And Edward, what happened to your son?"

An old man licked his dry lips before replying, "They mauled him to death—like animals."

Captain Picard swallowed before answering. "We're not here to defend these attacks. You've lived with this terror for many months, and we've only just found out about it. But Klingons are allies of the Federation, and the same laws protect them."

"But they have no laws!" protested Marta.

"Then they haven't been brought up as Klingons," answered Picard. "What do you really know about them? Nothing. Except that they attack you, seeking food. Have you ever left them food or tried to make peace?"

The old man, Edward, shook his head. "You are right, Oscaras. Let them go into the forest. After they've lost a few sons and daughters they may listen to reason."

"Perhaps we should speak to the captive," suggested Data.

A dark-skinned woman approached Data and sniffed him suspiciously. "What are you?" she asked.

"An android," he replied. "I was created by Doctor Singh—"

"Not now, Data," interrupted the captain. "We'll have plenty of time to get to know each other. I believe, President Oscaras, that we should see the captive as soon as possible."

"Come," said the bearded man. "I'll give you a quick tour of the compound on our way."

Oscaras led his visitors past the largest of the corrugated buildings, which seemed to Deanna like a fortress. "That building houses our replicator, subspace radio, science lab, and sickbay," he explained. "I don't believe there's anything in there that you aren't familiar with. Families have their own dwellings, and the younger unattached men and women live in dormitories on the other side of the square. That other large building is our communal dining hall, and it also serves as a courthouse and recreation room.

"In our original plan," he continued, "families were supposed to have houses and plots of land interspersed throughout the forest. Obviously, we had to abandon that idea. We are a little pressed for space, so families have been asked not to have any more children until we resolve this problem."

"Do you know how many Klingons live out there?" asked Riker, making a sweeping motion that took in the forest.

"They attack in small groups," said Oscaras, "and we've never seen more than a handful at a time."

"If the Klingons are the group we think they are," said Picard, "there would be slightly under fifty of them."

Oscaras gave a hollow laugh. "If there were fifty of them," he scoffed, "they would have killed us all by now."

He stopped outside a windowless corrugated shed that looked more beaten and weathered than any other building in the compound. The walls near the thick metal door bulged as if something inside had been trying to batter its way out.

"You keep him in here?" asked Beverly Crusher, clearly shocked.

"It's better than he deserves," answered Oscaras, scowling, "and certainly better than he's used to." The president of the colony lowered his voice to add, "If it had been left to the majority, the Klingon would have been executed for murder by now."

Picard frowned. "Capital punishment has been abandoned for centuries on Earth."

"If there were creatures like this on Earth," said Oscaras, "they would have to reinstate it. I warn you that the prisoner has been placed in restraints, but that's for his own safety. He threw himself against the walls with such force that we feared he might injure himself."

As Oscaras reached for the heavy bolt that locked the door Deanna saw Captain Picard and Data exchange glances, and Data nodded slightly. The android must have been given a secret order, she knew immediately. She had told herself to remain calm and nonjudgmental about anything she might see on this planet, but the raw emotions of hatred and terror emanating from the crude shed made her sick to her stomach. Involuntarily, she stepped back as Oscaras yanked the bolt and opened the door.

It was dark and foul-smelling inside the shack, like a primeval cave. Captain Picard wrinkled his regal nose but stepped forthrightly into the darkness. Oscaras motioned the others to stay back.

"There won't be room for all of you inside," he said.

"Let Doctor Crusher and Counselor Troi enter," ordered Riker. "Data, Ro, and I will remain here."

Doctor Crusher was already pushing her way inside, and Deanna reluctantly followed. The counselor's reluctance was not based on fear or disgust, but rather on the certainty that her opinion of human beings, who constituted half her heritage, was about to be downgraded.

"Let's have some light!" ordered Picard.

"Sorry," said Oscaras. He reached inside the doorway and grabbed a battery-operated lantern. He turned it on, then returned it to its hanger on the wall.

Deanna gasped as the light revealed the inhabitant of the decrepit shed. Against one rusted wall, restrained by straps and a crude straightjacket, sat a pathetic young Klingon surrounded by bits of rotting food and his own feces. He blinked and turned away from the unaccustomed light. Then he drew his thin, dirty knees up to his chest as if he was about to be beaten.

Picard swallowed hard, mustered a smile, and said, *"chay'. tlhlngan Hol Dajatlh'a'?"*

The Klingon blinked at him in amazement and

25

shook the strands of dark, matted hair from his face. Finally he lowered his legs slightly and seemed about to speak—but instead bared a set of jagged teeth and hissed.

Beverly Crusher looked twice as mad as the bound Klingon. "Release him immediately!" she ordered Oscaras. "This is no way to keep an animal, let alone a humanoid."

Oscaras poked his head in the door and mustered all the tact at his disposal as he replied, "I would advise against that, Doctor. He has bitten several of us, and he would instantly attempt to escape."

"Wouldn't you?" she snapped back. "Release him immediately so that I can examine him."

"You can make a preliminary examination while he's restrained," Oscaras countered. "Or may I suggest we stun him with a phaser first?"

Deanna watched the Klingon, who seemed to be quite interested in this exchange. Probably it was the first time he had seen anyone argue with his chief captor. His eyes, though reddened and wild, looked intelligent, and she judged his age to be about thirteen by Earth standards. Despite the filthy conditions of his imprisonment, he maintained a sort of primitive dignity—like photos she had seen of magnificent wild creatures that used to be housed in places like this on Earth, called zoos. She was certainly glad the captain had not brought Worf along. Seeing this, he would have throttled several of the colonists by now.

"I have a better idea," said Picard. "Let us beam him aboard the *Enterprise* where Doctor Crusher can examine him at her leisure in our sickbay. Also, we'll see if Lieutenant Worf can communicate with him."

"I'm afraid that's impossible," answered Oscaras. "He is due to be tried now that you are here. Also, we are hoping that some of his confederates will try to get him out. He howls when they begin drumming, so they know he's here."

"Do you refuse to release him in our custody?" asked Picard, as if clarifying the point rather than pressing it.

"I'm afraid I must," answered Oscaras, "for the moment. I'll take it up with the colonists, but the decision is mine."

Beverly Crusher looked angry enough to bite off Oscaras's head, but Picard flashed her a look that warned her to be calm. The captain was planning something, thought Deanna, and that kept her from adding her opinion to the matter.

The captain turned to the Klingon prisoner and said, *"pich vlghajbe'."*

Again, the boy blinked at the captain in surprise, as if one of these groomed and flat-headed savages couldn't possibly know his language. This reinforced in Deanna's mind the theory that the Klingons of Selva had raised themselves since they were small children, not knowing anyone else in the universe existed until the settlers arrived. Then their world and everything they knew had been turned completely on its head, and they had reacted violently.

"Lu'," the boy grunted.

Picard smiled slightly and left the shed. Beverly gave the boy an encouraging smile and followed the captain out, as did Deanna.

Oscaras did not look pleased. "What were you saying to him?" he asked accusingly.

"I will arrange Klingon language lessons for you," answered the captain testily. "In the meantime, I don't want any harm to befall that prisoner."

"You can rest assured of that," said Oscaras. "So what is our course of action?"

"We're going to return to the ship to discuss that,"

answered Picard. He tapped his communicator badge, which responded with a chirp. "Six to beam up."

"Aye, sir," answered the voice of Chief O'Brien.

Oscaras stepped back as his six interstellar visitors dematerialized on the spot.

Picard and party stepped quickly off the transporter pads, and the captain motioned to Data. "Take the controls," he ordered. "Get him up here immediately."

"Thank you." Beverly said with a sigh of relief. "I'll arrange a secured bed for him in sickbay."

O'Brien stepped away from the transporter console as Data took his place and entered the coordinates. "I am omitting his restraints," the android reported.

"Number One, phaser on light stun," ordered the captain.

The bearded first officer drew his phaser and checked its setting. They waited tensely while a scrawny, crouched figure materialized on the transporter platform. The Klingon's eyes stared wildly at them for a moment, then he realized that his restraints were gone. He leapt to his feet and bounded off the transporter platform with a swiftness that took everyone by surprise. He was almost out the doorway by the time Riker took aim and stunned him with a glowing ray of light. The young Klingon staggered for a moment, and Data rushed to catch him. The android lifted the unconscious boy in his arms as if he were an inconsequential piece of foam insulation.

"To sickbay," said Beverly, leading the way.

"Bridge to Picard," came the familiar voice of Geordi La Forge.

The captain tapped his communicator. "Picard here."

"President Oscaras wants to talk to you. He sounds awfully angry."

"Does he?" Picard smiled. "I'll take it in my ready room. Tell him to wait until I get there."

The captain strode out of the transporter room followed by Riker and Deanna Troi. That left only Chief O'Brien and Ensign Ro.

"What happened down there?" asked the ruddy-faced transporter operator.

Ensign Ro didn't hide the concern in her voice as she replied, "We may have chosen sides."

Captain Picard settled into the chair behind his desk and flicked on his viewscreen. The flustered face of Raul Oscaras glared at him.

"How dare you abduct our prisoner?"

"I'm sure I could find any number of regulations that would permit me to do what I did," replied the captain. "In fact, I could probably find some that would allow me to place *you* under arrest. Federation rules are quite strict on the treatment of prisoners, and it doesn't matter how angry you are at them."

President Oscaras's expression softened somewhat, but he remained defiant. "Captain, may I ask you how *you* are keeping the Klingon? He is either in restraints or under sedation, I know."

Picard frowned, "He's under the doctor's care. The fact of the matter is that *someone* must befriend that young Klingon. You are obviously not the ones to do it. There are a great many life-forms in that forest, and we have no way of knowing which are Klingons and which are sloths, chucks, or whatever else may be down there. You, in nine months of looking, haven't found their tribe. If you actually seek a resolution to this problem—and not just revenge—you had better start cooperating with us."

Looking humbled, Oscaras bowed his head. "You are right, Captain," he admitted. "We haven't gotten off to a very good start. I had hoped the visual record of the latest attack would be enough to show you what we are up against. Perhaps you got some idea from talking with our people today about how horrifying this has been for us. You live on a starship, and if you find something unpleasant, you simply pick up and go to another part of the galaxy. We can't do that. Our frustration is total."

"I realize that," said Picard, softening his own attitude. "You've been in a state of war, and war is dehumanizing. I can assure you that I have negotiated peace on a huge scale, between entire worlds, but that may have been easier than trying to solve this problem. We don't even know where to find the other combatants."

Oscaras held out his hands pleadingly. "Give us another chance, Captain," he asked. "Will you and your officers please come back for dinner tonight? You may keep the Klingon captive as long as you like. Nothing more will be said about it."

"Very well," said Picard. "We'll beam down in six hours. Out." The captain turned off his screen, then pressed another button. "Lieutenant Worf, will you please come in here?"

"Yes, sir," came the deep voice.

Already on the bridge, the Klingon entered the captain's ready room immediately. He stood waiting at attention.

"Please sit," said Picard. "Have you heard about what happened down on the planet?"

"Very little," answered Worf. "I understand that we brought the captured Klingon aboard and that he's in sickbay."

"He was caged like an animal," said Picard frankly.

The Klingon gritted his teeth and growled under his breath.

"I felt the same way," said Picard, "but now I'm

realizing that this handful of humans and Klingons has been at war with one another. I talked to people down there whose husbands, wives, and children were brutally murdered by the Klingons. The settlers have become desensitized and dehumanized. In all likelihood the Klingons have been brought up with no laws but those of their own survival. Have you talked to anyone on the High Council about this?"

"Yes"—Worf scowled—"I talked to Kang. As I feared, they don't wish to bring up the loss of the Kapor'At colonies. The records are sealed, the histories rewritten, and that's the way they want them to stay. I suspect there may be a way to secretly repatriate the survivors to the home worlds, but there will be no official help. No official acknowledgement."

"Then we're on our own." Picard nodded grimly. "Worf, you must befriend that boy down in sickbay and gain his trust. I believe he remembers some of the Klingon language, and the more that comes back to him, the better we'll be able to communicate. Doctor Crusher and Counselor Troi will give you all the help they can, but he'll never trust them as he will you. And you were right—you will have to go down to the planet and find all of them."

"Yes, Captain." Worf nodded. "I am ready."

"You're relieved of bridge duty and all other assignments for the duration of this mission. Let me know when you're ready to begin your search on the planet, and what you need. Dismissed."

"Yes, sir," said Worf, nodding. He stood, started for the door, then turned to say, "I have known what it is to be orphaned and cut off from my own people. To lose my laws and heritage. My adoptive parents returned them to me, and I will do the same for the survivors of Kapor'At."

"I have no doubt," said Picard. "Good luck."

* * *

Worf could hear the howls and screams emanating from sickbay when he was still several meters away from the door. He began to jog and reached the doorway just as Beverly Crusher tumbled backward into his arms. She nearly jabbed him with the hypo in her hand.

"Thank God you're here!" she gasped. "He broke out of his restraints."

Worf gently moved the doctor aside and strode into sickbay as another howl erupted. He saw a scrawny, dirty Klingon slashing his clawlike hands at two attendants who were trying to ward him off with trays. The crouching figure seemed determined to use screaming and sheer noise to keep his attackers at bay, and Worf marveled at his lung power.

His back was to Worf, and the elder Klingon was able to study the younger one for a second. He could almost sense the frightened youngster trying to figure out where he was and what he was going to do about it. He had decided for certain that he wasn't going to let any of them touch him.

Worf motioned the attendants back, then showed that he had a certain amount of lung power himself as he bellowed in his deepest voice, *"yitamchoH!"*

The adolescent Klingon whirled around and stared in amazement at something he had never seen before —an adult Klingon! His mouth gaped open between sunken cheeks, and he stumbled backward as Worf walked slowly toward him.

"Do you have a name?" Worf asked in Klingon.

The boy shook his head—not in answer but in disbelief, as if he couldn't conceive of another creature like himself, speaking a version of his tongue, in a place as strange as this. He lunged at one of the attendants and grabbed his tray. He held it in one hand and drummed on it with the other, his long fingernails beating a frenetic tattoo. The boy accompanied his drumming with howls and guttural groans, as if Worf was an evil spirit that could be driven away. The security officer stopped his advance, hoping that might stop the awful racket.

"Can you speak?" Worf asked with exasperation, "or only make noise?"

The boy stopped for a moment and muttered, "Am I dead?"

Worf laughed, and the unexpected sound of his laughter disarmed the young Klingon even more. It also caused him to increase his drumming and howling.

"Enough," Worf pleaded, still speaking Klingon. "We won't harm you, I promise."

"Or laugh at him either," Doctor Crusher suggested. "Just keep talking to him, as gently as possible."

The sight of the older Klingon and the red-haired female speaking to each other seemed to transfix the adolescent, and he stopped his frantic drumming. He waited, his frightened eyes shifting warily from one person to another.

"I am Worf," said the security officer, tapping his chest. "Do you have a name?"

"Turrok," answered the boy.

"Turrok," said Worf. "Welcome to the *Enterprise.*"

Chapter Three

THE STANDOFF CONTINUED—with Worf, Beverly, and two sickbay attendants on one side and a frightened, confused Klingon youth on the other. Turrok was armed only with his makeshift drum and a small metal tray, and the *Enterprise* personnel had hypos and phasers. But Worf was uncertain what to do next as the rawboned adolescent cowered before them.

"I can't keep talking," said Worf with frustration. "I don't think he understands half of what I'm saying. His language has been corrupted."

"Yours would be, too," answered Beverly, "if you had been tossed in the woods at the age of four. The more you talk to him and force him to speak, the more his language will come back to him. I don't want to sedate him, because that won't get us anywhere. However, I do need to clean him up and examine him."

"He seems healthy to me," Worf observed.

"These surroundings must seem very strange to him," said Beverly. She tapped her communicator badge. "Crusher to Picard."

"Picard here," answered the familiar clipped tones.

"Jean-Luc, our visitor is awake and very frightened. Worf has been able to communicate with him a little bit, and we know his name is Turrok."

"That's an excellent beginning," answered Picard. "Is there anything we can do to help?"

"Yes, I think there is," she replied. "Would you be able to clear the holodeck and set up a program running some sort of neutral forest setting?"

"Absolutely," answered the captain. "I'll send La Forge right now."

"When that's done," continued the doctor, "could you direct-beam myself, Lieutenant Worf, and Turrok there? It might also be a good idea to have Deanna Troi join us."

"Consider it done," answered Picard. "Maintain your positions."

"Oh, Jean-Luc," added Beverly, "could you also arrange to have some food and clean clothes there? He looks to be about two sizes down from Wesley."

"Anything to make our guest comfortable," said the captain. "We'll put a comm badge on his uniform so he will have access to the universal translator and understand all of us. Picard out."

"Are you hungry?" Worf asked the boy in Klingon.

Turrok blinked and stared at him for a moment.

"Food?" Worf elaborated.

Turrok nodded warily, his long, matted hair tumbling over his forehead.

"Keep talking," Beverly suggested. "Use as much Klingon vocabulary as you can. His childhood language and experiences are all in his mind, if we can just reawaken them."

"I have to gain his confidence first," said Worf.

Before the point could be debated further their bodies began to sparkle and disappear. Turrok dropped the tray and gripped his stomach in shock, then howled in fright. Before the cry was all the way out of his mouth he, Beverly, and Worf regenerated in the center of a cheery forest with the sun beaming through the gently waving branches of big oak trees and a stunning blue sky overhead.

Turrok spun around on his heels, hardly believing his good luck. He opened his mouth and cut loose with a trilling cry that sounded like a birdcall. He waited, but there was no answer.

"He's calling his comrades," said Worf.

Beverly replied, "But nobody's going to answer. He'll soon figure out he's not in his own forest."

From the trees, Geordi strolled into their midst carrying a large tray full of fruits and sandwiches. Behind him came Deanna Troi with a bundle of clothes under her arm. They both smiled warmly at the confused Klingon.

"Is this okay?" Geordi asked Worf.

The Klingon shrugged. "Set it down, and we'll see."

Geordi did as requested, making sure he didn't get too close to the wary youth. Deanna unfolded the gray tunic and pants she was carrying, then laid them on the ground.

"I think these will fit," she said.

"Eat," Worf told the boy in Klingon. He motioned to the food and the clothes. "It's all for you."

Cautiously Turrok knelt in front of the food and sniffed it. He finally took a peeled banana and stuffed the whole thing in his mouth, then began to do the same with a sandwich.

Geordi smiled. "Well, he eats like a Klingon."

Worf flashed his shipmate a quick glare, then returned his attention to the hungry boy. "His name is Turrok," he said. "His Klingon has been corrupted, and I'm not sure how much he understands of what I've been telling him."

Deanna smiled. "I think you're doing splendidly, Worf. I sense that his fear and distrust are diminishing. Coming here was a good idea."

"But how should I proceed?" asked the Klingon.

"Make friends," suggested the Betazoid. "That's all you can do."

"You have the holodeck as long as you need it," said Geordi. "This program is the Mount Gilead Park in central North America. If you stroll over that rise there, you'll find picnickers, a lake, and a reservoir. Nobody will bother you, but if you want to get rid of the people, just tell the computer. Above the dam there's a great place to catch crawdads."

"And take a bath?" suggested Beverly.

"Crawdads?" asked Worf uncertainly.

"Small freshwater crustaceans," said Geordi, holding his fingers a few centimeters apart.

"You're good at bonding with children," Deanna said encouragingly. "Later maybe you can introduce him to your son."

Worf heaved a deep sigh as he watched Turrok devouring the food. He wouldn't trust this wild creature with his boy for two seconds. "Perhaps you should leave us now," he muttered.

"Good luck," said Geordi, patting the Klingon on his massive back. "I'm going back to scanning his planet. There are some interesting things going on down there." Geordi strolled off into the trees.

"I can wait to examine him," said Beverly, "but call me as soon as he goes to sleep. Or if you need help."

"I will," said Worf.

Deanna seconded the sentiment, "Call me if you need anything at all."

Worf nodded again and watched the two women wander away into the holodeck woods. Then he turned and looked at the crouching boy, who was stuffing food in his mouth as if it would be taken away any moment. Turrok's wary eyes were never still as they scanned the forest for trouble.

He wiped food off his chin and stared at Worf. "No like them," he said, pointing after the departed humans. "Kill them."

Worf furrowed his huge brow, unsure if he had understood the broken Klingon correctly.

"Kill them," Turrok repeated. He stabbed his fist in the air as if holding a spear or a knife.

The elder Klingon shook his head. "They're my friends. My comrades."

Turrok made a motion with his hand over his ridged forehead as if to say they were different. Worf knelt down in front of the boy, who scurried several meters away. When he saw that the big Klingon wasn't going to do anything but look at him, he crawled back toward the food.

Worf let the boy resume eating, then asked, "Why do you want to kill them?" He made the same striking motion with his fist.

"Evil!" spat the boy. He pointed to the sky.

"But you take their food," said Worf, pointing toward the scraps on the tray. "Their food is not evil."

Turrok looked away as if he didn't want to acknowledge that point. "Balak say," he finally replied.

"Is Balak your leader? Is Balak chief?"

"Chief," nodded Turrok. He suddenly leapt to his feet and demanded, "I want to go home!"

"Home," nodded Worf, standing slowly. "What do you remember about your home? Before Balak, do you remember anything?"

"Before Balak?" asked the boy, frowning at the alien concept.

"You are a Klingon," said Worf forcefully. "You come from a proud heritage. You have a history. Do you remember your parents?"

"Parents?" asked Turrok, tasting the unfamiliar word.

"Computer," intoned Worf, "replace the humans in this simulation with Klingons. Klingon families."

"Request acknowledged," answered the feminine voice of the computer.

"Come," said Worf, reaching down to pick up the clean clothes. "Let's take a walk."

They strolled from the secluded part of the woods into a picnic area that offered a panoramic view of a small lake, as blue as cobalt and nestled in a beautiful circle of trees. Around the rustic tables and benches were dozens of Klingon families cooking food over barbecues, playing games, setting tables, and eating heartily. Worf might quarrel that the games these fake Klingons were playing were not as physical as those real Klingons would play, but the impression was what he wanted.

In a way, these humanlike Klingons in a human setting were more effective than real Klingons might have been. The children running around, the mothers and fathers feeding babies, everyone sharing the cooking—it was so idyllic it made his stomach turn, but it had the desired effect upon young Turrok. He stared in awe at the assembled paean to parenthood.

"You had a mother and father," said Worf, "like these. There are billions of Klingons all over the galaxy."

"Billions?" echoed the lad uncomprehendingly.

"Thousands," Worf replied, thinking that might be an easier concept to grasp. "You, Balak, and the others are not alone. We are many."

The boy shook his head as if rejecting the idea. Then he sat on his haunches and began to howl, a plaintive cry that seemed to beseech the heavens to help him. Worf crouched beside Turrok and waited until he finished.

"You have much to learn," he said. "All of you do. You must lead me to Balak and the others in your tribe."

Fighting tears, the boy motioned around the strange world. "They are not here," he replied.

"I know," said Worf. He sighed and looked at the small dam that helped to maintain the lake. "Come. Let's go catch some crawdads."

Captain Picard zipped his burgundy jacket shut and stepped onto the transporter platform. Will Riker, Data, and Ensign Ro followed him.

Ensign Ro turned to Riker and said, "I suggest you fasten your jacket, Commander. Our readings show it can be quite cold on Selva at night."

"Thank you, Ensign," replied Riker, doing as he was told. "You're becoming quite the expert."

"That's my job on this mission," Ro replied stiffly.

"We all need to become experts," said Picard. He glanced around to make sure that his small party was in place, then he nodded to Chief O'Brien. "Energize."

Once again they materialized in the public square of New Reykjavik, only this time darkness surrounded them and a fierce wind made them clutch their collars around their necks. Threatening mother-of-pearl clouds swirled over their heads. There were small lanterns beside the doors of each building, and giant searchlights were mounted on high standards in each corner of the compound. Some searchlights shone out over the walls, but most of them illuminated rows of squat, ugly buildings. All of the lights wobbled disconcertingly in the wind, creating eerie shadows that danced like ghosts throughout the village.

"I see what you mean about the cold," Riker said, shuddering.

"Without its proximity to the warm ocean currents," said Ro, "this village would be uninhabitable."

"These people have shelter," mused Riker, "but how can those Klingons live out there in the forest?"

Data replied, "If President Oscaras was accurate and not being denigrating when he said the Klingons burrow in the ground, that would afford them warmth and shelter."

"Where are the colonists?" asked Picard, surveying the deserted grounds.

A searchlight suddenly hit him full in face, blinding him. Picard, Ro, and Riker covered their eyes with their hands and staggered backward while Data peered curiously into the light.

"Extinguish that light!" ordered Picard. "You're blinding us!"

"Sorry!" called a voice. The light moved slowly away, and they saw that its operator was stationed in one of the turrets. "No one is allowed out after curfew without a pass. I suggest that you go to the dining hall."

"Thank you," Picard grumbled.

Fighting the wind, they made their way toward the communal building pointed out to them by Oscaras earlier in the day. Before they were halfway there they heard a strange rhythmic sound. At first the captain thought it was a door or something loose banging in the wind, but it was far too rapid for that. He stopped to listen, as did Data, Riker, and Ensign Ro. Whether the wind shifted or the noise simply increased in volume, it suddenly became as clear as his own shivery breathing. All around the compound, seemingly on every side, was the incessant sound of drumming.

They weren't the only ones to hear it, as the searchlight operators in the turrets began to probe the black forest with their lights. From the dining hall

Oscaras and a handful of men and women, phasers drawn, stepped into the blustery night. Oscaras nodded toward Picard in acknowledgement, but his attention—everyone's attention—was riveted on the hollow rapping that echoed in the darkness.

"How close are they?" Picard asked Data.

"Approximately thirty meters beyond the walls," answered the android. "They have the compound surrounded, and they are slowly moving as they drum. I believe they are using hollowed logs."

Oscaras and his armed guard strode up to the visitors. "They're waiting for their comrade to howl in response," the big man explained. "That's one reason I didn't want you to take him to your ship. Now they'll probably think we killed him."

"What will they do?" asked Riker.

"Your guess is as good as mine," said Oscaras. "They're not what you would call predictable."

Somewhere, muffled behind a closed door, a child cried. With the stormy sky over their heads, the wind buffeting everything, and shadows dancing to the bizarre beat, Picard couldn't fault anyone for being scared. He began to wonder how these people had kept their sanity. Perhaps they hadn't.

Suddenly there was the terrifying noise of loud clanging, as if metal had become part of the percussion. The guard in the eastern turret screamed, and his searchlight went dark with a crashing sound.

"They're throwing rocks!" Oscaras shouted. "Lights on turret two!"

The other guards tried to swivel their lights in that direction, but the gusting winds hampered their movements. By the time someone fixed a steady light on the darkened turret, demonic figures could be seen scurrying all over it.

"Breach on turret two!" Oscaras wailed, although no one seemed to have a clear idea what to do about it.

The president aimed his phasers in that direction, and a gleaming beam scorched the roof of the turret. Picard moved swiftly to intercept him. "Put your phasers on stun!" he ordered. "And let's get closer first."

Data, Riker, and Ro took that as an order, and they were soon jogging across the square toward the dark tower while drawing their own phasers. Picard reached the corner of the compound in time to see several slinky figures—each painted as black as the night—slip over the outside wall of the turret and disappear. Data reached the rope ladder under the guard post first and began to climb. Riker and Ro stood beneath him, phasers leveled, scanning the top of the wall. The drumming continued, but with every passing second it sounded farther away and less intimidating.

"Careful, Data!" Riker warned the android.

Data nodded, then lifted the small trapdoor beneath the turret and stuck his head into the guard post. A moment later he looked down and reported, "The attackers are gone. But we have a medical emergency."

Riker hit his combadge. "Riker to transporter room," he barked. "Stand by to beam one to sickbay."

Data disappeared into the elevated command post, and Picard began to scale the ladder with Raul Oscaras close behind him.

The captain passed through the trapdoor and saw Data crouching on the floor beside a figure lying prone and very still. The android unfastened his tricorder from the pouch on his belt and passed it over the man's body. Picard heard Oscaras lumbering up the ladder behind him, panting with his efforts, but he ignored him as he moved closer to the fallen man. The uncertain light from one of the other turrets suddenly focused with brutal clarity, and Picard swallowed hard as he saw the ugly red gash at the man's throat and the pool of blood oozing onto the rough-hewn floor.

"He is dead," said Data. "Cause of death—loss of blood and shock."

"Damn them to hell!" Oscaras bellowed, shaking both his fists at the sky. "That's *twelve* dead! Do you need more proof, Picard, that they're animals? Worse than animals, because animals don't kill for fun."

The captain started to say something, but there were no words in any language that could possibly do the dead man any good or make the situation any better.

"And I hold you personally responsible, Picard!" Oscaras accused him. "You stole my prisoner, and they thought he was dead. They've never been this bold before, attacking someone in the compound. But they had good reason—revenge. That's something both of us understand."

As if in answer to Oscaras's threat the dark forest erupted with frenzied drumming and inhuman howls of victory.

Chapter Four

TURROK LAUGHED with youthful exuberance as he sloshed through the cold knee-high water above the dam, chasing creatures that looked like tiny white lobsters. With impressive swiftness he plunged his arm into the water and came up with a squirming crustacean, which he promptly popped into his mouth and chewed with gusto. Worf, sitting on the bank, shook his head and reminded himself that the boy was really eating a fake crawdad generated in much the same way that the food slots generated different delicacies, but it was still disconcerting. Turrok had eaten about a dozen of the slimy creatures and showed no signs of stopping. If the youngster was ever reintroduced to Klingon civilization, thought Worf, he would certainly appreciate *ghargh*.

The boy stumbled backward and landed in water up to his shoulders, something he had also done about a dozen times. Laughing, he cupped the water in his hands and poured it over his head. Doctor Crusher would be pleased, thought Worf, that Turrok was getting his bath.

The youth fished around under the rocks and came up with another crayfish, which he held out to Worf. "For you!"

"Thank you," answered the adult, "but I ate before coming here."

Turrok looked at the crustacean and decided to save its simulated life. He tossed it back into the water. "Good place," he said, slapping the water like a little kid. "Not want to go home."

That was a new sentiment, and Worf furrowed his enormous brow. Klingon vocabulary had been coming back to Turrok at a rapid rate as they spoke. Worf was no expert on developmental psychology, but he knew that Turrok must have had a substantial vocabulary at the age of three or four, when he had been separated from his family on Kapor'At. He had started out using many terms unfamiliar to Worf, but now he was speaking almost entirely in Klingon. Counselor Troi would be pleased, because they were becoming fast friends. That left only one question—what to do next?

"We can't stay here," Worf answered, trying to think of a more plausible reason than that the place wasn't real. "We must find Balak and the others."

"Why?" asked Turrok, splashing water on his face.

"Because," said Worf, "you have been killing and stealing from the flat-heads, and that must stop." He used the boy's term for the settlers to make his point clear.

"Why?" the boy asked playfully.

If the boy was going to act like a recalcitrant child, Worf could act like a harried parent. "Because," he answered sternly, "if you don't help me find your tribe, I'll return you to the flat-heads in the village."

"No!" shrieked the boy. "They are evil! They beat me!"

"What have you done to deserve better treatment?"

46

asked Worf coldly. "You must learn to make peace with these people. I live and work with them, and they're the same as us, in most respects."

The boy stood, the water dripping off his scrawny body and his stringy hair. "If I take you to Balak," he said sheepishly, "you will teach me to be like you?"

"Yes," answered Worf, standing. "I will teach you to be Klingon. If you fight, you will fight with honor, not like an animal."

Turrok lowered his head and said glumly, "I can take you to Balak and the tribe, but they may kill you."

"Perhaps," agreed Worf. "But I will die like a Klingon, not an animal slinking in the bushes."

"I will miss this place," said Turrok, glancing around at the park.

"We'll come back here sometime," Worf promised with a smile. He held out his hand and pulled the youth from the pool. Then he handed him the gray tunic and pants. "You'll get along better with humans if you wear clothes."

Turrok laughed. "We only go naked because it frightens them."

Captain Picard sat in his ready room, dreading what he had to do next. He was overdue to make a report to Starfleet about his progress on Selva, such as it was. Information had been extremely sketchy when Admiral Bryant had assigned him the task of going to the planet to "sort out their problem." There were no unimportant Federation colonies, but this one was extremely small and had no strategic value, except that it was located near the disputed frontier of Romulan and Klingon space. That border was relatively peaceful now and had its own de facto neutral zone, of which the deserted Klingon colonies at Kapor'At were a part. New Reykjavik was the perfect size for a Federation colony in this sector—small and unassuming.

Except that this colony was at war and under seige. With an enemy that shouldn't be there and wasn't under the jurisdiction of any power in the universe. Even if the Klingon High Council hadn't disowned them, it was doubtful they could do anything to solve the problem. Only time could stop the bloodshed and heal the wounds on Selva, and time was a commodity the captain of the *Enterprise* seldom had in abundance.

He pressed the comm panel on his desk. "Picard to communications," he said. "Please contact Admiral Bryant on Starbase 73. When you have him, patch it to my ready room."

"Aye, sir," answered a pert young ensign. "Initiating subspace relay." After about a minute she reported, "Stand by, Captain, for Admiral Bryant."

A few seconds later the round, friendly face of one of the most respected admirals in Starfleet appeared on Picard's viewscreen. "Hello, Jean-Luc," he said, smiling.

"Hello, Admiral," the captain replied, returning the smile. "You are looking well."

"I haven't looked well in twenty years"—Bryant chuckled—"but it's nice of you to say so. So how are things on Selva? What was all the commotion about?"

Without embellishment Picard related their horrifying discoveries one by one, from their first briefing with President Oscaras to the murder of the guard only an hour before. Admiral Bryant listened in stunned silence.

"I had no idea," he said finally. "What's the matter with those people? Why didn't they tell us about this months ago?"

Picard shook his head and answered, "They want to be self-sufficient, and they thought they could handle it by themselves. Perhaps, too, they were afraid we'd shut down the colony."

"We still might," replied the admiral. "What's your recommendation?"

"It's dangerous, but if Lieutenant Worf can befriend the captive, he can lead us to the rest of the Klingons. From there we'll try to persuade them all to live in peace. If that fails, we'll have to relocate one or the other of the communities. Either way, we have to find the Klingons."

"That could take time," Bryant concluded. "I'll give you as much as I can."

"Thank you," replied the captain.

"Good luck. Bryant out."

The screen went dark, and Picard slumped back in his chair. At least there was no urgent business demanding their presence elsewhere. He touched the comm panel again and said, "Picard to Worf."

"Worf here," responded the familiar deep voice.

"How are you and our young friend doing?"

"As well as can be expected. He has agreed to lead me to the other Klingons."

"That's good news," replied Picard. "I would like to have a briefing in the observation lounge in one hour."

"May I bring Turrok?" asked Worf. "I'm afraid of leaving him alone or with anyone else."

"Why not?" answered Picard. "The sooner he gets used to us, the better. Lieutenant, who would you choose among the crew to accompany you and Turrok in search of the others?"

There was a pause, and the Klingon responded, "I wouldn't want to take a large party for fear of scaring them. I believe Data and Counselor Troi would be the most useful."

"Thank you," said Picard. "We will discuss this further in one hour."

* * *

Jean-Luc Picard, Will Riker, Data, Deanna Troi, Geordi La Forge, and Ensign Ro waited expectantly in the observation lounge as the door slid open and Worf entered with a young Klingon dressed in gray pants and tunic. A communications badge gleamed on his narrow chest. The boy hesitated in the doorway, and Worf had to nudge him to enter, but he finally did so. Everyone except Data smiled warmly, yet they were careful not to make any quick moves that might alarm him. The android was busy studying information on a hand-held computer terminal. Ensign Ro noticed that Worf tried to give the youngster some space, while standing close enough to grab him in an instant if he resorted to violence.

"Welcome, Turrok," said Picard, motioning to the oval table. "Will you please have a seat?"

Thanks to his increasing command of the Klingon language and the universal translator, the teenager understood what the captain had said. He looked at Worf in surprise.

"We are having a meeting," Worf explained. "Some of it may concern you, and you are free to be seated and listen. As long as you are wearing this badge, you will understand us." He pointed to the gleaming insignia.

Turrok nodded and rushed to an empty chair beside Captain Picard, who seemed pleased to have made a favorable impression on the youth. Turrok stared at the captain with fascination as he spoke.

"Now, let's begin this briefing," said Picard. He smiled at the boy. "Turrok has offered to lead Lieutenant Worf to the rest of the Klingons. It may be a risky mission, but it's a risk we have to take. Worf believes that Commander Data and Counselor Troi will be useful in helping him convince the Klingons to stop their attacks and make peace with the colonists. I agree, although I'm a bit concerned about the danger." The captain looked squarely at Deanna Troi, as did Will Riker.

The Betazoid smiled. "I'm sure I'll be safe with Data and Worf. If there's any danger, we can beam up to the *Enterprise.*"

"I'd like to go down to the planet with them," Geordi declared. "Ensign Ro and I have been running some simulations based on the data we've been collecting, and they've got a bad situation about a thousand kilometers offshore. If those tectonic plates shift any more, there's going to be some interesting seismic activity. And soon."

"I concur," said Data. "I have been studying their findings, and the planet is less stable than the colonists have reported."

"You can bring that up with President Oscaras in a few minutes," replied Picard. "He's waiting in my ready room. I'm sorry, Geordi, but I would prefer to keep you on board to run a level-three diagnostic while we have some extra time in orbit. If Ensign Ro has been working with you on this, perhaps we should station her in the settlement to monitor the situation from there. If they need any more equipment, we'll furnish it. How does that sit with you, Ensign?"

Ensign Ro straightened in her chair and replied, "Except for the fact that I sense hostility from them every time I'm down there, I welcome the opportunity to continue our observation." She didn't mention that Guinan had predicted this would happen.

Picard smiled sympathetically and added, "I'm sure you realize, Ensign, that your presence serves more than one purpose. Plus, I know from experience that you can handle yourself in a hostile situation, like the one you faced when you joined this crew."

Ro nodded, accepting the compliment. "Thank you, Captain."

With finality Picard slapped his hands on the table.

"Then it's settled—Worf, Data, and Troi will go with Turrok to make contact with the Klingons. And Ro will be stationed at New Reykjavik." He turned to his bearded first officer. "Number One, will you please fetch President Oscaras from my ready room?"

"Yes, sir," answered Riker, rising from his seat and striding out the door.

They waited, Ro smiling when she saw Turrok mimicking Worf by sitting as stiffly and quietly in his chair as possible. Worf gave him a slight smile of approval. But two Klingons—no matter how well behaved—were not exactly what Raul Oscaras wanted to see when he was ushered into the observation lounge.

"What's the meaning of *this?*" he snarled, pointing at the young Klingon.

Turrok bared his teeth and nearly bolted out of his seat, but Picard laid a comforting hand on the youth's shoulder. "You are welcome here," he said in Klingon. Then he glared at Oscaras and warned him, "You will behave yourself at least as well as this boy if you want our help."

Still glowering, the big human took a seat at the table. He sat stone-faced as Geordi explained to him what they had discovered about seismic activity offshore.

"That's a thousand kilometers away," Oscaras countered. "We know Selva isn't perfect, but neither is Earth or any other planet. Believe me, we made an exhaustive survey before selecting the location of our colony." He glanced at Turrok. "Maybe it wasn't exhaustive enough in some respects, but we thought all the life-form readings were indigenous animals. I don't see how an earthquake a thousand kilometers away is going to do us any harm."

"Be that as it may," said Picard, "we are stationing Ensign Ro in your settlement to continue to monitor the seismic activity." He went on to explain that Worf, Data, and Troi would undertake the dangerous mission of finding and befriending the other Klingons.

Oscaras looked incredulous. "If you want to send your crew out to die, that's your business," he muttered. "We've got a complete seismic lab, and we know exactly what's going on out there in the ocean. But more importantly, do you realize that not one single member of this away team is *human?*"

Now it was Picard's turn to look incredulous. "No," he answered, "I didn't. I thought I was sending down the four most valuable and capable crew members I could find. And if you have any complaints about their *performance,* I'll listen to them, but that's the last time I want to hear you complain about their origins. Do I make myself clear?"

"Perfectly," said Oscaras, rising to his feet. "I'd better go back and prepare my people for this. Daybreak is in a few hours. I presume you'll be starting then?"

"Prepare them well," growled Worf.

Oscaras made a perfunctory bow, adding, "I can find my own way to the transporter room. Until morning." He strode out the door.

Like everyone else, Ro sat in stunned silence for a moment until young Turrok summed up her impressions perfectly with a loud raspberry sound.

Steamy clouds of breath shot into the air as five bodies materialized in the gray village of New Reykjavik. If possible, thought Ensign Ro, dawn was even colder than night. Luckily, they were prepared— everyone except Data was bundled in a thick down jacket. Turrok seemed inordinately fond of his as he played with the zipper. Worf took a few cautious steps; this was his first visit to the planet's surface, and he looked as if he expected to be stoned. Data scanned the immediate vicinity with his tricorder while Ro assessed the empty public square and the forbidding walls that surrounded the village.

She took her pack off her back. "This is as far as I'm going," she told Deanna. "Would you like to trade assignments?"

"Not particularly," remarked the Betazoid.

Oscaras and a handful of colonists emerged from the communal dining hall and strode toward them. Seeing the humans, Turrok moved so close to Worf that he was almost inside his pocket. The humans stopped several meters from the party of two Klingons, two female humanoids, and an android.

"Good morning," said Oscaras, sounding very businesslike. "Have you had breakfast, or do you want to get started?"

"We have eaten," replied Worf.

Oscaras cupped his hand to his mouth and shouted to the guard in the turret by the gate, "Is the gate clear?"

"All clear!" cried the guard.

"Well, good luck," said Oscaras. "They should be in a good mood after having killed one of us last night."

Data ignored that remark and responded, "Our communicators are programmed to contact the *Enterprise*. They could be adjusted, but it might be convenient to have a communicator that could contact you directly."

"Good idea," answered Oscaras, taking a hand-held communicator from his pocket and giving it to the android. "If you find them and run into trouble, give us a call. Although I think you're being foolish, I really don't want to lose any of you."

"Do you have any other advice for us?" asked Deanna Troi.

"Yes," said the president. "If you run out of food,

everything on these trees is edible. If the water tastes alkaline, don't drink it. Shake out your clothes and boots, because there is a type of mantis that is very poisonous. And the chucks will attack if they feel threatened. Of course, I'm sure your guide knows all of this."

"Don't let them get your phasers," cautioned a tall blond man standing behind Oscaras.

Turrok was already edging toward the gate and trying to pull Worf with him. Deanna and Data began to follow them.

"We will keep you informed," Data called back.

There were no joyous waves or tearful sendoffs for Worf, Data, Troi, and Turrok. The guard in the tower by the gate threw a switch that opened the heavy metal door. With a feeling of dread Ro watched her companions depart, then turned to find herself alone with the colonists. She waited patiently until they saw fit to acknowledge her.

"Ensign Ro," said Oscaras, "normally, unattached women sleep in the dormitory, but a married couple has been gracious enough to let you have their quarters for your stay. We thought you might want your privacy."

Translated, thought Ro, nobody wanted to share a room with her. "I'll store my belongings there," she said, "but I'm eager to see the laboratory and seismic equipment."

Oscaras indicated a stern, dark-haired woman who was part of his entourage. "Doctor Drayton is the head of our science department, and you'll be working under her."

"The lab doesn't open until eight o'clock," said Drayton.

"That's very careless," responded Ro. "Considering the extent of the seismic activity, you should have

55

someone monitoring it at all times." She turned to Oscaras. "Give the married couple back their quarters. I'll sleep in the lab. Where is it?"

"Now just a minute," protested Drayton, "I'm in charge of that lab, and I give the orders."

Ro fixed her with a deadpan gaze and replied, "You can be in charge, and you can give all the orders you want—but *my* orders are to monitor seismic activity on this planet. You can assist me or not, but I won't let you hinder me. Where are the scanners? In that building over there?"

Shouldering her pack, the Bajoran strode off toward the second of the two largest buildings in the compound. Doctor Drayton moved to stop her, but Oscaras grasped the woman's arm. Ro could hear the end of their conversation:

"Let her go," said the president. "We need their cooperation, and if this is the price we have to pay, so be it. But Calvert, I want her observed both inside and outside the lab. I want to know who she talks to and what they talk about."

"Yes, sir," answered another man. "It won't be hard to keep track of *her.*"

A few meters away from the dull walls of the settlement the planet of Selva became an entirely different place. As big as Worf was, he felt like a flea on the back of a large, hairy dog—black trees stretched into what seemed like the stratosphere, their jade leaves obscuring all but slivers of pale sky. The trees were so closely spaced that it was impossible for him to walk without rubbing his shoulders against their trunks, and he soon found his shoulders were covered with a molasseslike sap that oozed from the thin bark. Remembering the words of Oscaras, he ran his finger along a trunk and put it to his tongue. The gum tasted sweet and acidic, although it smelled like cleaning fluid.

Turrok led the way, followed by Worf, Deanna Troi, and Data. The elder Klingon marveled at the brisk pace set by the younger, because he could find no trail in the damp humus that covered the forest floor. It felt as if they were alone and isolated, but they were hardly the only organisms in this dark cathedral. In the branches overhead things were moving—following them, chattering, clicking, and grunting. Worf imagined those were the sloths he had heard about, as well as birds. The tree trunks themselves were crawling with insects and other tiny creatures that made a parasitic livelihood off the free-flowing sap.

At one point Turrok stopped and peeled back a piece of bark that was already loose; he reached in and pulled out a dark grub that was about the size of a man's thumb.

The youngster offered the squirming larva to Worf. "Crawdad?"

The adult Klingon shook his head. The youth shrugged and popped it into his mouth. Then he headed on, chewing contentedly.

Suddenly Deanna gasped and stumbled backward, and Worf turned to see what had startled her. The partly decomposed leaves and twigs at their feet were undulating, as if something was poking its way up from underneath. Worf kicked away the debris with his boot and caught the tail end of a large rodent disappearing into a hole; two smaller animals scurried after it. Like everything in this forest, mother and babies were black and sleek.

Data had stopped behind Deanna. He studied the burrow for a moment, cocked his head, and suggested, "Those must be the chucks we have heard mentioned."

Deanna wrinkled her nose. "Handsome creatures, aren't they?"

"Do you think so?" asked Data. "I would categorize them as repulsive."

"I was joking," added the Betazoid.

"Heh, heh," responded Data flatly, obviously trying to be polite.

Worf looked up and saw Turrok some distance away, waving impatiently for them to follow. "Come," said Worf, shouldering his way through the thicket of tree trunks.

When they had caught up Data asked in Klingon, "Turrok, how do you know we are headed in the correct direction?"

The adolescent felt along one side of the nearest tree trunk and answered, "The sap runs greatest on the side facing the sea. Also, do you not smell the ocean?"

No, the three off-worlders shook their heads in unison.

"Well," said Turrok, "I do."

"But how will that allow you to find your camp?" asked Worf.

"That won't," answered Turrok, "but this will."

He searched the leafy ground until he found a broken branch, which he tested by whacking it several times against his palm. Then they walked a considerable distance until they found a suitable fallen log, one that time, insects, and animals had hollowed out.

"Mister Chuck," he said politely to the log, "please give me your home for my far voice." He tapped lightly on the log until a huge black rodent slithered out. It wrinkled its snout at the intruders and bared its considerable fangs. Worf was reaching for his phaser when the chuck apparently decided to grant the request. It burrowed into the decaying humus and was gone within seconds, despite its bulk.

Now Turrok began to pound in earnest on his found

drum. Tat-tat-tat, pause. Tat-tat-tat, pause. Tat-tat-tat, pause. The drumming caused the unseen but noisy animals over their heads to become strangely quiet, and the boy patiently repeated his signal many times, listening between the pauses for a response.

Finally, although it was barely perceptible in the vast forest, Worf heard the sound of two taps and a pause, repeated twice. Turrok answered with a complicated series of beats and pauses that reminded the lieutenant of the Morse code he had learned during his boyhood years on Earth. Worf glanced at Data and knew the android was analyzing and storing this primitive but effective form of communication and would be able to reproduce it perfectly.

Turrok finally stopped to listen. There was a long pause before the far drummer answered with a series of complex rhythms that evolved into a steady refrain that never varied. Like the ticking of a clock in a quiet room, it filled their senses. Turrok tossed down his stick and strode off in a slightly different direction, motioning the others to follow him. If one's hearing was acute enough, thought Worf, it would be a simple matter to follow the rhythmic beat home.

But Turrok didn't look particularly pleased. "Tribe is happy I'm alive," he said as they walked. "But not happy I bring you with me. Before day is over you may die, or you may kill."

After that pronouncement Deanna and Worf exchanged concerned glances, and the drumming deep in the forest sounded more ominous. But they walked steadily toward it, their legs marching instinctively to the far-off rhythm.

Chapter Five

ENSIGN RO STRAIGHTENED UP from the seismograph after having correlated its readings with a short-range scan of the ocean floor. There was no change, so she turned her attention to a concurrent analysis of the midwater zone. She noted how abruptly the waters close to shore dropped into the abyss, which was unusually shallow for such an extensive body of water. On this planet, she decided, the magma rising from underwater volcanoes was filling in the depths, not creating new islands and mountain ranges. That was okay, except that massive pelagic deposits could have an unknown effect on the tectonic plates.

Those plates, she knew, were like the cracked pieces of an eggshell. And they were almost as fragile. Worse than eggshells, these plates overlapped in several places, especially in that trouble spot a thousand kilometers offshore. Underneath the fragile crust, molten rock, or magma, was struggling to get out, pushed by forces deep in the planet's mantle. The trouble spot must be an underwater inferno, thought Ro. She had a dozen questions that could only be answered through long-term observation, such as: How much effect did all that heating and cooling have on the schistosity of the rock that formed the plates? Would they hold together in a major temblor, or would the egg split apart?

According to their records, the colonists had asked a lot of these same questions but hadn't come up with many answers. After discovering that the ocean couldn't support life they had moved on to more pressing matters. The ocean kept this part of the planet habitable, and that was all that mattered to them. Ro couldn't blame them—a proper study of the currents alone would keep an oceanographer busy for the rest of his life. Besides, there was only so much that could be gleaned from staring at digital readouts, graphs, and shifting vectors. Someday the citizens of Selva might have a fleet of bathyscaphes from which to probe the tumultuous ocean floor, but not today. When they couldn't safely walk fifty meters from their own gate, studying a region that was underwater and a thousand kilometers away was bound to be a low priority.

Ro could feel suspicious eyes on her all morning as various scientists reported to work. Some of them hadn't seemed to be doing very much, and she wondered if they had really come only to observe her. Of course, the building also housed the replicator, subspace radio, and sickbay, and workers in those departments might have been curious enough to stop by the lab. She wasn't particularly concerned or upset by the scrutiny. As Guinan had told her, she was the Other, in more ways than one. Lead by example, her friend had told her, and that was what she intended to do.

There was, however, one set of eyes that was more interesting than the others. They belonged to a small freckle-faced girl who was about twelve years old, by

Ro's reckoning. Despite her age, she obviously had come to work in the lab, because she was quite diligent about tending a number of plants growing in hydroponic splendor under ultraviolet lights. She wasn't just feeding them but measuring them, checking their temperature, and taking specimens and cultures, which she studied under a microscope. When Ro glanced back at one point the girl smiled. It was the first smile a colonist had seen fit to grant the Bajoran.

About midday several lab workers got up en masse and headed for the door. To lunch, Ro assumed. She knew quite well where the dining hall was—it was the only other good-sized building in the village—and she was prepared to go uninvited. But she wasn't prepared to *look* hungry. When everyone else returned she would go, Ro decided.

Then she saw the freckle-faced girl headed her way. "Hi," said the girl, bouncing to a stop in front of the seismograph console. "I'm Myra Calvert."

"Call me Ro," replied the Bajoran with a smile.

"They're not being very nice to you, are they?" asked Myra. "First they won't talk to you, then they won't tell you it's time to go to lunch."

"Well," replied the ensign, "if they won't talk to me, they can't very well tell me anything."

"Is it because you have those bumps on your head?" asked Myra. "What are you?"

"I'm Bajoran," said the visitor. "You've probably never heard of my race."

"Of course I have," scoffed Myra. "You were driven away from your homes by the Cardassians. Now you don't really have a home planet, and nobody will let you stay on theirs for very long."

Ro smiled, impressed. "That's right. You're very well informed."

Myra shrugged. "Everybody says I'm a prodigy.

The truth is, I just remember what I read. But I'm like you—nobody quite trusts me."

Ro nodded sympathetically. "That's their loss. What are you working on?"

"I'm studying to be a botanist," said the twelve-year-old proudly. "But it's tough—I can't go out in the forest to collect samples, and I already know more about the native plants than my teachers do. They want me to study Earth plants, but what fun is that when we're not on Earth?"

Ro said encouragingly, "I'm sure that someday you'll write the definitive study on the plant life of Selva."

"I hope so," sighed Myra. "Why did they send you down here—to watch for earthquakes?"

"I hope we're wrong to be so worried, but there's a definite trouble spot out there in the ocean."

Myra peered cautiously around the lab, but there was only one other worker besides the two of them. She lowered her voice to say, "They don't like to hear bad news around here. For months I've been trying to prove a theory I have, but they won't listen to me. I'm just a kid."

"What is it?" asked Ro. "I'll listen."

The girl was about to reply when a tall, blond-haired man entered the lab, apparently looking for her. "Myra!" he called in a stern voice.

"My dad," whispered the girl. "He's head of security." She called back, "I'm over here, talking to Ro!"

The man strode toward them but stopped several meters away, as if he didn't want to get too close. "I'm sure the ensign doesn't want to be bothered," he said. "Come along."

"She hasn't bothered me at all," answered the Bajoran. "I've found your daughter to be quite refreshing."

"Can Ro come to lunch with us?" asked Myra.

The man cleared his throat, as if that was the last thing he wanted, but he couldn't think of a good reason to refuse. "All right," he replied. "But we'll have to be quick about it. I've got to stay by the radio to see if the away team from the *Enterprise* runs into any trouble. They could meet up with those Klingons anytime."

"I don't want to be gone long either," said the slim Bajoran, rising from her seat. "I don't believe we've been introduced. I'm Ensign Ro."

"Gregg Calvert." The man nodded uncomfortably. "I see you've met Myra. She'll bend your ear, and if she becomes a problem—"

"Dad!" the girl protested. As if in revenge, she said to Ro, "Did I tell you my mom died a long time ago, and he's a single parent?"

"Myra!" growled Calvert. He smiled sheepishly at the visitor. "You'll know everything there is to know about us in the next ten minutes, if Myra has her way."

"That would be refreshing, too," said Ro.

Finally, thought Worf as they began to follow what looked like a path through the confusing mass of spindly trees. It led them to a stream that was about ten meters across; the rushing water looked surprisingly deep and treacherous, but there was a log that spanned the waterway. Turrok scampered across as if it were a boulevard, but Data held the log firmly as Deanna started slowly across.

"What are those white things at the bottom of the stream?" she asked.

"They appear to be shells," answered Data. "Perhaps a sort of freshwater mussel."

Worf followed Deanna across, and he was relieved to find that the black gum that coated the trunk offered excellent traction. He returned the favor and held the log for Data. All the while the distant drumming continued its eerie accompaniment, joined by the grunting and rustling of unseen wildlife overhead.

Data had the presence of mind to keep checking his tricorder as they walked, and he was the first to announce, "Several large life-forms moving our way."

Worf reluctantly drew his phaser. "Phasers on light stun," he ordered.

Deanna, who seldom handled a phaser, drew hers and checked the setting. As soon as Turrok saw the shiny weapons he bolted into the trees and disappeared.

"Wait!" called Worf. But there was no answer except for the ominous drums. There was also no sign of Turrok.

Deanna muttered, "How will we find them now?"

"I believe they will find us," answered Data, "and soon." He returned his tricorder to the case on his belt and drew his own phaser.

Suddenly there came what sounded like a stampede in the branches overhead as dozens of unseen creatures took flight. Within a matter of seconds dark shapes took their place, moving swiftly to encircle the travelers on the ground. Worf tried to remain calm and not make any threatening movements, but he knew the hovering figures could alight on them in less time than it would take to aim and fire their phasers. The drumming stopped, and falling leaves floated around them like a green snowstorm.

He tapped his communicator badge. "Worf to *Enterprise*," he breathed. "Stand by to beam three on my command."

"Acknowledged," responded a voice. "Locked on and standing by."

Deanna stepped closer to the big Klingon. "This

isn't fair," she said. "They're studying us, but we can barely see them."

"NuqueH!" barked Worf, shifting his attention from one figure to another. Leaves rustled as the branches filled with more wary observers.

"I count eleven," said Data. "Now thirteen."

Operating on sheer instinct, Worf held up his phaser and made a slow circle so that the beings in the trees could plainly see it. Then he returned the weapon to his jacket pocket and held up his empty hands. "We mean no harm!" he said in Klingon.

"Is that wise?" asked Data.

"We can't stand here forever," answered Worf. "They obviously fear the phasers too much to show themselves."

Deanna followed his example and pocketed her weapon, and Data did likewise. This gesture was answered by a guttural command in a language even the universal translator couldn't interpret, and a figure bounded out of the trees, landing two meters in front of Worf. The elder Klingon beheld a thin female of his own race who gaped at him as if he might be a ghost or a mirage. One by one more Klingons dropped from the trees until the strangers were entirely surrounded by a ragtag army of scrawny Klingons dressed in black animal skins.

One reached out to touch Data, and the android good-naturedly let himself be pawed. The teenage girl in front of Worf edged close enough to touch the bony ridges of his forehead. After determining that both he and his head were real, she touched the furrows of her own forehead and backed away, grinning. Another female crept toward Deanna and tried to touch her breasts, but she brushed the hand aside as politely as she could. The youths expressed themselves in primitive grunts that made Worf want to yell at them to act like Klingons, but he reminded himself that they didn't know how Klingons acted.

Several of the youths backed away as if frightened, and Worf turned to see Turrok being pushed toward the gathering by a youth who was at least a head taller than any of the others. He was probably about sixteen years old, thought Worf, the eldest of the castaways, and he would be considered big for an adult Klingon. Sinewy muscles flexed beneath his tight animal skins, and he glowered at Worf, all the while holding Turrok at arm's length. The younger boy looked terrified, and Worf could see that his Starfleet-issued clothes had been ripped in several places. The others practically scraped the ground at the approach of the larger boy, and there could be little doubt that he was Balak.

In guttural Klingon the sixteen-year-old growled, "Turrok returns, but he is infested by the flat-heads. Tonight he will take the Test of Evil!"

There were murmurings from the others that suggested to Worf this was more of a punishment than a homecoming. He stepped toward Balak and said in the simplest Klingon vocabulary he knew, "Turrok has been very brave. He was imprisoned and beaten and never disgraced himself. He deserves to be treated like a hero."

Balak sneered. "Only the dead are treated like heroes. Who are you? Pet of these flat-heads?"

Worf seethed under his breath, but he kept his composure. He knew the success of the entire mission —and many lives—depended on these next few seconds. "This is Data and Deanna Troi," he said, pointing to his companions. "I am Worf, and we've come from a great ship that journeys in the sky."

The girl who had touched him gasped and looked as if she was about to say something, but Balak shot her a glare that stilled her. "We have no need of you," he told the strangers. "Go away. Be thankful you live."

"You do have need of us," Worf countered. "You were not born here in this woods. You come from an empire of people like yourselves and me. We are called Klingons."

"An empire?" sneered Balak. "Cause your ship and your empire to rid our world of flat-heads. *Then* I welcome you."

"Excuse me," said Data in crisp Klingon, "you are incorrect to make war on humans, or flat-heads, as you call them. Klingons and humans are at peace everywhere in the galaxy except here."

Balak turned upon Data with rage. "Don't tell me what to do!" he screamed.

Like a panther he leapt upon the android, and he tried to choke him. Although his surprise attack knocked Data off balance, the android quickly recovered and forced the Klingon's hands away from his neck. Balak's face contorted with rage, pain, and amazement as the android easily held the strapping humanoid at bay.

"This will accomplish nothing," Data remarked with disapproval. "If I release you, do you promise not to attack us?"

"Knives! Knives!" screamed Balak.

All around them Worf, Deanna, and Data heard knives being drawn from sheaths. Before Worf could draw his phaser two youths grabbed Deanna and held knives to her throat. One of the weapons was a sharpened eating utensil, the other a crude stone blade, but both looked deadly.

Worf slapped his comm badge and bellowed, "Three to beam up. Energize!"

As the Klingons pressed their blades into Deanna's neck her molecules glimmered and evaporated. Another youth slashed his knife at Worf's back but stumbled to the ground, striking only air. Balak, released by the sudden disappearance of Data, sprawled to the ground.

Worf, Deanna, and Data materialized on a transporter platform aboard the *Enterprise*. Deanna, whose eyes were closed in anticipation of death, touched her throat and found it bleeding from a slight cut. Then she swallowed and began to breathe again.

Both Worf and Data rushed to her side. "Are you all right?" asked Data.

"I know I'm bleeding," she answered, "but I don't think it's bad."

"Your assessment is correct," answered the android. "The wound should heal without immediate medical attention."

Worf shook his head and looked downcast. "I have failed," he muttered. "They wouldn't listen."

Data cocked his head and remarked, "I believe this is not the easiest mission we have ever undertaken."

"What should we do next?" asked Deanna.

"We must go back," answered the android. "The sooner, the better, or we will have to find them without assistance."

"You don't have to go," Worf told the Betazoid. "It's too dangerous."

"Nonsense," smiled Deanna. "After the little exhibition we just put on, I'd like to see their faces. Besides, they probably won't try that again."

Worf turned to the stunned transporter operator and ordered, "Return us to the coordinates we just came from. And make sure the transporter controls are not left unattended—for even a second."

"Yes, sir," said the young officer with a gulp as Worf, Data, and Deanna stepped back on the pads. All three drew their phasers.

"Energize," commanded Worf.

For the second time in as many minutes the three

officers had their molecules scrambled and reassembled. Phasers leveled to fire, they whirled in every direction, but there was no sign of the feral Klingons. They stood alone in the regal forest of Selva.

Overhead some animal cackled at them with hooting laughter.

Chapter Six

DATA STUDIED HIS TRICORDER and reported, "Life-form readings are inconclusive, but I believe the Klingons are moving swiftly in an easterly direction. If we do likewise, we may be able to follow them."

"Lead the way," said Worf, pocketing his phaser.

Wasting no time on needless talk, Data, Worf, and Deanna plunged through the forest, guided only by Data's tricorder readings. The android strode swiftly and unerringly, although Worf and Deanna occasionally stumbled in the deep refuse that coated the forest floor. Several times Deanna had to run to catch up, and she wasn't certain how long she could keep up the pace. She was glad she had been working out diligently with Beverly Crusher in the *Enterprise*'s gymnasium.

They stopped only once, when a familiar voice sounded on their communicators: "Picard to away team."

"Worf here," answered the Klingon.

"Lieutenant," said the captain, "I've just received a

disturbing report from Transporter Room One. The operator said that you beamed there during an emergency, and that Counselor Troi was injured."

"I'm all right," Deanna replied for herself. "It was just a scratch."

"Have you made contact with the Klingons?" Picard asked.

"We have," answered Worf, "but we lost contact when we beamed up. We're attempting to relocate them now."

"Data," said the captain, "what exactly is your status?"

"We are in pursuit," answered the android. "I would not categorize our initial contact with the Klingons as successful. We talked briefly, then they attacked us."

"The problem is their leader," said Deanna. "I think he views us as a threat to his dominance."

"I see," replied Picard. "Don't take any unnecessary risks. There are other ways to handle this matter."

"We would be interested in hearing them," said Data, "but we must maintain our pursuit. We are in no danger at the present."

"Keep us informed," ordered the captain. "Picard out."

Data checked his tricorder and decided on a heading. He took one step and promptly vanished into a deep hole that had been covered with twigs and leaves.

"Data!" screamed Deanna, rushing to help the android. Her feet began to slip in the moist debris, and Worf grabbed her by the waist and hauled her back from the crumbling edge of the hole.

"Data!" barked the Klingon. "Can you hear me?"

"I am unhurt!" came a voice that sounded like it was at the bottom of a well. "I believe this pit was dug to catch animals, because there are several in here. In fact, two large chucks are gnawing on me as I speak. I may be forced to kill them. However, there is something else down here that is more disturbing."

"What?" asked Worf.

"A decomposed, partly eaten corpse."

Feeling his way, the Klingon crawled cautiously toward the obscured opening. "What is it?" he asked. "Human?"

"I cannot tell with one hundred percent certainty," responded the android, "but I believe it is Klingon."

"Damn them!" cursed Worf.

"Damn who?" asked Deanna.

"Whoever would dig a trap like this, then not check it."

The Betazoid remarked, "We shouldn't jump to conclusions. The Klingons could have put one of their own down there as punishment. I think Balak is capable of that."

Data's voice echoed. "This pit is deep, more than five meters down. The walls and the floor are smooth, which would indicate that sophisticated digging equipment was used. Perhaps even a phaser."

"The colonists," growled Worf. "Who else could it be? Should we bring the body out?"

"I fail to see what purpose that would serve," answered Data. "The body is unrecognizable. However, *I* would like to come out."

Lying on the ground, Worf wrapped one brawny arm around the nearest tree trunk and extended his other arm into the pit. For added support Deanna gripped the Klingon's feet and braced her legs against two tree trunks. She saw Worf grimace as Data climbed his arm like a rope, then she saw the android's hands extend out of the pit and grip the Klingon's shoulder. The hands moved up Worf's torso until Data could swing one leg over the edge and extricate himself from the hole.

Regaining his feet, Data suggested they look for sticks to clear away the debris that obscured the deadly trap. After the hole was cleared Worf turned on his flashlight and peered into the forbidding darkness. Deanna looked over his shoulder and saw a skeletal face peering up at them, guarded by a fat rodent perched in its hair. She quickly turned away.

"And the colonists claim they're civilized," said Worf.

Data peered curiously at his tricorder and tapped it several times with his finger. "The fall seems to have damaged my tricorder," he reported. "They are probably out of tricorder range, and electronic devices are frightening to the Klingons. Perhaps we should proceed without a tricorder. My directional memory retains their general heading."

Deanna mustered a smile. "Maybe they'll help us by playing their drums."

"Perhaps," said Data. "More likely they will attack us again."

"Let's proceed," said Worf.

Giving the deadly pit a wide berth, the three off-worlders continued deeper into the primeval forest. This time, however, their pace was slow and cautious.

Quite to her surprise, Ensign Ro enjoyed her lunch with Myra Calvert and her father, Gregg. The food itself was quite good, which was no great surprise considering it came from the same sort of replicator used on the *Enterprise*. The difference, explained Myra, was that the colonists used the replicator to create raw commodities, such as onions and rice, which they cooked using traditional methods. All of this was in preparation for the day when they would be able to farm their land as they had envisioned. Myra hoped to contribute to that future by discovering the tastiest and most nutritious native vegetables and grains.

Although Gregg Calvert said very little during the meal, it was obvious that he loved his daughter very much. He deferred to her and was as proud as a parent could be of a twelve-year-old child who was undoubtedly smarter than he. Ro said even less during the meal and was content to listen to Myra explain the workings of the colony, mixed with a good deal of family history. Her father and mother had met aboard the *Icarus,* a scientific vessel charged with the exploration of asteroid belts that posed a threat to commercial shipping. Gregg had been in charge of security, which wasn't much of a job on a scientific vessel, while his wife Janna did the dangerous work of charting the asteroids from a shuttlecraft. A mere two years after Myra's birth something had happened to the stabilizers on Janna's shuttlecraft; it plowed into an asteroid, with all hands lost.

Sickened by the loss of his wife, Gregg turned his back on space travel and returned with his young daughter to Earth. After a few aimless years he fell under the sway of Raul Oscaras and his promises of a meaningful life in a self-sufficient colony on an unexplored world. With the assurance of a long but one-way journey to their new home, Gregg took the job of security chief for the colony of New Reykjavik. That job had turned into a nightmare, he wasn't ashamed to admit to the visitor. He himself had been wounded in the second attack, before the settlers had thought to arm themselves with phasers. If it hadn't been for a fully equipped sickbay, he told the Bajoran, Myra would be an orphan.

Left unsaid in his account was his impression that Captain Picard's approach to the problem was dead wrong. Ro could tell he wanted to take an army of soldiers into the forest and wipe out the Klingons before they caused any more grief. She found it hard to blame him, having known many Bajora who felt the same way about Cardassians.

Back at the seismograph, she found it hard to concentrate on the job at hand, mainly because nothing had changed out there, a thousand kilometers away in the lifeless ocean. Ro felt an irrational impulse to get out of her seat and walk the twenty kilometers or so to the sea, just to look at it. Not that she would be able to see anything beneath its surface, but staring at instruments and readouts wasn't doing much to assuage her fears of the powerful forces that were grinding away on this young planet. After only half a day in New Reykjavik she could understand why the colonists were testy and tense. Waiting was hell, and that was all any of them were doing.

As darkness filtered through the somber forest the drums began to beat again. Data was in the lead, and he cocked his head, listened for a moment, then changed direction entirely. Deanna Troi was glad to be moving on a solid heading, because they had been virtually blind since Data's tricorder had been broken. The sun had been no directional help, because it was impossible to see except when it was directly overhead; then it was just an intermittent twinkle between the dense leaves.

They had been moving rather slowly since Data's fall into the hidden pit, and the Betazoid did not feel tired. She couldn't explain why, but it almost seemed *necessary* to wander around the forest for several hours, as if they couldn't possibly understand these Klingons until they understood their world.

There had been no complaints, and Worf's impatience and anger over the failure of their initial contact had evaporated. There was something soothing about the dark trees, the chirping of birds and animals overhead, and the rustling of moist leaves under their feet. Even the drumming seemed to be in tune with the rhythms of the planet. Suddenly Deanna knew why the colonists had chosen Selva for their home. They had wandered around the same forest—while the Klingons hid from them—and they had felt it welcome them and take them in. More than ever, Deanna sensed the necessity and rightness of their mission. This was a planet that needed living creatures, because it didn't seem to have enough of its own.

The body in the pit was the only discordant note in everything they had seen and heard. There was something wrong with it, something that didn't fit her impressions of either the Klingons or the colonists. Death was not the thing that didn't fit—death was surely a part of this world. It was the carelessness and heartlessness of that particular death that shocked her. It had even shocked Worf, who had seen more than his share of death. She couldn't envision either of the warring groups digging a trap like that, then abandoning it. The Betazoid resolved to find the answer to this disturbing mystery even if she had to question every person who lived on the planet.

Their pace quickened, both because it was getting darker and because the drums were getting louder. There was also something remarkable ahead of them, the first irregularity in the unchanging canopy of trees since they had passed the stream that morning. Just ahead of them the trees ended and a hill began. But it wasn't an ordinary hill—it was a steep mound of dirt with trees growing upon it that were mere saplings.

"This is unusual," observed Data as he trod up the side of the mound. "This is the first elevation we have seen. It is also perfectly oval. I would say someone built it."

"Built a pile of dirt?" asked Worf skeptically.

"Such things are not unknown," answered Data. "On Earth early humans built extremely complex mounds, some in the shape of serpents. They were found along the northern part of the Ohio River."

"What were they used for?" asked Deanna.

"Burial," answered the android. "To show a ruler's greatness. Because of their size and visibility, there is some speculation they were constructed to communicate with beings in the sky. If this was a natural hill, the trees would be as tall as those in the forest. They clearly are not."

"S-s-h-h," cautioned Worf. "Listen."

They held their breath—the drumming was getting louder.

"They are coming closer," said Data. "They may be coming here."

"We're too visible on this mound," said Worf, scurrying down the side of it. "Let's get back to the trees."

Data and Deanna followed him, and they crouched at the edge of the darkening forest.

"This is a good place for observation," whispered Data. "The way Turrok could smell the ocean, we can surmise that their sense of smell is highly developed, so the two of you need to remain upwind from them."

No one else spoke as slow, funereal drumming filled the clearing. In the fading light they saw a solemn procession emerge from the forest. There were two drummers in the lead, followed by six marchers who were carrying what appeared to be a wooden cage over their heads. Then came two more who were holding a rope; the rope was tied to the neck of a forlorn figure who walked alone and appeared to have his hands tied behind his back. Ten or so youngsters followed him, making a total of about twenty, and they were led by an imposing figure who stood at least a head taller than the rest and banged on a scrap of metal with a knife.

To the beat of the drums the procession climbed the mound until they reached the top, where they stood silhouetted against the red sky. The drummers stopped drumming, and the marchers set down the cage so that it was standing on end. It was impossible to see their faces, but Deanna knew that the bound prisoner was Turrok, and she also knew the tall one with the knife was Balak. The others formed a tight circle around the two of them and the cage.

With great ritual Balak held the knife over his head and intoned in Klingon, "Knife-god, giver of Death and Truth, tell us if Turrok is infected with Evil. Taste his blood and tell us. If he is innocent, let him live. If he is evil, *kill him!*"

The others cheered and grunted their approval. Then the drummers began beating a wild tattoo, and the young Klingons around the circle clapped their hands to the tempo. Balak cut the rope from Turrok's neck and hands, then grabbed the boy and thrust him into the cage, latching it after him. The big Klingon raised the knife high over his head, as if he was about to summarily execute the boy, and Deanna gasped and held her breath. But Balak plunged the knife into the side of the cage, where its deadly blade stuck fast—pointing toward the shivering figure.

The powerfully built Klingon grabbed the cage and turned it over on the ground. Then he shoved it toward the Klingon beside him, and each person in turn rolled and spun the cage, passing it from one to the other. The drums beat faster and faster, and the cage whirled around the circle with the youth falling against the knife countless times.

Worf growled and jumped to his feet, but Data restrained him. "He may already be dead," whispered the android. "We risk alienating them forever if we disturb their ritual."

Worf nodded and looked away.

Finally Balak caught the cage in his powerful arms, and the drumming and the ceremony abruptly stopped. Many hands reached forward to rip open the cage and pull the blood-smeared body out, and Deanna waited breathlessly for their pronouncement.

A girl shouted, "He lives! He lives!"

There were even louder cheers, and Turrok was lifted high into the air like a conquering hero, although he seemed to have barely enough strength to lift his arm. As the drums beat a joyous refrain twenty laughing youths carried the survivor of the test down from the mound and into the forest. Balak stood alone on the hill, retrieving his knife from the cage. He wiped it across his chest, then sniffed the air for a moment, as if something was amiss. Was it only her imagination, wondered Deanna, or did he look squarely in their direction? Finally the big Klingon sheathed his knife, grabbed the cage, and ran after his fellows.

"Balak will have to be dealt with," Data observed.

"Yes," grunted Worf angrily. "He will have to be dealt with."

"How?" murmured Deanna, shaking her head. "How will we ever get them to lay down their weapons and live peacefully?"

"To gain their confidence," said Data, "one of us could take their Test of Evil. If we assume this mound is the spiritual center of their existence, we should set up camp here and wait for them." He rose to his feet and strode toward the top of the knoll.

Deanna looked at Worf and shrugged. "I haven't got any better ideas. Have you?"

The Klingon muttered, "Yes, but they all involve smashing Balak in the mouth." He grabbed his pack

and climbed after the android, and the Betazoid
followed.

Ensign Ro looked at the tiny barred window over
the weather maps along the wall and saw that night
had fallen on this part of Selva. She had no feeling
that her work had ended, even though all the other
technicians had left their stations in the lab. The
Bajoran had spent the last hour rigging up an audio
alarm on the seismograph so that it would awaken her
if there was a sizable jump in the readings. She had
also focused two scanners on the troublesome ocean
bed and was recording every grain of sand that
shifted. Without staying awake for twenty-four hours,
that was the best she could do, and she intended to
sleep right beside her equipment on a cot she had
requisitioned from the replicator room.

She heard people walking on the floor above her in
the stillness of the prefab building, and she knew that
Gregg Calvert's personnel were standing guard at the
communications console. She also knew that the
replicator on the same floor was manned around the
clock, providing for the 212 colonists, somewhat
against their will. Those hollow footsteps were as
much company as she needed until Myra returned—
if she ever did. The girl had left after lunch to attend
classes, but she had promised to return as soon as she
could. Ro could imagine the many explanations for
her not returning, and she hoped the stifling atmosphere of New Reykjavik would change. Myra and the
other children deserved better.

The pressurized metal door whooshed open, and Ro
turned, expecting to see Myra. Instead she saw the
head of the lab, Doctor Louise Drayton. The small,
dark-haired woman strode toward her, looking as if
she wanted to chew her head off and spit out the
bumps. The formidable doctor had stayed away all

day, but Ro hadn't kidded herself into thinking she would never confront the woman again.

Drayton pointed to the cot and snapped, "What's the meaning of this?"

"It's to sleep on," answered Ro, turning her attention to the midzone scanner.

"You can't turn my lab into a flophouse!" the doctor hissed, kicking the cot and flipping it onto its side.

"Flophouse is a term I'm unfamiliar with," Ro answered dryly.

The woman sneered. "That's right—you're not human. Why did they send you here? To rub our noses in it?"

"I appreciate this lesson in colorful terran language," said Ro, "but I have work to do. Does your visit have a point?"

"Yes"—the woman frowned—"it has a point. I've been ordered to put up with you, but there isn't a helluva lot they can do to me if I don't. Still, I have a lab to run, and morale is bad enough around here as it is—so I'm going to try to get along. We just need to work out some ground rules."

"What kind of ground rules?" asked Ro.

Drayton took a deep breath to calm herself, then continued. "If you don't openly defy me and weaken my authority, I'll bend the rules to suit you. There are good reasons for not sleeping in this lab, but if you insist, I'll change the rules to allow it. I only ask that you consult me before you take action on your own."

Ro nodded. "Very well. I'll consult you, but I won't let you interfere with my mission."

The small woman smiled grimly and replied, "I won't let you interfere with mine either. Good night."

Doctor Drayton ambled slowly around the lab, checking on a few experiments and computer screens as she went. She stopped to pick up a rubber glove that had fallen on the floor and dropped it disdainfully into a trash receptacle. Ensign Ro watched the dark-haired woman until the outer door clanged shut behind her, and she wondered if this would be their only confrontation.

Deanna Troi tried to get comfortable on the sleeping pad atop the hard earth of the mound. A few meters away, Worf snored contentedly, and Data sat on his haunches, staring alternately at the stars and at the pitch-black forest. It wasn't that she was cold; her paper-thin sleeping bag had a microscopic heating element based on nanotechnology that kept her body temperature at a perfect ninety-eight degrees, even in extremities like toes and fingers. But unlike Worf, she preferred soft bedding. Had they been sleeping in the forest, it occurred to her, she could have augmented the sleeping pad with a mattress of decomposing leaves and twigs. Tomorrow night, she promised herself, she'd collect some extra bedding before it got dark, but she wasn't going to poke around in those woods now.

As if reading her mind—or, more likely, hearing her toss and turn—Data remarked, "You could return to the ship, Counselor, for your sleep period. I will alert you when the Klingons return."

"That's kind of you," Deanna replied, rolling onto her back. "But I prefer to stay here with you and Worf. If I slept in my own bed tonight, I couldn't face those lost young people. I'm having a hard time empathizing with them, and maybe this will help. What do you suppose they're doing?"

"I certainly hope they are attending to Turrok's wounds," the android answered. "I believe if his initial contact with the knife changed its angle sufficiently, subsequent wounds would be mostly superficial."

"Don't talk about it"—she shuddered—"please. I

really despair that we're going to be able to get through to them and change their way of life. Unless we abduct them, as we did with Turrok."

"That is an alternative," Data replied, "but it is preferable that sentient beings make their own decisions. Do you not agree?"

"I agree, Data. Keep reminding me of that, all right?"

"As you wish." The android nodded. "How often should I remind you?"

"Good night, Data."

"Good night, Counselor."

No one returned to the lab that night, and eventually Ensign Ro couldn't keep her eyes open or stare at readouts any longer. Thinking about the Calvert family and Doctor Drayton, the ensign made a trip to the lavatory, then stretched out on her simple cot. There had to be an interesting story behind Doctor Drayton's presence in this far-flung colony, and Ro resolved to ask Myra about it the next time she saw her.

The night was quiet, although there had been intermittent drumming that sounded far away. Even the animals in the forest and the footsteps overhead sounded unreal and far removed. Despite her fears and worries and the glaring lights of the laboratory, sleep overcame the Bajoran in due course.

She had no idea what time it was when she awoke, and she was slightly disoriented for a moment. But Ro certainly knew *what* had awakened her, as she could feel something crawling on her chest under her tunic. In her confused state she did what anybody would do and slapped at her chest to brush it off. Immediately there was a sharp, stinging pain that took her breath away, and she gasped. Now she knew she was in some kind of trouble as she carefully sat up in her cot.

Ro had never been much for proper uniform etiquette, and her collar was open as usual. Her determined calm was shattered by a deep, throbbing pain between her breasts. Alarmed, she ripped at her top, then screamed as something crawled down her stomach and bit her again.

Leaping to her feet, she shook the scraps of her top, and a jade-green creature that looked like a stick with legs tumbled to the floor. Under normal circumstances Ro would never take the life of any living thing, but she didn't want to let the giant insect get away before she could find out what it was. She stomped it with her boot just as it began to jump. With desperation she ground it into the floor.

Ro could hear footsteps pounding above her, and she knew her second scream had been loud enough to attract attention. Suddenly her thumping heart, throbbing chest pains, and the panicked footsteps overhead all melded into one giant drumbeat that pummeled her brain. The Bajoran staggered around the lab; the blood vessels inside her head felt as if they might explode, and bizarre lights and shapes assaulted her senses. She knew she was hallucinating, but she felt as though the crushed insect had wormed its way into her brain. She wasn't even aware that she was screaming.

Weird, hollow voices shouted at her, and arms grabbed her, but she struggled with these new demons. "Sickbay!" she heard someone yell—maybe it was she. Pain and lights exploded in her head and rushed down her body, and she felt she was melting and igniting simultaneously.

She knew she was dying.

Chapter Seven

RO PLUNGED UNDER the brackish green water and felt herself gasping for air. She flailed in terror as the thick liquid flowed over her and pressed against her chest—it pushed and pushed until the pain was excruciating. She held her breath and tried to kick her way out, but the water was like syrup and pulled her deeper with every desperate movement. She was going to die! It was just a matter of what would get her first—the lack of air, the chest pains, or the wispy tentacles pulling her deeper. She screamed and screamed, not thinking how strange it was to be doing that underwater, but still the sticky liquid pulled her deeper. Deeper into darkness.

Then she saw lights spinning somewhere above her, like bodies in a transporter, shifting and flowing in and out of reality. She swam desperately toward the lights until she suddenly found herself walking, then running. She had to run, because they were chasing her—giant skull-faced Cardassians! They were giant because she was a little girl again, running for her life. The gaunt creatures caught her and threw her to the ground; she screamed and kicked and cried, because this was real! This had happened before! She screwed her eyes shut as they carried her away, because she knew the nightmarish vision that was about to come next.

There he was—her compassionate father, a leader of her people—beaten, bleeding, and kneeling on the ground. Seeing her, he shook like an animal awakened from a long sleep, staggered to his feet, and yelled in rage, "No!" The Cardassians glared at him, their black eyes rimmed by bone. Then they swarmed around him and struck him down again and again. The little girl struggled and turned away, but she couldn't shut out the sickening blows. Mercifully, she felt herself collapsing again into darkness.

When she awoke, arms were still holding her. No, not arms, restraints. She was strapped to an examination table in a modern sickbay with a screenful of readouts blinking and blipping reassuringly behind her.

"Ro!" a small voice called. "You're awake!" Grinning down at her was the cheery face of Myra Calvert, and it reminded her of the girl she had once been—before she'd lived through the nightmarish visions in her memory.

"I'm awake," sighed the Bajoran, "but I seem to be strapped down. What happened?"

"You were going crazy," said Myra, clearly impressed by what she had seen. "Full-scale hallucinations. They had to strap you down, or you would've hurt yourself and probably everybody else. I've never heard anybody scream like that."

Above the girl's face hovered another familiar face, and their red hair seemed to blend in Ro's blurred vision.

"Hi." Doctor Beverly Crusher smiled. "Good to have you back."

"Am I on the *Enterprise?*" asked Ro.

"No, you're in the settlement sickbay," answered Beverly. "They know more about these mantis bites than I do. Of course, I know more about Bajoran physiology than they do. So between the two of us, we managed to pull you through."

"Do I have to stay in restraints?"

"I don't know," said Crusher. "You're lucid now, but the effects of the venom might come back. Let me ask Doctor Freleng. He's out in the hall with Captain Picard."

Beverly vanished, but her small assistant stayed by Ro's bedside. "You're lucky," remarked Myra. "You got bitten twice, and nobody's survived *two* bites from a pit mantis."

"That's what bit me?" asked Ro groggily. "A pit mantis? It was something that crawled under my shirt."

"Yeah." Myra frowned. "That was weird. We have pressurized doors around here to keep those things out. I'll have to check the cages to make sure none of our specimens escaped."

"How long have I been . . . here?"

"About six hours," answered Myra. "It's just break-fast time."

Ro wanted to ask more, but a young man she didn't know came striding up to her bedside, followed by Beverly Crusher and a grinning Captain Picard.

"I'm Doctor Freleng," said the young man, peering through a scope into her eyes. "Oh, yes, you look excellent. I'll have to take Doctor Crusher's word for it that your vital signs are what they ought to be."

"Almost," offered Beverly. "That must be quite a powerful neurotoxin."

"It is." Freleng nodded. "If we could get out to catch more of those mantises, maybe we could develop an antidote. Right now every reaction is different.

One member of a scouting party died instantaneously. But when President Oscaras was bitten he just sat around in a stupor all day, smiling blissfully. Here, I think it's safe to take off the restraints."

While the young doctor unbuckled the straps around Ro's chest and limbs Captain Picard moved closer. "Hello, Ensign," he said sympathetically. "That must have been quite an experience."

She mustered a smile. "I wouldn't care to repeat it."

Picard glanced at Freleng. "With the doctor's permission," he said, "we can take you back to the *Enterprise* to recuperate in more familiar surroundings."

Gratefully, Ensign Ro rubbed her chafed wrists. Her muscles felt sore and wrung out, as if she had been exercising all night. "Thank you, Captain," she said, "but I really have to keep track of the seismic readings."

"Commander La Forge is downstairs now," answered Picard. "After what you went through, I think you should take it easy today."

"I insist on it," added Doctor Freleng. "You'll be weak for at least twenty-four hours. You can take a little nourishment, but after that you should try to sleep. This is as good a place as any."

"Can I be Ro's nurse?" Myra asked eagerly. "Please?"

The two doctors exchanged amused glances. "I see no reason why not," answered Freleng. "There's no medication we can give her—just food and rest. I have to make a report to Doctor Drayton."

"Doctor Drayton?" asked Ro, trying to hide the curiosity in her voice. "What has she got to do with this?"

Freleng replied, "She's the colony's entomologist. She keeps a record of all serious bug bites, and the pit mantis is a special project of hers."

Ro slumped back on the bed, suddenly feeling a little sicker.

At daybreak Worf bolted out of his thermal sleeping bag. He could tell by the tingling on the hairs of his neck that something was wrong, but the forest looked serene, if somewhat eerie. A milky white fog obscured both the bottoms and the tops of the trees, making the black trunks look like the bars of some gigantic prison. In the fog the mound was like an island held captive. Data sat calmly on the slope, studying the forest with the same detachment with which he studied his console on the bridge of the *Enterprise.* A few meters away Deanna Troi slept, curled up in a tight ball.

"They're out there, aren't they?" asked Worf.

"Yes," said Data, "they have been watching us for approximately thirty-five minutes. I assume they have not developed a plan for dealing with our presence here."

"That makes us even," grumbled Worf. "How many do you think there are?"

"At present, no more than eight. But others have been steadily joining the original group that discovered us."

Worf stood, straining to see them in the shrouded forest. He finally gave up and decided he would have to take Data's word for it. "Let's hail them," he suggested.

"We must exhibit patience," the android replied. "We are in command of perhaps the only thing they value—this mound, which I believe they built. We must trade them command of this mound for their acceptance and friendship."

"So we're going to wait here until they ask us to leave?"

"Precisely," answered Data.

Worf trod to the edge of the slope and relieved himself in the cold, misty air.

"Stop!" screamed an anguished voice from the forest. A scruffy female—the same one who had brazenly touched Worf's head—stepped out of the fog and spoke in Klingon: "Do not defile our sacred place! What do you want?"

Data whispered, "That was a clever maneuver."

Nodding to Data, Worf responded to the girl in Klingon. "We want your friendship! We will remain here until you accept us as friends. As Turrok did."

There was some incomprehensible muttering and discussion. Worf could only imagine that Balak was still sleeping in his cave somewhere, and nobody was eager to awaken him. Worf was relieved that several of the older castaways still had a rudimentary command of the Klingon language. It hadn't helped much so far, but communication was crucial. Deanna Troi rolled over in her sleeping bag and was watching him.

"Is Turrok well this morning?" Worf asked the girl at the bottom of the slope.

"He lives!" she called. "The knife-god said Turrok not evil. Maybe you are not evil, but you come from flat-heads."

"Am I a flat-head?" answered Worf. "You touched my crown yesterday—I am like you. We are brothers and sisters, not enemies. Everywhere but here we live in peace and respect with humans. There is no reason to be enemies."

The girl turned and spoke to unseen youths in the forest.

"You're doing very well," Deanna whispered encouragingly to Worf. "I think we can reason with her."

"Until she pulls her knife," muttered the Klingon. He called out, "Can we sit together to discuss this? We have food!"

"I will come," said the girl, "but I not command others."

"Anyone who wants to come is welcome!" called Worf. He turned to Deanna and Data and said under his breath, "Find whatever food you can in your packs."

They began digging out protein bars, biscuits, and reconstituted food that was heated by twisting its special chemical packaging. Although he didn't normally eat, Data was carrying the bulk of their supplies, enough for two weeks under ideal circumstances. Food would be no problem, thought Worf, as long as the *Enterprise* was in orbit.

When he looked down the female and three bedraggled but brave boys were headed up the slope, their hands gripping the hilts of their crude knives. They looked wary, but their nostrils flared at the scent of unusual food, and that buried their fear and spurred them on. Data twisted a packet of cherry cobbler to mix the chemicals that would heat it, and his apparently violent action caused the girl and her companions to crouch in fear.

"There is no danger," Worf assured them. "He is only heating the food for you."

"Heating?" asked one boy.

"With food they have magic," the girl said, as if she had told them this on many occasions, without it sinking in. "They make food from air," she added.

Interesting, thought Worf, considering how close her uneducated guess was to the truth. Molecular synthesis from patterns stored in a computer could reasonably be called "making food out of air." Worf was glad to see a certain amount of native intelligence and quest for knowledge in these young Klingons, even if the trappings of civilization were gone.

Counselor Troi stepped to Worf's side and unfolded her hand to show him a comm badge. "I'd like to put this on the girl," she explained, "so she can understand me. Will you explain the universal translator to her and tell her it's not harmful—that we all wear them?"

"Of course," agreed the Klingon. Pointing to his own comm badge, Worf turned to the girl and spoke in Klingon. "We would like you to wear this as a token of friendship. It will allow you to understand all of us, and it will not harm you."

The skinny girl shrank back for a moment, but Deanna's smiling face won her over. She stood still as Deanna fastened the insignia to the inside strap of her furry garment. "Inside," said the Betazoid, "so Balak won't see it."

The girl blinked in amazement at comprehending the flat-head language for the first time.

"What do you normally eat?" asked Deanna.

The amazed youngster opened her mouth to speak but couldn't find the proper word. So she reached down and grabbed a few blades of wild grass, which she stuffed into her mouth with little enthusiasm. Then she pinched the crude fur she was wearing as if to say she had eaten its previous owner, too.

"I see," answered the Betazoid. She held out a protein bar made of nutritious fruits, nuts, and grains. "Try this."

The female Klingon edged closer, then snatched the treat from her hand. She devoured it selfishly while her three comrades made grunting sounds and looked as if they would steal it from her.

"There is sufficient to go around," said Data, handing out another batch of snack bars. They were gone in seconds, and the young Klingons were soon looking around, trying to figure out what else amid the packs and equipment was edible.

"I am Worf," the elder Klingon told the frightened guests. "What are your names?"

"Wolm," said the girl with a smile, apparently pleased that they had similar-sounding names. She pointed to her three companions. "Pojra, Krell, and Maltak." The young Klingons nodded and smiled warily as they heard their names pronounced.

Data opened the packet of cherry cobbler and distributed bites of it to the four Klingons. "You will like this," he said. "Most humanoids enjoy food that is sweet."

By the way they gulped it down, thought Worf, they enjoyed it, all right. He thought this was a good time to ask the most pertinent question: "If the colonists *gave* you food like this, would you stop attacking them?"

Wolm looked at her comrades before replying, but it was obvious they weren't going to venture an opinion. They were too busy eating and looking about nervously, waiting for something terrible to happen that would end the handouts.

"I would," said the girl warily. "But we have laws—not allow us."

Worf growled, "You have Balak, you mean."

"He is the voice of the laws," she said defensively.

"Where is Balak now?" asked Deanna.

"Seeing the goddess," Wolm answered.

"The goddess?" asked the Betazoid. "Can you tell me more about that?"

Wolm had other things on her mind. She pointed to the empty cobbler wrapper and demanded, "More of that."

Worf spotted eight more scrawny Klingons creeping out of the forest and starting up the mound. He could see them rubbing their mouths and licking their lips. As Deanna and Data rushed to dispense snacks to all of them the Klingon tapped his communicator badge.

"Worf to *Enterprise*."

"Riker here," came the concerned voice of the first officer. "Are you in any danger?"

"Only of running out of food," answered Worf. "Can you beam down fifteen full-course meals to these coordinates?"

The amusement in Riker's voice was evident as he asked, "Any particular kind?"

"I don't think it matters," said Worf. "We may need to request more food later."

There was a pause, and Riker responded, "We just relayed your request to Transporter Room Three. With all that hiking around in the fresh air you must have worked up quite an appetite."

Not appreciating the joke, Worf scowled. "Have you ever heard the proverb: 'The way to a Klingon's heart is through his stomach'?"

"No," chuckled Riker, "I hadn't heard that."

"It's true," Worf said gravely.

"Your food should be there momentarily," the commander assured him. "On a more serious note, look out for any thin, green insects about a decimeter in length. There's a type of mantis down there that's very poisonous—one of them nearly killed Ensign Ro last night. But she seems to be recovering."

"That's terrible," said Deanna Troi, overhearing. "President Oscaras warned us about the mantises, but I thought people would be safe in the village."

"Apparently not," answered Riker. "The captain is in the village, too, and you might want to contact him when you have the chance. I'll let him know you're serving breakfast down there."

"Thank you," replied Worf. "Away team out."

When the Klingon looked down he saw Wolm staring at him. The girl smiled, and he thought for a moment that she could be pretty—given a couple more years, a little fattening up, and lots of soap and water. A second later he grew angry at himself for these thoughts, until he realized that such thinking couldn't be avoided. These survivors might once have been children, but they weren't children any longer. They were on the threshold of becoming adults, and it was up to him, a cultured Betazoid, and an android to see that they became responsible Klingons instead of bloodthirsty brigands. If left on their own, they might breed an entire clan of Balaks.

Fifteen steaming plates of food materialized on the ground, which only reinforced Wolm's claim that the flat-heads made food out of thin air. That didn't keep the dozen Klingons from attacking it, and their ravenous hunger quickly turned to ravenous gluttony. They ate as though they weren't sure they would ever eat again, and they fought like dogs over scraps and bones. Disgusted at their savagery and discouraged by the enormity of the task ahead of him, Worf wandered to the other side of the mound. He watched the fog dissipate with the first rays of morning, releasing the vast forest from its prison. He was standing there when Deanna Troi strolled to his side.

"They're almost done with the food," she said. "What do you think we should do next?"

"I want to see Turrok," answered Worf, "and make sure he's recovering. After that, I would welcome suggestions."

"It's one thing to buy their loyalty with food," said Deanna. "It's another thing to earn it. What do you think of Data's idea about taking their Test of Evil?"

"Do we sink to their level," asked Worf, scowling, "or do we make them rise to ours?" He shook his head as if he didn't have an answer. "What most disturbs me is that Klingons have a propensity to behave like savages. Would Betazoids or humans be like this after spending a few years in the woods? I think not."

"You should read more Betazoid and human history," Deanna remarked. "What makes our job hard is that they have no frame of reference except for this bizarre existence they've cobbled together from a few childhood memories and a daily struggle for survival. I think you should be proud of them for the way they've survived and formed a society without any guidelines."

Worf frowned. "I'll reserve my opinion until I find out more about their society."

The peaceful morning was suddenly broken by the pounding of a lone drum, which permeated the forest like the fog. The staccato drumbeats were in code; Wolm, Pojra, Krell, Maltak, and the others waited breathlessly. Worf was impressed because it looked as if nothing would stop their voracious eating. Carrying as much food as they could grab, they began to scamper away.

Gnawing on a drumstick, Wolm started down the mound. "We must go," she said. "Balak is back."

"We will go with you," offered Worf.

"No!" she cautioned. "We tell him you here. He will want to come."

"Wolm!" called Data. "Tell Balak that I wish to take the Test of Evil to prove our sincerity."

She blinked in amazement, as if she never expected to hear anyone *offer* to take the deadly test. "I tell him," she promised. She bounded down the hill and was gone.

Worf, Deanna, and Data looked around at the remains of fifteen meals and an uncounted number of snacks and packaged foods. They began to pick up the plates, most of which had been licked clean, along with wrappers, bones, and other bits of refuse. They stacked everything in a pile, then Worf drew his phaser, cranked up the setting to eleven, and vaporized the garbage.

"Maybe we should ask Guinan to come down here," remarked Deanna.

"May I ask why?" queried Data.

Deanna smiled. "Because we seem to have opened up the first restaurant on Selva."

Worf growled, "I fail to see the humor in this situation. They need more than food."

Data cocked his head and remarked, "There is something that interests them in addition to food."

"Besides looting and killing, what?" asked Worf.

The android tapped his comm badge. "Data to *Enterprise.*"

"Riker here," came the response. "Don't tell me you need more food already."

"No," answered Data, "we need gifts. I believe the replicator is capable of producing a variety of drums and musical instruments. I would like to requisition twenty percussive instruments, such as snare drums, kettledrums, tambourines, maracas, marimbas, rattles, and gongs."

"All right." Riker laughed. "What are you going to do, form a marching band?"

"I have no doubt that would be possible given enough time," said Data, "but our immediate purpose is to make friends."

"I'll check the replicator to see how many of those instruments we have in memory," Riker promised. "You'll have them as soon as we can make them."

"Thank you, Commander," replied the android. "Data out."

Deanna Troi shook her head. "I'm not so sure the settlers are going to appreciate this."

Myra Calvert took the glass of apple juice away from her patient's lips and scolded her. "The doctor said you should sleep. Why don't you?"

Ensign Ro didn't want to tell the girl she couldn't sleep because she kept wondering if the mantis attack had been an accident. Myra was hardly the person to be burdened with such suspicions. Who could she tell? President Oscaras? Captain Picard? No matter whom she told, it was bound to create an uproar that would only further strain the relationship between the *Enterprise* crew and the colonists. Besides, she was hardly the first person to be bitten by a pit mantis; that much was clear. It was entirely possible that the insect had found its own way down her shirt, and her unfamiliarity with the life-forms of Selva had caused her to react in the worst possible way.

"Myra," asked Ro, "does the laboratory have any sort of visual system or automatic log that records who enters and exits? And at what times?"

"No," answered the girl. "Why do you ask?"

"No reason," sighed the Bajoran, slumping back in her bed. "I don't remember what happened to me, and I just wondered if there was a visual record."

Myra rolled her eyes. "Believe me, Ro, you wouldn't want to see what you went through. The only place we have any monitoring equipment is outside, on the perimeter. But it still doesn't give us enough warning."

"Let's talk about something else," said Ro, trying to sound cheerful. "Tell me about Doctor Drayton. I only met her once."

"Doctor Louise Drayton," Myra began, sounding eerily like a computer, "born in Ottawa fifty-three years ago. Achieved her doctorate in entomology at the Academy of Science on Arcturus IV. She's been all over the galaxy, and my dad was a little surprised when someone with her credentials decided to sign onto this colony. But like all of us, she gets the first crack at classifying the flora and fauna of Selva."

Ro tried to sound conversational as she asked, "Did she lose a husband, or someone close to her, in one of the attacks?"

Myra looked old beyond her years as she replied, "Ro, everyone has lost somebody close in these attacks. This is a small town. Doctor Drayton got a knife in her shoulder while she was out collecting specimens, but that didn't stop her. She'd be out there now if it wasn't forbidden. Most of the settlers wouldn't leave the compound for anything."

Ro sighed aloud. She had to remember that she was living in a colony full of scarred people, both emotionally and physically. It reminded her too much of the refugee camps where she had grown up—the camps she had escaped in order to join Starfleet. Had she met Louise Drayton two years ago instead of now—in a place racked with violence—she might have met an entirely different woman. She was also beginning to think it was foolish and paranoid to blame a bug bite on a person.

Gratefully, her reverie was broken by a pleasant, deep voice. "Can I come in?" asked Gregg Calvert from the doorway.

"Daddy!" cried Myra with delight.

Ro waved weakly to him. "Please do."

As the handsome blond man approached the bed Myra exclaimed proudly, "It was my dad who saved you!"

"Was it?" responded the Bajoran. She rewarded him with the best smile she could muster under the circumstances. "Thank you."

He shrugged, blushing in that peculiar human way that Ro found fascinating. "I didn't do anything but carry you up here."

"And look at the marks you left on him," said Myra accusingly as she pointed out three scratches on his cheek.

The ensign frowned. "Did I do that? I'm sorry."

Gregg smiled, "I haven't been scratched by a woman in a long time."

With that remark Ro didn't have to muster a smile—it came easily. The look between them lingered until Gregg glanced at the chronometer on his wrist.

"I only wanted to see how you were doing," he said. "President Oscaras has called a meeting, and I have to be there. Is Myra taking good care of you?"

"The best."

"I hope you'll be well enough to have dinner with us," said the security chief. "Until then."

"Thanks for everything," said Ro.

The tall blond man strode out of sickbay, and both females gazed after him.

Myra beamed. "I think he likes you."

"You're very lucky," said Ro, thinking about her own father and the horrible way he had died. The hallucinatory vision of it was fresh in her mind—only it wasn't just a hallucination.

She wanted to change the subject. "Yesterday," she began, "before all this commotion, you started to tell me about a theory of yours. You said it was bad news, and no one wanted to accept it."

"Oh, yeah!" exclaimed Myra. "I first wondered about this when I came across a tree out in the forest that had been knocked over by lightning. This was before we knew about the Klingons, when we could travel wherever we wanted. Anyway, this was the biggest trunk I've ever seen around here, which is probably why it got hit by lightning. Like any kid, I counted the rings on the trunk, and there were only ninety of them."

"All right," nodded Ro, failing to see the significance of this discovery.

"Don't you get it?" asked Myra. "That was the

biggest tree on this part of the planet, and it was only ninety years old. A year on Selva is actually fifty-two days longer than a year on Earth, but they're close enough for comparison. Ever since then I've been looking around to find something older than ninety years, but I haven't found it yet."

Ro sat up in bed, intrigued. "Are you saying that all that vegetation out there is only ninety years old?"

"Yes," said Myra. "Don't let the size of those trees fool you—they grow fast, up to half a meter a year. A lot of us have been trying to figure out why there isn't more diversity in both plant and animal life around here. I mean, there's plenty of stuff growing and living in the forest, but not as much as you would think. My theory is that something—or someone—wiped everything out about ninety years ago. But no one wants to hear that."

"Have you tried carbon dating and molecular analysis?" asked Ro.

"Of course," said Myra, slightly hurt. "Are you going to act like a grownup and not believe me because I'm only twelve years old?"

"No," said Ro, smiling and settling back in her bed. "I believe you. But if you're right, and that same thing happens again—"

"Yep," said the girl. "This whole colony—and the Klingons, too—we're history."

Ro lay back in her bed, staring at the corrugated ceiling and thinking. Finally she asked, "There aren't any mountains or geological formations we can study, are there?"

"Nope," answered the girl. "This whole area is like a clean slate, and that's what's scary."

"Tomorrow," said Ro, "I want to take a trip to the ocean."

"Right." The girl chuckled. "It'd be easier if you said you wanted to take a trip to Earth. Nobody is going to let us travel those twenty kilometers to the ocean."

With determination Ro said, "I'll talk to your father, President Oscaras, and Captain Picard about it. We've got the *Enterprise* in orbit—we don't have to walk there."

"Wow!" gushed Myra. "I hadn't thought about transporting there. If you promise to get some sleep, I'll go soften up my dad."

"All right," sighed Ro, suddenly feeling very weary. Myra's disturbing theory had given her something bigger to worry about than angry colonists and poisonous bugs, and that freed the part of her mind that was forcing her to stay awake. Before the girl had left her bedside, sleep overcame Ensign Ro.

Chapter Eight

WORF WATCHED DATA with a slight smile. The android banged on a tambourine a few times and held it to his ear, as if measuring its resonance. Then he tried the maracas, which appeared to have been made from genuine gourds in a time-honored tradition—before having been scanned and stored in the replicator's memory for resurrection hundreds of years later. Many of the instruments seemed to be of museum quality, except for the snare drums and kettledrums, which sparkled with brand-new chrome. All in all, thought Worf, the *Enterprise* had sent them an impressive collection of terran percussive instruments, with a set of Vulcan gongs thrown in for good measure.

Data picked up a pair of drumsticks and clacked them together. "Shall I summon the Klingons?" he asked Worf and Deanna.

"Which code will you use?" asked Worf.

"The most recent one we heard, which Balak used to summon the others. I have also assimilated the code Turrok used to announce our presence, as well as various responses and the Test of Evil rhythm. Would you like me to teach them to you?"

"Not right now," said Deanna with a smile. "Perhaps we should contact Captain Picard before we renew our acquaintance with Balak."

"Agreed," nodded Worf. He pressed his comm badge. "Worf to Captain Picard."

"Picard here," answered the familiar clipped tones. "Where are you, Lieutenant?"

"That," said Worf, "we do not know for sure. We took a rather circuitous route to get here. We're standing on a large mound that Data believes the survivors built for spiritual purposes. We witnessed a ceremony they held here last night, and we know they consider this a sacred place. This morning we fed twelve of them breakfast, and we have requisitioned drums and other musical instruments from the *Enterprise* to give to them as presents."

"It sounds like you're making progress," said Picard. "But don't hesitate to come back to the village if there's any danger. Also, watch out for a certain type of mantis."

"We heard about Ensign Ro," said Deanna. "How is she?"

"Resting. But it was touch and go."

"Captain," said the Betazoid, "we found something disturbing yesterday. A pit, which was apparently dug for the express purpose of trapping animals. Inside the pit there was a dead Klingon, badly decomposed. Would you ask President Oscaras if they've been digging pits out here to trap the Klingons?"

"He's standing right beside me," said Picard, "and I can tell by the look on his face that he doesn't know what you're talking about."

A gruff voice insisted, "We've never done any such thing! I'll bet you those savages did it themselves."

Worf grumbled under his breath, but it was Data

who responded. "They could not have dug this pit without sophisticated equipment or phasers."

"You don't know what they're capable of," muttered Oscaras. "And they've stolen a lot of stuff from us."

"I was just curious," said Deanna Troi. To Worf she looked more than curious—she looked troubled.

Picard asked, "Do you need more people or any other assistance?"

"None at the moment," said Worf. "Data has learned their drum code and is about to summon them."

"Good luck," replied Picard. "Out."

Worf heaved a sigh and turned to the android. "You might as well try it."

"I think I shall use the kettledrum," Data remarked, picking up the largest of the drums as if it were weightless. "It produces more volume and a deeper timbre."

Data set the large drum in front of him and began to beat a complex rhythm that vibrated the very earth they stood upon. Worf glanced toward the forest, wondering how this new overture would be received. By this time, he thought, the adolescents must realize that the strangers were determined to gain their trust. But would they ever realize that the rewards of friendship were greater than those of hatred? As he listened to the deafening drum Worf thought about his own family and the pain and humiliation they had suffered due to political machinations. So-called civilized Klingons fought and killed among themselves for far less worthy reasons than hunger and survival. Perhaps he was wrong to think of the castaways as savages. At least they were noble in their desires.

Then he thought of Balak, and he felt his jaw

tightening. Balak was a type of Klingon he recognized well—one who ruled through intimidation and strength. Not only that, but he had proclaimed himself the voice of the laws, which meant that to question him was to question what little order they had in their lives. It wasn't surprising that Balak was both the biggest and the oldest of the survivors—he had spent the most time with "civilized" Klingons before being uprooted by the Romulans.

Thinking of Romulans made Worf's stomach clench in knots. Whatever else he thought of Balak and the others, he had to remember they were brothers in one respect: The Romulans had ripped them from their families and turned them into orphans.

Data stopped drumming, and they heard a faraway drummer answer them in a burst of staccato tones. Then the forest was quiet, except for the cawing complaint of some bird that seemed to resent having its morning interrupted with all that pounding.

"Balak is coming," said the android.

"How do you know it's Balak?" asked Deanna.

Data replied, "Each one has a signature code. I have only just learned this, based on Balak's response. I think he is angry that I used his signature."

Worf grumbled, "As you said, we have to deal with Balak."

They waited anxiously, peering at the forest. The mysterious mound was one of the few vantage points that offered a clear view of Selva's gray sky. The sun rose over an ocean of jade treetops, but it was little more than a yellow wave rippling through the cloud cover. By noon, thought Worf, the fog would burn off. Until then the sky was shrouded in a muted haze that matched his mood.

First came the drumming—the same steady marching beat they had heard the previous sundown. Then the drummers emerged from the forest, followed by the bearers of the wicker cage that was used for the Test of Evil. There was no prisoner following them, only Turrok, supported between two larger boys who half carried him while he tried valiantly to walk. Then came Balak, followed by the rest of the tribe, which numbered about a dozen. The leader of the castaways did not looked pleased, thought Worf, as he clanged his knife on his scrap of metal. He looked exactly like a Klingon whose leadership was being challenged.

As they climbed the mound Worf and Deanna picked up the various gifts and were prepared to distribute them. Only Data seemed to sense that this process wasn't going to be as easy as it looked, and he remained immobile, poised for whatever happened. The youths gazed curiously at the strange instruments, and some even smiled; but no one broke ranks to take them from the strangers' outstretched hands.

Balak looked at the assembled instruments and scowled. In Klingon he said, "You give us food, then toys. Do you think we are children?"

"No," said Worf, "we want to be friends."

"We have *laws!*" growled the strapping teenager, as if they were the only ones in the universe who did. "You must prove yourselves worthy."

"We will," answered Data. "I am prepared to take the Test of Evil."

Balak declared, "*Each* of you must take a test." He pointed to Deanna. "She will take the Test of Finding."

Deanna shook her head and said to Data, "I can't agree to that, because I don't know what that is."

"Let us say nothing until we know more," suggested the android. Deanna nodded her agreement.

Balak glowered at Worf. "Your test will be *me.*"

This was something Worf understood, and he tried not to smile. He saw Wolm and Turrok nod encouragingly to him from the back of the pack. To make certain of Balak's intentions, he asked, "Do you mean a fight?"

Balak nodded as if he was looking forward to it.

"I won't fight you to the death," said Worf. "We're here to make friends, not kill each other."

Balak held his hands up and wiggled his fingers.

Now Worf smiled. "Bare hands, yes."

Data asked, "In what order shall we take these tests?"

"You first," said Balak. "If anyone fails, you go away. Or we will kill you."

The three strangers looked at one another as if this didn't leave them much choice. To clarify the bargain, Worf asked, "If we pass these tests, will you accept us and let us live among you?"

Balak looked somewhat shaken by that idea, but Wolm bravely proclaimed, "Yes! That is fair."

"There is no law," protested Balak.

The girl declared, "If they take test, they claim reward. It is law! When Turrok pass Test of Evil, we take him back. When I pass Test of Finding, I become a lawmaker. If Worf fights you and wins, we take him into tribe."

"He won't win," muttered Balak.

"Fair is fair," Wolm reiterated.

"All right," grumbled Balak. "Form the circle. All of you!" He glared at Worf and Deanna as if they were expected to join in the barbaric Test of Evil.

All of them formed a circle while the drummers began a slow beating. Worf saw one of the drummers eyeing the new snare drum enviously, but he apparently knew this wasn't the time to interrupt the ceremony. In one respect these Klingons were like any others, thought Worf—they loved ceremony and formality. The big Klingon grabbed the cage himself and set it upright, and Data stepped into it as if he were

John Vornholt

walking into a turbolift. The young Klingons were
quite amazed by Data's stalwart bravery.

Balak held the knife over his head and snarled,
"Knife-god, giver of Death and Truth, tell us if this
flat-head is Evil. Taste his blood and tell us. If he is
innocent, he lives. If he is evil, kill him!"

This time there was nothing haphazard about the
way he plunged the knife into the cage. He wedged it
forcefully between the strongest bars, with the blade
pointing at the android's midsection. Then he latched
the door securely while Data looked on with a total
lack of expression. Grunting with the effort, Balak
grabbed the cage between two brawny arms and
turned it over several times as Data stumbled around
inside.

The drummers beat wildly as each member of the
circle turned the cage over on the ground and shoved
it to the person beside him. Balak let the ceremony go
on until everyone was sweating and grunting from
exertion, then he grabbed the cage and—unlike the
night before—rolled it down the side of the mound.
There were gasps from the young Klingons as the cage
clattered all the way to the bottom and bounced into
the trees.

Worf noted that the cage was strong and well made.
Though damaged, it did not disintegrate as Worf
would have expected.

The Klingons looked in terror at Worf and Deanna,
certain they would react violently to the death of their
friend. But the strangers waited patiently as Data
extricated himself from the crushed cage. His uniform
was ripped to shreds, but the android was none the
worse for wear as he picked up what was left of the
receptacle and carried it up the mound.

"Quite exhilarating," he said to Balak, dropping the
lump of wicker at his feet.

"*Qapla'!*" shouted Wolm, raising her fist in the air.

Others joined in her cheer, and it was obvious the newcomers were picking up supporters. Turrok laughed out loud.

Balak shook with rage. "How did you—never mind." He turned upon Deanna. "You are next—the Test of Finding."

"I will explain it," said Wolm, stepping forward. "I can speak with Deanna."

Balak nodded reluctantly.

"Deanna," said the young female, "this is test of cleverness. Test for women. We cannot be stronger than men, but we are smarter. You must run into woods and hide. If men cannot find you, then you pass Test of Finding."

"Hide-and-seek," remarked Troi. "Very well. How much time do I have?"

"One thousand drumbeats."

The Betazoid glanced at Data, who nodded, giving his approval. It wasn't much time, thought Deanna, but she didn't need more than that. "I'm ready," she said.

In guttural language Balak spoke to the males under his command, and they stood crouched, ready to run at his order. Deanna watched him for a sign of when to begin, and he finally motioned to the lead drummer, who banged one deliberate beat. A little over a second later he banged another, and Deanna was already halfway down the mound. By the time they sounded the fifth beat she had dashed into the trees.

She ran until she was sure she was out of sight, then she listened, trying to get an approximate timing of the drumbeats. She pressed her communicator badge.

"Troi to transporter room. Lock onto my signal and beam me up immediately."

"Locking on," replied the Irish-tinged voice of Chief O'Brien. "Energizing."

As excited voices and crashing footsteps sounded

behind her Counselor Troi transported to a hiding place where the young Klingons would never think of looking. She regenerated on the platform in Transporter Room Three.

"Hello, Counselor," said Chief O'Brien. "Shall I notify Commander Riker that you're here?"

"That won't be necessary," said Deanna, stepping down from the platform. "I'm only going to be here about twenty minutes. So, how are Keiko and the baby?"

O'Brien gave her a quizzical look. "They're fine. The little one's getting her first tooth, we think. Um, aren't you supposed to be taming a bunch of murderous Klingons?"

Deanna smiled. "That's exactly what I'm doing. Well, actually I'm playing hide-and-seek, but it's all part of winning their confidence. How long have I been here?"

"About a minute," said O'Brien. "Let's see, thus far I've beamed down fifteen full-course meals and twenty musical instruments, and now you're playing hide-and-seek. Are you sure this assignment is that dangerous?"

Deanna lifted her chin. "Do you see this scratch on my neck?" she asked. "You weren't on duty yesterday when we beamed up, but this comes from two Klingons who tried to slit my throat."

"I see." O'Brien nodded, still looking confused. "Well, I'm glad they decided to play hide-and-seek instead."

"Me, too," sighed the Betazoid.

They chatted amiably for the remaining time, and Deanna bid the transporter chief good-bye to return to the planet, to the same coordinates from which she had been transported. Instead of the steady counting beat she heard calls and a rapid tattoo. She assumed that meant the test was over, and she strolled out of the forest and up the mound. The counselor noticed with satisfaction the angry expressions on the faces of Balak and several of the other males. Wolm and the females were grinning.

"She wins Test of Finding!" proclaimed Wolm. "Deanna proves herself worthy!"

Worf smiled at the Betazoid. "Well done." Then he gazed at Balak and said in Klingon, "It is time for my test."

The young Klingon dropped into a crouch and circled warily around the adult. "You use tricks," he accused.

"No tricks," grunted Worf, dropping into a wrestler's stance.

The drummers began to pound a rhythm that matched the cautious dance of the combatants, and everyone else fanned out around them. Deanna found herself holding her breath, watching intently as the brawny Klingons sized each other up and waited for an opening. Worf was slightly taller, but both humanoids were broad-shouldered and thickly muscled.

Because of the dirt and animal skins that covered him, Balak looked fiercer, and there was no denying that he was twenty years younger. Instinctively they bared their teeth at each other, and Deanna wondered if the lack of weapons really guaranteed that both would survive. She swallowed dryly, trying to content herself with the fact that Doctor Crusher and the *Enterprise* sickbay were only a call away.

Balak lunged first, grabbing Worf's tunic and trying to hurl him to the ground. Worf struck Balak's arms and face, but the swiftness of the attack had caught him off balance. The younger Klingon drove forward, his legs pumping, and Worf reeled backward, flattening young saplings as he went. The elder Klingon dropped into a crouch and dug his head into Balak's midsection, momentarily lifting the youth off the ground. They locked arms, grunting like bull moose, and Worf staggered to his full height. Grimacing, he freed one hand and jabbed Balak in the stomach, which led to a flurry of blows between the two behemoths. The drummers went wild in an ecstasy that tried to match the pummeling.

Worf drew first blood with a vicious chop to Balak's nose, and the younger Klingon bellowed in rage and boxed Worf's ears with two beefy fists. This stunned the lieutenant, who dropped to one knee, and Balak kicked him in the mouth and sent him sprawling. Worf had barely crawled to his knees before the younger Klingon sprawled on top of him and pushed his face into the dirt. Worf was in an awkward position that reminded Deanna of amateur wrestlers she had seen on Earth. He tried to move, crablike, but Balak used his considerable weight to pin him down on his chest. He wormed his hand under Worf's face and tried to tear off his nose.

Worf howled with pain, and his mouth filled with dirt as he twisted away from Balak's grasp. Deanna took a nervous step forward before realizing there was nothing she could do. She looked at Data, whose hand was poised over his communicator badge.

The younger Klingon clasped his hands over his head to finish his foe with a two-handed chop to the neck. But Worf sprang forward at the last second, tossing Balak the way a bucking bronco tosses a rider. He rolled on his back and swung his legs around, tripping the youngster. Both their faces were bloody as they staggered to their feet. Worf didn't waste a second as he charged and buried his head in Balak's stomach. Now it was the younger Klingon who was reeling backward as Worf propelled him with his pumping legs. The action was so swift that one young Klingon couldn't get out of the way, and the two hulks slammed into him; all three went tumbling over the edge of the mound.

All the way down the hill Balak and Worf lunged for each other, but neither one could get his footing. They kept rolling until they ended up in a thicket at the edge of the trees, and the third Klingon scurried out of the way. With fingers mauling each other's faces the combatants staggered to their feet. Both were bleeding from numerous cuts and panting from exertion, but they locked arms once again. Deanna gnawed on her lower lip. It was a draw, and she wanted to stop it—but she didn't know how. Neither did they.

While Balak tried again to wrestle his older foe to the ground Worf mustered a final burst of strength and drove Balak's head backward into a low-hanging tree branch. The crack of the breaking branch was louder than either of the drums, and the strapping youth stumbled forward, his eyes glassy. Worf crouched to pounce on him, but Balak was already dropping to the ground. When he collapsed the drums abruptly stopped, and the spectators stared in awe.

Worf staggered a few meters away and fell to his knees. The closest observer was the one who had tumbled down the hill with them, and he rushed to Balak's side. Worf wasn't too concerned, because he could see the youth's chest heaving. His skull was hard—he would live. Worf did wonder if each breath Balak took was as painful as his own. He had been injured often enough to know that his ribs were severely bruised, if not broken, and he didn't want to think what his face looked like. But he was still smiling as Data and Deanna knelt beside him.

"Do you need medical attention?" asked Data. His hand was poised over his comm badge.

Worf's answer came in gasps. "Don't . . . call . . . the *Enterprise.* I'll live."

"You need first aid at least," said Deanna, reaching into her pack.

Worf brushed her hand away and tried to get control of his breathing. "Leave the cuts and bruises," he whispered. "Let the others see them . . . and remember."

Wolm, Turrok, and a few others slowly approached Worf. They looked confused and uncertain, as if the entire order of their existence had been overturned.

"You beat him," Turrok muttered, as if such a thing was impossible.

"He is a worthy opponent," breathed Worf.

Up on the mound some of the Klingons knew what to do. They picked up the rattles, tambourines, and maracas and were making a racket that was enough to wake the dead. The noise did, in fact, wake Balak, who shook himself awake and rolled over, holding his bloody head.

He looked at Worf and laughed. "Good fight!"

Worf nodded, a painful grin stretching across his lumpy face. "Very good," he agreed.

When the two big Klingons laughed everyone laughed, and then the remaining Klingons picked up the new instruments and banged them for hours.

Chapter Nine

"WHAT IS THAT awful noise?" muttered Raul Oscaras. "Damn those savages—can't they ever give it a rest?"

Even Captain Picard had to admit that the noise that had been coming from the forest all afternoon— though muted by distance—was enough to jangle anyone's nerves. He didn't want to admit that his people had been responsible for introducing new instruments to the feral Klingons, so he just nodded his head in silent agreement.

This meeting of the inner circle of New Reykjavik had lasted almost all day, having begun in midmorning with a discussion of local issues. Then it had adjourned for a leisurely lunch, during which Picard had fielded questions about the *Enterprise*'s ports of call and various adventures. Normally he hated having to regale an audience with tales that seemed astounding to them but were for him day-to-day occurrences aboard a starship. But Picard felt sorry for these landlocked colonists who couldn't even live the life they had envisioned for themselves. He put his personal wishes aside and told them about the various phenomena he had witnessed since taking the helm of the *Enterprise.*

Everyone was attentive—President Oscaras, Vice-president Aryapour, Doctor Freleng, Security Chief Calvert, Communications Chief Jansing—except for an intense dark-haired woman who was introduced to him as Doctor Louise Drayton, head of the Science Department. She seemed unusually distracted and uninterested, which miffed him slightly because the others were hanging on every word. It also intrigued him, and he couldn't help but wonder what was going on in her life that was so preoccupying.

Lunch finally ended, however, and Captain Picard was getting ready to excuse himself and return to his ship when he was interrupted by the blond-haired security chief.

"One thing, sir," said Gregg Calvert. "I talked to my daughter and Ensign Ro this morning, and they would like to make a trip to the seashore tomorrow. Even though it's only twenty kilometers, hiking there is impossible while the renegades are active. But if you were willing to beam a small party aboard your ship, then to the ocean, we could accomplish the trip with a minimum of danger."

"I insist upon going with them," declared Louise Drayton. "I've been trying to organize a trip there for three months, but nobody around here has any stomach for it."

Since these were the first words the scientist had spoken the entire day, Picard looked at her with interest. Perhaps boredom was the reason for her dour expression, and he couldn't blame her for that. He also couldn't think of a good reason to refuse, and Ensign Ro must have thought the trip was important or she wouldn't have requested it.

"Very well," he answered. "Assemble your party in the square at oh-nine hundred hours tomorrow morning. But please keep it small." The captain stood with finality. "Let's hope we have an uneventful night."

The young Klingons had romped atop their mound for at least two hours, trying out all the musical instruments and all the ways the bells, bangs, and gongs could harmonize. Deanna was impressed by one facet of their society—there was no fighting over possession of the instruments. They shared them equally, although it was clear that the two boys who had been the lead drummers in the Test of Evil were by far the most gifted and energetic musicians of the group. It seemed to Deanna that they could make the chrome drums sing.

As the others danced and played Balak contented himself with trying to repair the cage damaged during Data's Test of Evil. Worf and Data sat with Turrok and examined the strange black poultices that had been applied to the wounds inflicted in his Test of Evil the previous night. They pronounced the holistic remedies effective, although they did nothing to alleviate the boy's obvious pain. Deanna mainly observed—and counted.

The tribe consisted of twenty-one individuals— fourteen males and seven females—the oldest being Balak, and the youngest being Turrok or perhaps one of the other smaller adolescents. That meant that over half of the forty-eight children stashed away on the Klingon freighter had not survived the crash landing and this rugged existence. One of the missing was undoubtedly out there in the forest, rotting at the bottom of a skillfully dug pit.

When he had finished tying the cage together Balak retrieved his knife and shouted, "We go to hutch!"

The procession quickly reformed and marched down the mound and into the trees, but the beating was subdued compared to the joyous dancing music of a few minutes earlier. It was, thought Deanna, as if entering the forest was a solemn occasion, like entering a great public hall. The mound was their place to frolic and rule; in the forest they acted as if they were still guests.

They walked over a trail that she felt certain she could remember again, unless it became too thick with debris. The wind had strengthened, and miniature cyclones were chasing leaves between the tree trunks, shooting them across the trail. A real storm could all but obliterate the path, thought Deanna, and a storm seemed to be building in the charcoal clouds that swirled above the treetops.

Without fanfare the procession came to a stop. Some of the adolescents shinnied up trees, as if going to guard posts, and they took their new instruments with them. The rest of them watched Balak expectantly. Deanna was glad to see that he was still their leader. The gracious way he had accepted them after being bested by Worf had raised him in everyone's esteem.

At the base of a tree Balak lifted a piece of hand-woven material with leaves and twigs stitched into it for camouflage. It revealed a large, dark burrow that plunged into the ground at about a seventy-degree angle. He promptly dropped to all fours and crawled in. The others looked at Worf, making it clear that he was expected to follow, but Data stepped in front of him and the dark muddy chute.

"Lieutenant," he said matter-of-factly, "my infra-red vision allows me to see better in the darkness. Would you and Counselor Troi follow me?"

"Certainly, sir," Worf agreed with obvious relief.

One by one Data and Worf ventured into the narrow opening and disappeared. Because this was only a larger variation of a chuck burrow, Deanna was forced to get on all fours and scurry like a rodent. She held her breath against the overpowering stench of rotting loam and furry roots. The roots held onto as much dirt as they could, but some still tumbled into her hair and eyes. Finally Troi closed her eyes, because there was no reason to keep them open in the pitch-black tunnel.

Hearing Worf ahead of her gave Deanna some comfort: If *he* could fit, so could she. Nevertheless, as she scraped along the dark mud in a sea of blackness Deanna fought the claustrophobic impulse to put her legs in reverse and escape that earthen tomb.

The tunnel probably only stretched ten meters or so, but the relief she felt in tumbling into a chamber where she could stand was immense. After brushing some of the dirt out of her hair she stretched her arms over her head and felt the root system there, too. They were under the trees, she thought with wonder.

"Is there no light?" asked Worf.

"Maybe some," muttered Balak, somewhere in the blackness.

She heard what sounded like a stick gently tapping, and a column of gray light swirled down the center of the chamber from a shaft that had been carved through the roots. It wasn't much, and the feeble rays of light couldn't be said to illuminate the hovel; but any light was welcome under the circumstances. Deanna looked up and saw a twisting root system that formed a material like sod—dense and vast enough to keep loose dirt and moderate rainwater at bay, she supposed.

The light shaft was operated by a wooden rod that opened a small trapdoor on the surface. That meant, thought Deanna with alarm, that these people lived and slept in blackness when they were sheltered after dark.

As her eyes adjusted to the dim light she saw Data inspecting a collection of thick clamlike shells stacked neatly against a wall. She recognized them as being similar to those in the stream they had crossed. Some of the shells were whole, and some had been broken into smaller shards for use as tools. Mixed in with the shells were silver eating utensils, thermal cups, empty equipment pouches, and other souvenirs from raids on the colonists. In another corner several drums were neatly stacked.

"What are the shells used for?" asked Data.

Balak shrugged. "Digging, eating, everything. Very useful."

Deanna saw Worf inspecting the earthy surroundings until he discovered a place where he could stand upright. The chamber wasn't very big—perhaps twelve by twelve meters—but it would house the whole tribe if they didn't mind a little togetherness, she decided.

"Is this your only hutch?" asked Worf.

"No," said Balak with a laugh. "That would be stupid. We have many—keep hidden from flat-heads."

Worf removed a tubular instrument from his jacket and showed it to Balak. "Have you ever seen a flashlight before?"

"Yes," muttered the big teenager. "But it went out. I left light-god at ocean hutch."

"Can I use mine?" asked Worf. "I can get more, for everybody."

"Yes, yes," agreed Balak. "Light indoors—I remember it! When I was little there was a place called nursery—we had light. Long time ago. Can't remember it too much." He shook his head sadly, and for a moment, thought Deanna, he looked like the little boy he must once have been.

Worf's flashlight lit up the crude mud chamber as well as someone might care to see it, thought Deanna. She saw a chuck scurry away in a far corner, and the stack of shells rattled. Deanna was suddenly depressed by the realization that this hovel was their home, and they had been fighting to protect it.

A voice broke into her thoughts: "Picard to away team."

Data answered, "Away team here."

"Data, what is your current status?" asked the captain.

"The mission is going satisfactorily," answered the android. "We have been accepted by Balak, leader of the Klingons, and we are standing with him now in one of their underground shelters."

"May we speak freely?" asked Picard.

"Yes, sir," answered Data. "Thus far only Turrok and a female named Wolm are wearing comm badges. Balak will not be able to understand us."

"I wanted to inform you that we are transporting a small party of colonists to the seashore tomorrow morning. This probably wouldn't be the time or place to mix the two parties."

"Understood," answered Data. "We will remain here and continue gaining their confidence."

"Excellent," said Picard. "Out."

Balak was staring at them curiously. "That your god? Tell you what to do?"

"Only metaphorically speaking," answered Data, "not mythologically."

The flashlight did little to warm the mud hole, and Deanna shivered and said, "I would like to sleep outside. I've been looking forward to lying on all those leaves."

"I will accompany you," said Data. To Balak he explained in Klingon, "Counselor Troi and I are going outside. Perhaps Lieutenant Worf would like to remain inside with you."

Worf looked forlornly at the grim surroundings but said only, "I may take a walk later."

Deanna noticed a second entrance, but she preferred to traverse the one she had just come down. Who knew where the other one went? Data followed politely behind her.

"Use roots to pull yourself up!" Balak called after them.

The young Klingon smiled and tapped Worf's shoulder. "Storm coming. You better off here."

"I hope so," said Worf doubtfully.

Balak looked up the light shaft to study a microscopic bit of sky. "Yes, a storm," he smiled. "Good night to see goddess."

"Goddess?" asked Worf. "You mentioned her before."

"Not now, quiet," cautioned Balak. "Goddess for me now—you later."

After giving Data and Deanna enough time to reach the surface Balak shouted up the chute, and Wolm, Turrok, and several of the others came scuffling down, their new musical instruments in tow.

Worf sat with them by the light of his flashlight and answered their questions, marveling at how intelligent they were. He described the great Klingon Empire—all the fantastic cities that encompassed dozens of planets and the noble ships that plied the space between them. Then he talked a little about the Federation and the hard-won friendship between that loosely knit body and the empire. They couldn't grasp the concept of spaceships very well, but they all remembered—in disjointed bits and images—a place that was different than the forest, a place that sounded like the cities Worf described.

Several youths came and went through the tunnel, gathering things for dinner: giant larvae, various greens, mussels, dried chuck meat, and some stale peanut butter sandwiches that were presented without comment along with everything else. Worf added a few delicacies from his pack, and the communal dinner grew to a respectable size before everyone grabbed a shell and waited to be served by Wolm. She did an astounding job of apportioning the meager helpings.

Worf noticed that at least half the tribe was topside, keeping guard, he assumed, or sleeping in other hutches. After dinner he excused himself to see his comrades, and Wolm and Turrok looked sadly after him, as if he might not return. The others were too busy inspecting the flashlight and enjoying the novelty of having light after dark.

On the surface Worf gratefully breathed cold air splashed with rain and whipped by a substantial wind. It was darker than below, but not so claustrophobic, so uncomfortably like being buried alive. He spied the light of another flashlight, lowered his head against the drizzle, and strode toward it.

Deanna was huddled in her sleeping bag under a tree trunk. She looked drenched and tired but determined to tough it out. Data stood a few meters away, peering up into dark branches; he looked thoughtful and content.

"Hello, Lieutenant," he said, not turning around. "Does it remain dry in the hutch?"

"So far," replied Worf. "Drier than up here."

Deanna shook her head. "I'm sorry," she said. "I know it's irrational, but I can't stay down there."

"Counselor, may I make a suggestion?" said Worf sympathetically. "Why don't you return to the ship and give a full report to Captain Picard? I believe that, given time, we can convince the survivors to make peace with the colonists. But there's no telling how many days it may take."

"I agree," said Data. "There is no reason for you to stay here tonight."

Deanna stood, relief spreading across her face. "You won't think I'm a—what did Wesley used to say?—a wimp?"

"No," answered Worf, "and if you don't care to go, I will. I think Captain Picard would value your assessment more than mine."

Deanna smiled. "Besides, you don't want him to see your face until it heals a bit."

Worf self-consciously touched his bruises and cleared his throat. "Please tell the captain that if we adhere to our present course of action, we may be able to persuade the survivors to accompany us to the settlement. But I don't want to request it until I know they will accept the idea."

"Counselor," added Data, "please stress to the captain that we are not in physical danger."

"I will," she promised. "Is there anything else we should tell him?"

"There is," Worf whispered. "Balak said earlier that tonight would be a good night for him to visit the goddess. When I pressed him for information, he would tell me nothing more about this goddess."

Deanna recalled something. "Wolm mentioned that he was seeing the goddess last night. But it could be something as simple as an altar or another mound."

"We should follow him," Worf declared.

"*I* should follow him," Data replied. "No offense, Lieutenant, but he may smell you, hear you, or otherwise detect your presence. In this darkness I will be able to see him clearly and follow him, and you would have difficulty. Also, I do not sleep and can watch the exit."

"Very well," grumbled Worf. "Then I'm going back down there to try to sleep. I think it would be a show of good faith."

Now it was Deanna's turn to be sympathetic. "I'll

beam down a few more flashlights for you, some food, and a couple more sleeping bags," she offered.

Worf managed a smile. "That would be useful."

Data glanced around the murky forest and declared, "My vision algorithms are adjusted for optimum performance. If Balak goes somewhere tonight, I will follow."

Worf went back down into the hutch and talked with Turrok, Wolm, and a few of the others for a short time. Then the relative peace of the burrow began to soothe him. Turrok cuddled into his chest, Wolm cuddled into his back, and he found himself drifting off to sleep. The dim flashlight shone in a far corner for some time, then was extinguished. Before slipping into oblivion Worf was aware that people were going in and out of the burrow, and he recognized an effective revolving guard system. He slept contentedly after that, his nose getting used to the dark smells of earth and unwashed bodies.

On the surface Data stood as still as one of the silent tree trunks. The wind had died down, and the rain had lessened to a misty drizzle. He knew there were guards in the trees, but their attention was on the forest itself, especially in the direction of the village. His attention was on the camouflaged flap that hid the entrance to the hutch.

The guards had long since changed their shift when the trapdoor moved and a large figure clambered out. Data knew it was Balak, but he didn't deviate from his impression of a tree. The big Klingon made some clicking noises, and his subordinates in the branches clicked back. Then he loped off into the forest. Data moved swiftly after him, shifting to absolute stillness when he thought he had attracted the attention of a guard, then stepping briskly in pursuit.

Balak was not trying to be circumspect—he was skipping along in the dark woods like a little boy heading home from school. He stopped to sniff the breeze several times, and once he whirled abruptly on his heel. But Data had stopped in time and was doing his impression of a tree trunk. Balak scrutinized the blackness for a moment, then hurried on. The android discreetly kept his distance until the Klingon stopped to make a cawing sound that shook the branches.

Both he and Data stood perfectly still, waiting. Finally a voice floated on the misty breeze, calling in Klingon, "Come! Come, my follower! Come to me!"

Data recognized the amplified female voice for what it was, but he assumed that Balak might have heard it as the haunting voice of a goddess beckoning him. The big teenager plodded through the woods after the mysterious voice, and it repeated the refrain of "Come to me!" several times. The sophisticated sound system maintained a good level over a considerable distance, noted Data.

A frosty white light bounced between the trees, and Balak crept toward it. The Klingon's cautious stance showed that he was poised for danger, and Data thought it wise to fall back a few more steps. The light could be coming from any number of sources, thought the android, but it was probably a halogen lantern covered by some sort of gauzy material. He had to admit that its ghostly dancing between the stark tree trunks was hypnotic. The lighting effect was heightened by the natural occurrence of little cyclones that tossed leaves in their wake like black confetti.

"Come forward, Balak!" said a voice that was stern and deep-throated, but very feminine.

The youth edged forward, his hands held upright as if in repentance. "I—I have returned, Goddess!" he stammered. He made whimpering sounds of obedience and fear.

"You have not done what I told you!" thundered the voice. "I told you to *kill* the flat-heads. Now you take them into your hutch!"

Data focused on the wavering light and could make out the silhouette of a feminine shape that accompanied the voice. She seemed to be swaying back and forth in the light, her presence more obscuring than enlightening. He wanted to creep closer, but Balak stood between them, and he saw no way to get around the terrified Klingon without attracting his attention.

"They passed the tests," Balak whimpered. "Test of Evil, of Finding, of Strength—each one passed! They give us food and drums—"

"Stop!" blasted the voice. A whoosh of cold air swept around him, and Data quickly realized why. The female was walking toward them and wielding a glowing whiplike weapon—a *displacer!* Some credited the displacer to the Romulans, some to the Ferengi, but they were outlawed in the Federation as a weapon of torture. All the light in the forest seemed to swirl around the sizzling snakelike coil as it flicked menacingly from side to side in front of the goddess.

Data wondered how much voltage the weapon was capable of delivering. It appeared snakelike because the tip had enough artificial intelligence to direct its own attack, if the user so wished. Wielding the displacer also changed the air pressure around it, which, Data had read, made for some exquisite tortures. He would have liked to examine the displacer more than the people in front of him, but he forced his attention back to Balak. Despite his fear, the Klingon was creeping toward the glowing goddess and her weapon of punishment.

"I'm sorry, I'm sorry!" he blubbered. "I need deliverance! Deliverance!"

The goddess moaned, "So you shall have it."

Like an avenging angel she strode through the

darkness with the lasso of light rippling over her head. She cracked the displacer in front of the cowering Klingon, and he reacted as if he'd been punched by an invisible fist. He rolled to his left and tried to stand. She gave the coil the merest flick, but it was enough to knock the air out of his stomach and send him writhing to the ground. The woman stood over him, victorious. She was wearing a long black cloak under which she appeared to be naked.

Data couldn't see much more, because the halogen lantern in the trees had been extinguished. The only light in the oppressive forest was the displacer, sizzling and curling around Balak's legs. It wrapped itself around his ankle and gave the appendage a tug. Balak yelped in pain.

"Deliverance, deliverance," he was still babbling.

"You will kill them," the woman insisted. "Or I will kill you."

"Deliverance!" he rasped, getting up to his knees.

He reached for her, not as a man reaches for a religious icon, but as a man reaches for a woman. The goddess laughed, but she didn't fight off his advances. The displacer curled around his thigh and gave him a jolt of electricity in a sensitive spot. He whimpered— with pain or pleasure, it was hard for Data to tell. The woman laughed hoarsely, then circled his neck with the glowing whip.

Still as a tree trunk, the android watched impassionately as the Klingon and the goddess dropped to the damp humus and coupled as lovers do. Then he heard a noise behind him.

Data whirled to see another young Klingon holding a long kitchen knife.

Chapter Ten

THE YOUNG KLINGON looked nervous as he waved the knife at Data, motioning him away from the couple writhing on the ground thirty meters in front of them. The android didn't fear the sharpened kitchen blade, but he didn't wish to do anything that would reveal his presence to Balak and the mysterious goddess. Certainly he had no interest in watching them engage in sex, although he was disappointed that he had to leave before getting a closer look at her displacer weapon. Data nodded in agreement and walked as quietly as possible away from the scene.

The young Klingon followed warily behind him, never sheathing his knife, and they were soon far enough away from the lovers to talk.

"I congratulate you," the android said in Klingon. "You trailed me without my knowledge."

"I saw you pass under me," said the boy in a yodeling voice that was struggling through puberty. "We leave Balak alone—when he with goddess."

"Who is the goddess?" Data queried.

131

"The goddess is"—the boy stammered—"the goddess is . . . spirit from the forest!"

"That is incorrect," said Data. "The goddess is a flesh-and-blood humanoid like yourself. She possesses a common halogen lantern and an uncommon weapon called a displacer."

"You lie!" hissed the Klingon. "She is holy. She show us how to fight flat-heads."

Data observed, "That is apparently not all she is showing you."

Data sensed the boy running at him and turned in time to catch his wrist, with the knife blade a few centimeters from his chest. The youth grimaced, groaned, and struggled to free himself, but the android held him implacably.

"You do not attack a being for merely stating the obvious," said Data. "If I turn you loose, do you promise to put your knife away? We are returning to the hutch, as you wish."

The Klingon grunted in agreement, and he soon had use of his arm again. He rubbed his wrist and glowered at the android, but he finally returned the knife to his belt.

"How long has Balak been seeing this goddess?" asked Data.

"I not know," muttered the youth. "He not talk with us about it except to say, 'The goddess say the flat-heads are coming out tomorrow.' Or she tell us where to steal knives and food."

"I see," said Data. "That is a very useful ally. Do the rest of you engage in sex, as do Balak and the goddess?"

"No!" exclaimed the boy, looking aghast at the idea, and somewhat embarrassed. If Data read humanoid reaction correctly, the thought had occurred to the young Klingon, but he was fighting the disturbing impulse of procreation. Given another year or two, Data thought, he might think differently. He had seen enough of humanoid sexuality to know it was a powerful drive.

Data asked, "Is Balak the only person from the tribe who visits the goddess in the forest?"

"Yes," said the boy, furrowing his thick brow in thought. "That not fair, is it?"

"From your perspective, no," answered Data. "What is your name?"

"Lupo," answered the boy proudly.

"Lupo," Data repeated. "I am Data. I do not wish to alarm you, but your existence in this forest is accidental. It will not last much longer. We are introducing new concepts into your society, so is the goddess, and so are the colonists, whether they wish to or not. You must be prepared to learn new ways and have your conceptions destroyed. Do you understand?"

The boy swallowed hard and shook his head, but he looked as if he understood all too well.

"Those large rodents," said Data. "Have you ever seen baby or newborn chucks?"

The boy nodded yes.

"Then you may appreciate hearing where they come from," continued the android, stepping between the black tree trunks. "Inside the female is an organ called a womb."

"Womb," the Klingon repeated, following the android. In a few seconds their voices were muted by the endless columns within the immense black cathedral.

Captain Picard rubbed his eyes and touched his cup to see if his Earl Grey tea had cooled to the point where he could drink it. He didn't want to sip the tea, he wanted to take a healthy slug.

Assembled before him in his personal quarters were Commander Data, Deanna Troi, and Lieutenant

Worf, but all eyes were riveted upon Data, who was just finishing a detailed but dispassionate account of two people making love. One of them was actually referred to as a goddess, but that didn't cheer Captain Picard any. He had been fast asleep when an urgent call had come from Worf to have a meeting with their part of the away team. Data had a story that had to be told, Worf had insisted. It certainly did, thought the captain glumly.

Deanna Troi looked every bit as amazed as the captain felt. They had already discussed the progress of the mission, and she had assured him they had been accepted and were safe among the feral Klingons. But that was before they knew that a woman was influencing these vulnerable young people. This was a development no one had foreseen.

Deanna shook her head with disbelief. "You say this goddess insisted that he kill the settlers, then she seduced him?"

"That is the order of occurrence," agreed Data. "Then another Klingon trailed me and forced me to leave at knifepoint."

"Captain," said Worf urgently, "we must determine the identity of this 'goddess.'"

The captain's lips tightened, and he cleared his throat. "Romulan," he murmured. "Data, you said her weapon was Romulan?"

The android responded, "Of possible Romulan origin. Others have attributed the displacer to the Ferengi secret police. Believed to have originated from a design called the Viper, which was used by Romulans until 2320."

"That's enough," said Picard, "to make me worried. Officially, the Romulans vacated this sector in exchange for the Klingons vacating Kapor'At, where those youngsters are from. But did they really leave?"

The captain picked up his cup and crossed to the

porthole, where he could see the steady gaze of a million suns. But the opaque clarity of space didn't help him see Romulans any more clearly.

He took a sip of tea and continued. "What we have here is a sort of de facto neutral zone between the Romulans and the Klingons. Free space, or so the Federation was led to believe. But what if the Romulans have never left? They wouldn't dare leave a ship in orbit, even cloaked, because they wouldn't be able to use their transporter with the cloaking up. Romulans, however, are not above using hidden bases, or spies."

"That is quite possible," Data agreed. "Seventy-three percent of the ocean area is unscanned and unmapped, and the terrestrial surface is scanned infrequently. A small outpost, properly shielded, might go undiscovered for years on Selva."

"The Klingons did," Deanna added.

Worf heaved his massive shoulders. "Captain," he began, "we must overcome the influence of this 'goddess.' To lessen the risks, I volunteer to stay alone."

"Lieutenant, if you were overpowered in your sleep, then what?" asked Picard. He heaved a sigh. "I have Ensign Ro in sickbay down there and the three of you living in a mud hovel. We committed ourselves to saving lives, and so we must. At oh-nine hundred I am conducting the party of colonists to the seashore via transporter. I'll appraise Ensign Ro of the situation at that time. Please consider your safety first in everything you do. Dismissed."

Worf, Deanna, and Data strode out of the captain's quarters toward the turbolift. Deanna Troi was trying to figure out how to counter the influence of this love goddess. Clearly, sex was an unstable element to unleash on the impressionable Klingons, so childlike on one hand and so violently unpredictable on the other. This mission needed time and patience, but she had the uneasy feeling that both were running out.

They stepped out of the turbolift and headed for the transporter room. Data glanced at Deanna and queried, "Are you returning to the planet with us, Counselor?"

"Yes." She smiled gamely. "I left my gear down there. I don't know what made me think I would be getting a good night's sleep tonight."

The door to the transporter room whooshed open, and they strode toward the transporter platform.

"This goddess business is maddening," grumbled Worf. "Who would goad them into attacking the settlers?"

"Unknown," answered Data, centering himself on a pad, "but the probabilities favor a spy planted among the colonists. That would be the most effective method for the Romulans to influence events on Selva without tipping their hand."

Worf nodded and muttered, "It doesn't take much to make a Romulan look human."

"That could also explain the pit we discovered," said Deanna, thinking of the decomposed Klingon at the bottom.

"Quite possibly," agreed Data. He checked to see that his companions were situated, then he nodded to the transporter operator. "Energize."

When they materialized in the woods the only things they noticed were the rapt silence and utter darkness. The trees seemed still, as if the guards and the animals had all fallen asleep. They found their pile of sleeping bags and equipment under the tree where they had left them, but the lanterns were gone. Upon seeing that, Worf drew his phaser—but his eyes hadn't adjusted from the light on the ship, and he was all but blind.

Data moved swiftly to the entrance of the hutch and stopped, his head making minute adjustments for the benefit of his short-range sensors. "We are alone," he proclaimed. "The guards who were above ground have vacated their posts. We could search the hutch, but I believe all its occupants are gone as well."

Worf knelt down at the entrance to the burrow. "Turrok!" he called. "Wolm!" No answer came from within the dark earth.

"Damn!" cursed Deanna, putting her fists on her hips.

Worf jumped to his feet, cupped his hand to his mouth, and yelled, "Balak!"

"There is no point in shouting," said Data. "They are out of earshot, or I would have picked them up on my internal sensors. Also, I do not believe Balak would answer you."

Worf muttered, "That's all right. We can track Turrok and Wolm by their comm badges."

"No, we cannot," Data corrected him. The android bent down, brushed away some damp leaves, and picked up two comm badges. One of them had a small patch of black animal fur still sticking to it.

Deanna shook her head glumly. "We should never have left the planet."

"In hindsight, that would appear to have been an error," agreed Data. "We can surmise that Balak returned with instructions from the goddess, saw that we were gone, and decided to leave the area. Had we been here, there might have been a confrontation. Leaving was by far his easiest course of action."

"Now we're back to square one," sighed Deanna. "We have to find them again."

At some distance a rapid but brief tattoo of drumbeats sounded, and Data cocked his head in that direction. "To the east," he reported, "toward the ocean."

"We'll follow you," said Worf with determination. He reached down and grabbed a big handful of their gear. Deanna and Data grabbed what was left, and the trio stepped cautiously into the immense darkness of the forest.

Ensign Ro looked out the second-floor window of sickbay and saw the first glimmerings of dawn striking the corrugated metal fence. New Reykjavik could be so beautiful, she thought to herself, but there was nothing beautiful about a wall designed to keep other people out. There was nothing beautiful about a people who had a paradise to explore yet cowered in a metal enclosure.

The trees, which loomed over the fence like giant celery stalks, were honestly beautiful, but even they had an unsettling mystery about them. Were they really no older than ninety years, as Myra thought? Ro wasn't a botanist, but she had thought it was peculiar the way they were all about the same height. That quality reminded the Bajoran of a Christmas tree farm she had seen during her training days at Starfleet Academy. Perfect trees in perfect rows—all the same height. It didn't look natural then, either.

Ro sighed, thinking she was getting too paranoid and suspicious. She had been warned about the mantis bites, so she couldn't blame anyone for that. On the good side, she had made two friends—Myra and her father, Gregg—and two friends in two days was pretty good for Ro. Only Doctor Drayton had shown any overt hostility toward her, but she was probably just another control freak who resented her moving into her lab. Ro was gradually learning to stomach those types.

She felt like someone who had slept for fifteen hours, which she had, and she was raring to do something. She wondered what time Myra and Gregg awoke. Maybe she could locate the family in time to have breakfast with them before their outing at the beach.

"I'm checking out," she told the orderly on duty. "Will you please thank Doctor Freleng and everyone for my care? I owe you all my life."

"Here, dearie," said the older lady, "button up your shirt collar so they don't crawl in there again."

"Good advice," Ro agreed, letting the woman button her collar. She was wearing the plain brown clothing of the settlers and found it extremely comfortable. Another reason to like New Reykjavik, she decided. She had thought about changing back into her Starfleet uniform, but then she remembered Guinan's words on the night before her trip to Selva: "Conquer their fear of the Other." It was time to become one of them. Nevertheless, her communicator badge was stuck securely on her breast pocket.

Ro stepped out into the bracing cold of the early morning and gripped the homespun jacket tightly around her shoulders. Her breath came in steaming spurts, intermingled with the early morning fog. She sensed rather than saw eyes peering at her from the guard stations in the corners of the compound, and she stood perfectly still to give them a good long look. Then she walked purposefully across the compound toward the square.

In the square she remembered seeing a map and directory of people's homes carved into a wooden plaque by someone who obviously had a lot of time on his hands. That was the shame of this place, she thought—they were too busy hating to conduct their lives.

She checked the directory and located the Calvert unit in the southwest corner. Walking the deserted metal streets was oddly soothing, and she could smell cooking fumes coming from a few of the apartments. The cold rows of one-story dwellings would have been oppressive if the main streets hadn't been left broad and spacious. For what reason that had been done, Ro didn't know, because walking was the only form of transportation they had in New Reykjavik. She passed only one colonist, a woman returning home from guard duty. Bleary-eyed, the woman smiled at Ro, noticing the familiar clothes, not the unfamiliar face. Ro smiled back, and the woman didn't stop to take a second look until the Bajoran was well past her.

A camera swiveled to watch her as she approached the door and pushed the buzzer. "State your business," said a synthesized voice.

"Ensign Ro to see Myra and Gregg Calvert," she replied.

"Ro!" called a friendlier voice on the intercom. It was Myra. "Wait there, we have the manual bolt on the door."

Ro waited at least a minute. When she heard the bolt snapping back and the door opening she looked down to where she expected to see Myra. Instead she found herself staring into Gregg Calvert's muscular chest, which he quickly hid by buttoning his brown shirt.

"Sorry." He smiled. "Myra wasn't as together as she thought she was. Please come in."

He stepped back and allowed her to enter an apartment that was doing its best not to look like an army barracks. But it was losing. Despite the personalized touch of some unusual plants, family photographs, and limp curtains, it looked about as homey as what it was—several metal utility shacks welded together. It reminded her of the places where the Bajora lived. The difference was, she reminded her-

140

self, that the Bajora lived in makeshift housing out of desperation—the humans lived here by choice. She didn't know for whom to feel sorrier.

"I wondered if I would be in time to have breakfast with you," she explained, trying to sound cheerful.

"Sure," he answered. "How are you feeling?"

"Terrific!" she exclaimed, stretching her arms over her head. "I feel like walking the twenty kilometers to the ocean."

"Not too many people would give you odds on getting there," Gregg said glumly. Then he forced himself to be upbeat. "This is a great favor your captain is doing us. There's only so much you can tell about an ocean by looking at sensors. I sent the *Enterprise* some coordinates of tide pools that Doctor Drayton wanted to see, so that's where we'll go."

"Does anything live in the ocean?"

"That's a matter of opinion," chirped a voice behind them. Myra bounded into the makeshift living room. "You'll see when we get there. *I* think it's alive, but Doctor Drayton's not sure. Of course, we can't agree whether it's animal or vegetable, either."

"We were planning to eat at the dining hall," Gregg told the ensign. "Is that all right?"

"Lead on," said Ro, smiling.

It was perfectly all right with Ensign Ro, but not so all right with Louise Drayton, whom they met outside the community building. She didn't say anything, but Ro felt the hostility bristling from her, just as it had the night before the mantis bite. Having survived a brush with death and the hallucinatory weirdness of her own mind, the Bajoran was in a mood to be forgiving. She had even convinced herself that the mantis bite was an accident, although she was curious to hear Doctor Drayton's opinion of it.

Ro studied the compact, dark-haired woman, think-

141

ing she didn't look her fifty-three years. Her personal dynamism made her seem youthful, spritelike, despite her tough attitude. Ro had no problem with outspoken and opinionated people, because she was one of them herself. But bigotry rankled her, because her people and family had suffered so much from it. That made it even harder to accept the fact that an intelligent woman like Doctor Drayton wouldn't give her a chance, for no apparent reason except bigotry. She resolved to make a project out of Drayton, thinking that if she could win her over, she could win over any of the colonists.

But she couldn't resist asking Drayton the foremost question on her mind. As they filed into the cafeteria line Ro remarked, "That mantis bite really gave me a scare, I can tell you. Myra tells me you're an expert on the pit mantis. I would welcome hearing anything you could tell me about it."

"I'm sorry," muttered Doctor Drayton, looking sheepish for the first time. "That bite might have been my fault. I don't know how, but one of the mantises escaped from its terrarium. They're devilishly clever, and strong. They've bitten and punched holes through several tough grades of metal screen."

Drayton averted her eyes from Ro's. "I can't help liking them," she admitted. "That's probably why I keep too many of them. They're highly venomous but, fortunately, very territorial—they never travel in swarms. I don't think a person would last long if bitten by a swarm of them. I call this species a pit mantis because it has a heat-sensitive pit above its mandible, something like a pit viper."

Drayton caught herself, as if she was talking too much. "I do apologize for your illness," she said, "although I *did* tell you the lab was unsafe for sleeping."

"How close to death was I?" asked Ro with frank curiosity.

"That was an adult female that bit you," replied Drayton, as if that meant something very serious.

"Bit her *twice!*" Myra interjected from behind them.

Drayton nodded. "Thank you, Myra. That certainly would have killed a child or a person in less than perfect health. I'm not a medical doctor, but I understand your ship's doctor did an excellent job keeping your blood pressure and temperature in acceptable ranges . . . for your species."

"That she did," agreed Gregg Calvert. "We were all impressed with Doctor Crusher."

Ro smiled, her outlook brightening by the moment. It was her turn at the food counter, and she gratefully took a large portion of hot cereal and a dish of applesauce. There were a few rude stares from the kitchen workers and other diners, but not too many. Ro felt she was making progress, at least by her own measure.

"I'm looking forward to seeing the ocean," Ro remarked as they took their seats at a family-style picnic table. "I've been studying it for days now, but that's not like seeing it with your own eyes."

Gregg chuckled. "Myra and Doctor Drayton wax rhapsodic about that ocean, but it looks sort of eerie and barren to me."

"Dad, it can't support life, but it does!" countered Myra. "That's what's so neat about it. Doctor Drayton, please pass the butter."

"Here, child," muttered Drayton. "There may be life in that ocean, or rather on top of it."

"Under it, too," said Ro. "There's some impressive seismic activity in those depths. I know it must look like a lot of brackish water to you, Gregg, but that ocean is one of Selva's main tourist attractions. That's what I feel like—a tourist. I just want to see the sights."

Everyone chuckled, even Louise Drayton. Ro took a big bite of cereal and munched it happily.

"The euphoric feeling after a bite from a pit mantis is one of its most curious aftereffects," observed Drayton. "Enjoy it while it lasts, Ensign Ro."

"I guess I do feel pretty good," said the Bajoran. She finished the rest of her food in record time. "I'm going to get seconds," she announced.

"Increased appetite," nodded Louise Drayton. "Typical."

"I'll go," said Gregg, standing quickly. "I'm hungry this morning, too, and it didn't take a bug bite. I agree with you, Ro, it'll be nice to see something besides these four walls."

"That reminds me," said Louise Drayton, wiping her mouth, "I haven't packed. How much time do we have?"

"Half an hour," answered Gregg. "Please don't bring too much, Doctor—a canteen, a tricorder, some specimen jars. We may have to move quickly. Oh, and bring your phaser." He looked pointedly at Ro. "Everyone but Myra will be armed."

That took some of the luster off the morning, and Ro thought about protesting. Then she remembered the man who'd been overpowered in the guard tower a couple nights earlier. "Set to stun," she replied.

"Ensign, you look great in our clothes," said Gregg with a sly smile. "But I'm glad you're wearing your communicator badge, in case we have to contact your ship."

"You don't take much for granted, do you?" asked Ro.

"No," said Gregg Calvert. He took her bowl. "I'll be right back."

144

Myra beamed at Ro. "He likes you."

Drayton stood brusquely and declared, "I'll join you in the square at nine o'clock." She stomped off.

Myra looked after the departed entomologist and giggled. She whispered even lower, "I think *she* likes my dad, too, but she's never done anything about it. I know he'd be surprised to hear it. I like you better, anyway."

Ro mildly scolded the girl. "You shouldn't take such an active interest in your father's personal life."

Myra shrugged. "Why not? What else is there to do around here?"

Gregg Calvert returned to the table, set down the plates, and brushed a strand of blond hair off his forehead. "I'll let you two finish breakfast," he said. "I want to make sure your ship has the right coordinates."

"You're really nervous about this, aren't you?" asked Ro.

Gregg replied, "I'm just the head of security taking his daughter, our most distinguished scientist, and a visiting Starfleet officer into the territory of savages who try to kill us on sight. Why should I be nervous?"

"We'll be fine," Ro said encouragingly. Perhaps, she mused, she judged these settlers too harshly for their apparent bigotry—she knew all too well how the constant fear of attack could to do terrible things to a community's collective psyche. The Bajoran checked to make sure that her comm badge was securely fixed to the rough fabric over her heart.

"We won't be alone," she assured him.

Five minutes before the rendezvous time Ensign Ro, Gregg and Myra Calvert, and Doctor Drayton were gathered in the town square of New Reykjavik, eagerly awaiting their molecular transport. Doctor Drayton was wearing a backpack stuffed with so much equipment that she looked ready to topple over, but her determined jaw made it obvious she was bringing whatever she wanted. She also had a Type II pistol phaser strapped to her waist. Myra carried a tricorder, and Gregg had a medikit and survival gear strapped to his back. He also wore a holstered phaser on his belt.

In contrast, Ro had decided to be a real tourist. She brought nothing but her communicator badge, personal phaser slipped unobtrusively into her pocket, and a smile. There was no piece of equipment she could carry that would tell her anything more about the tectonic plates a thousand kilometers offshore, and she had no wish to collect specimens—not if they were anything like the pit mantis. She was merely going to look at the ocean and do something very unscientific—that is, to see if she could get any impressions from it.

Ro's cheerful mood was cut short by a booming voice. "Don't hesitate to defend yourselves!" called Raul Oscaras, striding toward them across the green. "For God's sake, be careful. We can't afford to lose anyone else."

"We will," sighed Gregg Calvert, who didn't need to be reminded about the danger.

Oscaras turned to Ensign Ro and warned, "I'm holding you responsible for the fate of this party, because this trip was your idea."

"We might as well take advantage of the *Enterprise,*" she replied. Whether her good mood was an aftereffect of the mantis bite or merely relief at still being alive, Ro didn't care—she wasn't going to let anyone bring her down, especially not the blustery president of New Reykjavik.

"Just watch yourselves," said Oscaras. "You have my permission to leave."

Ro shook her head in amazement at the self-importance of the man but said nothing. She was relieved when a familiar voice sounded over her communicator:

"Captain Picard to Ensign Ro."

She tapped the badge and answered, "Ro here."

"How many in your party?" asked the captain.

"Four, counting myself."

"Then perhaps I'll join you," said Captain Picard. "Are you ready to beam aboard?"

"Yes," she said quickly.

Their bodies dematerialized into swirls of glittering molecules.

Chapter Eleven

ENSIGN RO, Myra and Gregg Calvert, and Doctor Drayton rematerialized in Transporter Room Three aboard the *Enterprise.* They were met by Chief O'Brien and Captain Picard, who was dressed to travel in a warm-looking suede jacket. He welcomed them with a smile.

"Wow!" said Myra, gaping at a transporter facility the crew of the Enterprise took for granted. "Can we look around?"

Captain Picard stepped jauntily aboard the platform. "Perhaps later," he replied. "At the moment most of the crew is performing diagnostic tests and maintenance."

"Can we get on to the ocean?" asked Louise Drayton impatiently. "I don't want to waste a second."

"Very well," said Picard, centering himself on a transporter pad. "Chief O'Brien, you have the coordinates."

The chief nodded. "Locked in. If you want to come back quickly, don't hesitate to call."

"We shan't," answered Picard. "Energize."

A dull hum suffused the room, and the five people in the chamber evaporated into shafts of light.

They materialized on a black beach with copper-colored waves washing ashore at a leisurely pace. The polished ebony pebbles crunched loudly under his feet as Captain Picard took a few hesitant steps along the beach. A wave splashed ashore and dumped some reddish scum atop Picard's boot; the substance instantly coalesced, like mercury, clinging to itself. It slid off the toe of his boot into the coarse black sand, leaving a gray trail where the black shoe polish had been.

"Hey!" exclaimed Picard, jumping back in alarm.

"Oh, yes," said Doctor Drayton, "the sea foam is acidic. Don't let it get on you."

"Also alive and sentient!" yelled Myra, jogging down the beach toward an archway of black rock that jutted from the forest and disappeared into the churning sea, forming a natural bridge between the two elements.

"Myra! Wait for the rest of us!" called Gregg like a worried parent. He trod after her and was quickly followed by Ensign Ro.

Drayton shook her head at Picard, muttering, "That child. She thinks the pond scum you see on the waves is sentient. I will admit our tests show it may have a hive mind, like bees and ants. But how much thinking it does is open to debate."

"What do you think?" asked Picard.

"I think it's a remarkable organism," answered Drayton, "and we need to camp out here for a year to study it. We have quite a world here, and we don't know one fifth of what there is to know about it. Come along to the tide pools, and you will see for yourself."

They trod along the beach toward the immense, jagged archway, and Picard tried to reconcile colors that seemed in the wrong places: a black beach and forest, a copper-red sea, and a sickly green sky. The only healthy green was at the very tops of the trees, and the trees seemed to be slinking back from the ocean, as if they knew its waters were deadly. It was peculiar to see the lazy red waves washing ashore to deposit clumps of mysterious sea life that oozed into the black pebbles as quickly as they could. Picard glanced at the white patch on his boot, now bleached bone white.

They stepped under an ebony archway that had been carved by waves from solid black rock that must have been the same material as the beach. Even now it crumbled away over their heads, a victim of the higher splashes of acidic sea foam, and Picard dashed under it. He saw Ro and the Calverts gathered around a few shallow pools that had been carved from a solid shelf of ebony rock. With a stick Myra was poking at the sea foam that had been trapped there when the tide rushed out.

The foam contracted into a floating lump when she put the stick near it. If she actually touched the substance with the stick it struck back, splashing and oozing and melting away bark.

"It's got to be animal," she said to Doctor Drayton. "Plants don't act like that."

"Ever seen a Venus flytrap?" scoffed Drayton. "There are many plants that recoil and react to stimuli."

"It's more like sea anemone," countered Myra. "And that's classified as an animal. If it's intelligent in this small amount, what's it like when a big glob of it gets together?"

"Depends," answered Drayton.

While they argued the point Picard glanced at the other members of the party. Gregg Calvert was alert, surveying the jungle, his hand close to his holster. He didn't seem to be enjoying the outing at all, but he was doing it for his daughter. Ro was wide-eyed, taking in the unique flora and fauna. She did not seem herself, thought Picard, but she didn't appear ill. He decided it was time to fill her in on all that had transpired.

Picard ambled to Ro's side and remarked, "This black rock is volcanic, isn't it?"

"Yes," she answered. "Raw molten lava from the belly of this planet. Isn't it magnificent?"

"Very lovely." Picard frowned and lowered his voice. "Ensign, while you were sleeping off your unfortunate insect bite Commander Data witnessed something very odd. Balak, the leader of the Klingons, went to see a goddess in the woods, and he had sex with her."

That got Ro's full attention, and she blinked at the captain. "Are you speaking in the metaphysical sense?" she asked.

"Not at all," replied Picard. "This was a real woman in every sense, but she was passing herself off as a goddess in order to influence these young Klingons. You must be on the lookout for this woman —she could be one of the colonists."

Instinctively Ro looked away from the captain's hawklike features and peered at Doctor Drayton. The doctor was peering back, an enigmatic smile on her face.

"Captain Picard," said Drayton, rising and taking his arm, "let me show you some amazing insects that live in this sand."

"They can live here despite that acidic sea foam?" asked Picard.

"They have adapted," she explained. "They are beetles that have developed a calcium shell. Too much acid and they suffocate, but the sea foam seems to slide around them. It does not attack. There may be a symbiotic relationship, as the beetles finish specks of food the acid can't and keep the beach clean."

While Drayton commandeered the captain and Myra made notes on her tricorder about the sudsy creature in the tide pools, Ro stared at the ocean. It looked like an endless pool of blood sloshing back and forth in a steamy cauldron. The waves performed a mute dance under a somber sky—no birds flew over them, nor did fish leap from one to the other.

Ro was not one given to fits of imagination, but she could almost envision the great slabs of crust on the ocean bottom, all being forced upward by seething molten lava. This sea was dead because it was fighting a losing battle against underwater continents that wanted supremacy over Selva. It was a very young planet, indeed.

She turned back to look at Gregg Calvert and his joyous daughter. Ro couldn't help but wonder if anyone—Klingon or human—should be on this planet. It obviously hadn't come close to developing any sort of high-level life on its own. The species she had encountered, like the pit mantis and the sea scum, were extremely dangerous. The amount of habitable land was small, although destined to get larger. It might be a pretty nice place, she thought, if you could come back in a couple million years.

She looked back at the sea, wondering if it had really lost the war already. Perhaps Selva would develop into an aquatic planet, and the sea foam would evolve into a sentient being, not just the far-flung appendages of a hive mind. That would mean, she thought abruptly, that the land masses in existence now would be flooded. It could happen, given the forces at work—great floods were part of the creation mythology of many races.

Ensign Ro's thoughts were abruptly cut short by a

horrible screeching sound from the forest, and she turned around to see a scrawny young Klingon running toward them. Another lithe figure bounded after him, but when he saw the settlers he dashed back into the obscurity of the forest. The first ragged Klingon rushed onward, staggering as he came, and Gregg Calvert drew his phaser.

"Hold your fire!" ordered Picard. "There's only one, and he's unarmed."

But Picard talked to the wrong colonist, because Louise Drayton calmly drew her phaser and took dead aim. Before she could shoot, Ensign Ro flung a sinewy arm into her face and blocked her vision. She grabbed the phaser with her other hand and pulled it out of the doctor's grasp.

"What are you doing?" shrieked Drayton.

"The captain said not to shoot," snapped Ro. On impulse she checked the doctor's phaser. It was set to kill. She reset it to light stun.

"When we get back," she told Drayton coldly, "I'll show you how to set these things for stun."

Louise Drayton glared at her for a moment, then looked away.

The young Klingon finally realized he was no longer being chased, and he slumped to the black sand, breathing heavily. His exhaustion didn't seem nearly as bad as the deep cuts and gashes that covered his emaciated body. Ro and Picard rushed toward him while the colonists hung back.

"Turrok!" said the captain, recognizing the boy as he got closer. Kneeling down to put his arm around Turrok's shoulders, Picard was relieved to see that most of the gashes and wounds were healing and not as fresh as they looked from a distance.

Ro drew her phaser and stood guard over them, glancing both at the forest and behind her at the settlers, not sure where trouble would come first.

"You must go," gasped Turrok in Klingon. "Leave now. *They* are in the forest."

"How many?" asked Picard in Klingon.

"All," rasped Turrok. "Balak says to attack . . . and kill."

Ro shifted uneasily. "I see more of them, sir. At the edge of the forest."

Picard didn't wait to see them. He tapped his comm badge and announced, "Picard to transporter room. Five to beam up." He glanced at Turrok. "Make that six."

O'Brien's response was drowned out by a shriek from the forest, and about a dozen young Klingons rushed toward them, wielding knives of various lengths. Ro, Picard, and Turrok were much closer to the mob than the Calverts, and the strapping youth in the lead was upon them in seconds. Ro aimed and fired a dazzling beam that spun the big Klingon around and dropped him to the ground at their feet.

"Energize!" Picard shouted.

From the forest Wolm could see the swirling lights that engulfed the humans and whisked them away to their magic land, that mysterious thing they called a "ship." Her comrades just stopped and stared at the strange apparitions. Then she saw Balak lying unconscious on the black beach. Wolm touched her swollen cheek where Balak had hit her the night before after stealing her pretty badge. Then she drew her knife.

The lithe Klingon dashed between the others before they even had a chance to see her. She crouched over Balak's stunned body, gripped her knife in both hands, and plunged it deep into his chest. The big Klingon gave an involuntary gasp and went to sleep forever as blood gushed over the hilt of the knife and Wolm's fist.

"Wolm!" screamed a large boy named Maltz. He grabbed the girl and tossed her away from the body.

The other warriors, Balak's closest allies and henchmen, just stared at the girl and their dead leader, unbelieving and uncomprehending. Maltz bent down and shook Balak's limp shoulders, calling his name, but he could see the waterfall of blood tumbling over his ribs, seeping into the black pebbles of the beach. Balak was no more. The younger members of the tribe stumbled out of the forest, looking numb and confused. The shreds of order that were left in their society had suddenly vanished.

Wolm crawled back to the body and retrieved her weapon. She stood and shook the knife over the fallen leader. "He had to die!" she proclaimed. "He wanted to kill flat-heads and never make peace. That is not way to live! We cannot kill and kill and kill. They have much to offer, and they give it freely. We will learn to fly ships, make food out of air, and change into stars!"

Maltz snarled at her, "You will take Test of Truth!"

Wolm stood defiantly and brushed back her scraggly hair. "I will take it," she declared. "But you know I am true."

"The goddess will be angry," warned another.

"Let goddess punish me!" snapped the female. "I never see goddess. No one sees goddess but Balak."

"I saw her," said one young Klingon. "Last night. What if we not see her again?"

Wolm crossed her scrawny arms and said determinedly, "Then we make our own decisions."

Chapter Twelve

Myra Calvert got a brief tour of the *Enterprise* after all, with Geordi trying to keep up with her as Captain Picard, Ensign Ro, Gregg Calvert, and Doctor Drayton assembled in sickbay. Turrok lay on the examination table, and Doctor Crusher cleaned and sealed some of the wounds that hadn't healed properly. Captain Picard stood with the others at a respectful distance, waiting to ask questions.

"Captain," said Gregg Calvert, "can you find out how they knew where we were going to be? Sometimes I think they must be psychic."

Picard held up his hand, demanding patience. "Turrok saved our lives by warning us," he explained. "At least he prevented another tragic incident. How is he, Beverly?"

The doctor scowled. "Considerably worse for wear than when he left here a few days ago. As you can see, he's been stabbed numerous times, beaten up, and apparently marched to exhaustion. If you want to question him, do it gently. He's mildly sedated, so you may have to repeat your questions." Crusher looked pointedly at Gregg Calvert and Louise Drayton. "Don't say or do anything that would upset him."

"We won't," said Gregg. "I just want to understand how they knew."

Picard leaned over the boy and placed a comm badge on the bandages that covered his thin chest. Turrok, who had been gazing at the ceiling, took a second to focus on the captain. "Captain," he said with a sigh of relief.

"Please rest," said Picard with a sympathetic smile. "I want to thank you for saving our lives."

"Balak," murmured the young Klingon, shaking his head. "He was wrong. Worf, Troi, and Data—they enter our hutch. They join with us. Wolm and I are so happy—killing was over. Then Balak go to see the goddess." Turrok squirmed on the table, and Captain Picard gently touched his shoulder.

"Don't upset yourself," said Picard. "You're safe here. We're all safe."

"Who is this Balak?" asked Gregg Calvert.

"Their leader," said Louise Drayton. "Let him go on."

"What happened after Balak saw the goddess?" asked Picard.

"Before he go we were friends," said Turrok. "When he come back he want to kill flat-heads again. He said he knew where they would be in the morning."

Gregg interjected, "The goddess told him that?"

Turrok nodded. "Goddess right before. And Worf, Troi, and Data were gone. We could not talk to Balak—he dragged us out of hutch and hit us. Took badges from me and Wolm. We walk all night to get there—to the rainbow rock and little pools."

"Damn!" cursed Gregg. "They were tipped off!"

Beverly Crusher shot him a glare, and Picard gently patted the boy's shoulder. "You got away from them and warned us?" he asked.

Turrok nodded, and he seemed to be fighting back tears. It took a magnificent act of courage, thought Picard, to rebel against the only authority he had ever known in order to prevent more bloodshed.

"You rest now," Picard told the adolescent. "Worf, Troi, and Data will find your friends and make peace again."

When Picard pulled his hand away Turrok gripped his sleeve urgently. "Captain?" he asked.

"Yes."

"Can see forest on your ship?"

"Forest?" asked Picard, looking quizzically at Beverly.

"The holodeck," she offered.

"Certainly," agreed the captain with a smile. "I'm sure Doctor Crusher can find someone to take you there."

Worf prowled the top of the mound impatiently, keeping an eye on the forest that surrounded the island of dirt. Deanna Troi knelt at the far end of the mound, taking an inventory of their foodstuffs and supplies. Data was prowling the forest, keeping his sensors open for the Klingons.

The night before had been a lost cause, thought Worf. After an hour of tromping through the pitch-black forest to locate the source of the intermittent drumbeats they heard, they had decided on another course of action. The youths would return to their sacred mound at some point, and Data was certain he could find its location.

So they had rested for a couple hours until light trickled through the thick leaves, then set out for the mound, which was swiftly becoming their base of operations. The inactivity was frustrating to Worf, but even Data agreed that it was more logical to let the Klingons come to them than to wander around the vast forest looking for them.

Worf saw something move among the tree trunks, and he stopped to peer into the shadowy cathedral under the vast canopy of leaves. Between the row of trees a figure was moving so fluidly—yet so perfectly upright—that it could only be Data. Seconds later the android stepped from the forest and strode up the mound. Worf relaxed, and Deanna Troi rose to her feet.

"They are coming," said Data. He pointed behind him. "They are not traveling through the trees as they often do during daylight, but they are marching slowly, talking. I heard their voices before I sensed them."

"When will they be here?" asked Deanna.

"Estimated time of arrival," said Data, "is sixteen point five minutes, given their current pace."

"What is our plan?" asked the Betazoid.

"The way to a Klingon's heart is through his stomach," reiterated Worf. "We should call the *Enterprise* and put in an order for lunch—for thirty."

Deanna nodded. "I have some requisitions to make, anyway," she said. "I'll order the food and tell them to keep it waiting for our signal."

"Very well," said Data. "But I must suggest, after what I saw last night, that they may try to attack and kill us."

Worf turned to Deanna. "Have the transporter room stand by. If you call them, it is to send the food. If I call them, it's to beam us up immediately."

Captain Picard stood in the turbolift with Ensign Ro, Gregg Calvert, and Doctor Drayton. Geordi was meeting them in the transporter room with Myra, and the small party was beaming back to New Reykjavik. They had seen the beach, as they had set out to do, but they had seen things they didn't want to see. Picard was both encouraged and discouraged by the morning's events. On one hand, they had obviously won over Turrok, who risked his life and his whole existence to warn them. On the other hand, without the warning, they would have been cut to pieces by Balak and his charging warriors. Picard was concerned that both the colonists and the Klingons had to be won over one-at-a-time, and he wondered if they would have the time to do that.

Gregg Calvert was still shaking his head over Turrok's revelation. "Never," he muttered, "in my wildest nightmares did I think there was a spy—a traitor!—among the colonists."

"How can you be so sure it's one of the colonists?" asked Picard. "We feel a hidden Romulan base is also a possibility."

"Because this goddess *knew* where we were going to be this morning," snapped Gregg. "Either the goddess is a colonist, or someone from the colony is in contact with the hidden base. Either way, there's a spy in our midst. This explains how the Klingons knew our weaknesses, and where our parties were going to be. Thank god she didn't give them phasers."

"That would have tipped you off," said Ro. "You would have never found out about this if Worf and our people hadn't befriended them."

Gregg nodded resolutely and declared, "You have an ally now, Captain, I can tell you. We must make friends with as many of the Klingons as we can, however we can."

The turbolift door whooshed open, and Captain Picard led the way. "I wish *you* were in charge of New Reykjavik instead of Raul Oscaras," remarked Picard. "But do what you can to stop the violence."

Calvert nodded. "I'll try at least as hard as that poor boy Turrok. And to think we had him chained to a wall only a few days ago."

"The Golden Rule remains the best guidance in these matters," said Picard. "Do unto others as you would have them do unto you."

"Daddy!" cried Myra Calvert as the door to the transporter room opened. She and Geordi were waiting inside.

"We had a great tour," said Myra, grinning. "Although I told them they should be raising some fresh vegetables, because the replicator food just doesn't cut it. There are some important enzymes missing."

Geordi laughed. "If you ever send this child to Starfleet Academy, will you please let us know, so that we can arrange a transfer when she graduates?"

"I will," answered Gregg Calvert, hugging his daughter. He told her somberly, "I've learned some things, too."

"Riker to Picard," came a concerned voice.

The captain tapped his comm badge. "What is it, Number One?"

"Admiral Bryant wishes to speak with you. He says it's urgent."

Picard furrowed his brow. "Put him through."

"Captain Picard," said an authoritative voice. "Why aren't you on visual?"

"I'm down in Transporter Room Three," answered the captain, "with some visitors from Selva. If we need a secured channel, I can be in my ready room in a few moments."

"No, this concerns them, too," answered the admiral. "I hate to do this, but I'm going to have to pull you away from Selva for another mission. I'm sure you know about the war between the Aretians and the Pargites over the Aretian solar system. We've had a diplomatic team there for months, and we've finally achieved a breakthrough—they've agreed to let *us* chart the solar system and divide it equitably. We have to move quickly before this agreement falls apart."

Captain Picard cleared his throat uncomfortably and replied, "This is a rather tense time in our current mission. Is there another ship that could do the charting?"

"You're the closest ship," answered Admiral Bryant, "and both parties have faith in the reputation of the *Enterprise*. At warp speed the Aretian system is only six hours away from your present position, and I've promised you will be there in ten."

"Yes, sir," Picard said firmly. "Do I have complete autonomy with regard to the charting procedure?"

"Complete autonomy. You'll draw up the boundaries, and they've agreed to abide by them. There are several disputed moons and asteroids, and I'll have the background material sent to you. Obviously, you can return to Selva as soon as possible. I leave it up to you whether you want to leave personnel on Selva while you're gone. Not to belittle the two hundred or so people on Selva, but billions of lives are at stake in the Aretian system."

Picard nodded resolutely. "I understand perfectly, Admiral. We'll be there in ten hours."

"The conference is taking place at the Polar Auditorium on Pargite. Bryant out."

Louise Drayton scoffed, "So the *Enterprise* is leaving in four hours? That just about shows the depth of your commitment."

Picard stiffened to attention and declared, "You are wrong, Doctor Drayton. We are committed to peace wherever we go, but the *Enterprise* is always a visitor, an outsider, and we cannot instill values that don't exist. Everyone can think of reasons to hate and spill blood, but only a few can think of reasons to make peace. If you and those poor castaways want to kill each other, we can't stop you. *You* have to be committed to ending the bloodshed."

"We understand perfectly," said Gregg Calvert, lifting his little girl in his brawny arms. "I'm only one person, but I swear I'm going to do everything I can to bring peace to my world."

Louise Drayton followed them onto the platform, averting her eyes from the gaze of Ensign Ro. The Bajoran was deeply disturbed about Drayton's argument with the captain—the woman almost seemed determined to cause trouble. The ensign shook her head and joined the others on the platform, reluctant to be leaving the *Enterprise.* She had a premonition that something terrible was about to happen. All signs were pointing that way.

Worf finally heard the slow drumbeat throbbing in the forest. Then the voices, most of them angry. The procession wound slowly through the stark tree trunks, a single line of mourners led by the drummers and their hollow logs. In the center of the line walked six Klingons close together, holding Balak's body over their head; they were followed by the last members of the tribe, who seemed to be arguing about something.

The big Klingon stared in amazement, along with Deanna Troi. He hadn't expected a funeral procession, and he strained to see who was being carried in the upraised arms.

"It is Balak," said Data. "He appears to be dead."

The procession was headed their way, and they had already been spotted. Wary eyes darted in their direction, and Worf motioned his comrades off the mound to give them their holy place. Wolm and some of the older survivors were arguing at the rear, but they took on a respectful silence upon seeing Worf, Data, and

Deanna. The crew members stood at the bottom of the mound as the youngsters struggled to carry Balak's limp body up the incline. When they started to drop the heavy burden Worf sprinted up the hill and grabbed Balak by the shoulders. With the big Klingon's aid they carried the dead sixteen-year-old to the top of the mound.

"Go now," Maltz snarled at Worf.

Worf looked at the youngster, unable to decide what to do or say that would help to express his feelings and close the gap between them.

"Go now!" yelled Maltz.

Then Wolm turned to him, and he saw that one side of her face was horribly bruised. She whispered under her breath, "Go, Worf. All will be well."

Worf nodded. He reached into his jacket pocket and produced a handful of communicator badges, which he set reverently on the moist earth. "These are for you," he said. Wolm mustered a slight smile.

When Worf jogged down the hill to join Deanna and Data the android informed him, "Captain Picard has requested that we return to the *Enterprise*. This would appear to be a good time to leave them alone."

The lieutenant nodded and tapped his communicator badge. "Three to beam up."

Two minutes later the three members of the away team were standing in Captain Picard's ready room. Also in attendance was Will Riker, who was being briefed on the new mission along with recent events on Selva. Like the others, Deanna listened quietly as Picard outlined the situation in the Aretian system. Then she listened as Data related in detail their activities since transporting back to the planet the night before. The account ended at the funeral procession for Balak, about whose death they knew nothing.

The captain sighed troubledly and asked the android, "How would you characterize your progress with the Klingons?"

"Satisfactory," answered Data. "Although unfortunate, the death of Balak will probably work to our advantage."

"I see," muttered Picard. "I still don't feel right about leaving you on Selva while we're surveying the Aretian system. President Oscaras will not guarantee your safety, and I don't think he could even if he wanted to. Can you bid them farewell temporarily without endangering the mission?"

Deanna could tell that both Worf and Data were considering their responses, but she couldn't help but to blurt out, "Captain, I believe the progress we have made needs continued reinforcement. To leave now would be a mistake unless there is a clear danger. And I don't believe any of us feel threatened."

"Thank you, Counselor." Picard frowned. "That only complicates the situation. I'm saying that I don't trust *either* of the parties down there, and that's why I'm concerned. The Aretian system is six hours away, so the earliest we can return is in twelve hours. Unless you use the colonists' subspace radio system, you'll be out of contact with the ship."

Worf replied, "We understand that, Captain. Still, we do not want to leave when we are so close to solving the problem."

The captain slapped the arms of his chair and declared, "Then you'll remain on Selva. The *Enterprise* leaves orbit at fifteen hundred for the Aretian system. Once there, I will propose leaving Commander Riker, La Forge, and several shuttlecraft to do the actual charting while we return here. That's the only way we can possibly be in two places at once."

Deanna smiled at Worf and found the big Klingon smiling back.

"Won't we need Counselor Troi on the diplomatic mission?" asked Riker.

"I think not," answered the captain. "The Pargites and Aretians are ready for peace, providing their solar system can be divided in a fair and equitable manner. Ensign Ro should stay as well." He looked squarely at the dispassionate android. "Data, I'm only leaving four crew members on Selva, but they aren't four crew members I would care to lose. I'm counting on you to make the safety of the away team your prime consideration."

"Understood, Captain."

Ensign Ro sat stiffly in the guest chair in President Oscaras's office while Gregg Calvert paced the cramped enclosure from the bookshelf to the tiny window. Outside the window a crew of construction workers was welding together another galvanized corrugated rabbit warren. Raul Oscaras was self-importantly directing the work while Gregg Calvert fumed. He had requested a meeting at least an hour ago and had been kept waiting ever since. Ensign Ro stayed with him because she wanted to see how Oscaras would respond to calls for peace from his own security chief.

Finally the president swaggered into his office, huffing and puffing and wiping sweat from the back of his neck with a rag. He collapsed into his overstuffed executive chair.

"Okay, Calvert, you have my undivided attention," he said with a sigh. "What's so important?"

"Only two things," answered the tall blond man, fighting to keep his anger in check. "Today I found out we have a spy in our midst, someone who's been secretly meeting with the Klingons and giving them information about our defenses and our movements."

Oscaras responded with a booming laugh. "That's

preposterous!" he said. "Nobody would dare venture out there by himself. And what would be the point of it? He would be signing his own death certificate."

Gregg leaned across the bearded man's desk. "As to the point of it, I don't know," he admitted. "But the spy is not just taking a stroll out there—*she* is masquerading as a goddess, using a halogen lantern and some kind of Romulan whip. She had sex with the leader of the Klingons."

"Please!" scoffed the president. "You've been reading too many Gothic romances. A person from this community—a woman, you say—goes out alone disguised as a Romulan goddess? She befriends the Klingons, has sex with them, and tells them what we're doing?"

"More than that," said Calvert. "According to an eyewitness from the *Enterprise,* she encouraged them to attack us."

"Again, to what purpose?" growled Oscaras, the humor fading from his chubby face. "How did she get outside, past the guards? And why would somebody arrange an attack on her own friends and neighbors?"

"I don't know," muttered Gregg. "But take this morning as an example. We were beamed to a specific place on the beach, twenty kilometers from here, and we weren't there fifteen minutes before we were attacked. We weren't making any noise or doing anything to draw their attention. How did they know we were there? Don't tell me they were just in the neighborhood!"

Oscaras glanced suspiciously at Ro. "Well, members of the *Enterprise* crew are with the Klingons, and we did send the coordinates to the *Enterprise* well in advance. That's at least one other explanation."

"But the same thing has happened time and time again!" Gregg protested. "Before the *Enterprise* got here."

"Save your breath, Gregg," said Ro, standing. "President Oscaras isn't interested in the roots of this problem or its solution. He wants to keep the hatred going so that he can maintain a dictatorship over a terrified community."

The burly man nearly jumped over his desk, he was so angry. He pointed a chubby finger at Ro and warned her, "I don't need any advice from a Bajoran. You don't even have a home to protect. I asked for help from Starfleet, and all I get are a bunch of nonhumans who want to make friends with the savages and camp out in the woods. Ask any member of this community, and he'll tell you exactly what we need to solve this problem—a couple hundred armed men and the determination to hunt down every last one of those heathens!"

"I don't believe that's the solution anymore," said Gregg softly.

"Okay," growled Oscaras, "if you've got a better solution, I'd be willing to hear it. But if it's a good idea, you should've told me months ago."

"It is a good idea," answered Gregg, "but we weren't ready for it months ago. We should make friends with the Klingons, as the *Enterprise* is trying to do."

Oscaras looked as if he was going to turn purple with rage, and his eyes shifted accusingly from Gregg Calvert to Ensign Ro. "She turned your head, didn't she?" he sneered. "Not a bad-looking woman, despite those things on her head. In some respects I don't blame you, Calvert. You and Ro are free to do whatever you want, but you're relieved of duty as security chief."

"No!" growled the blond man, slamming his palms on the president's desk, causing Oscaras to flinch. "It has nothing to do with Ro—I saw with my own eyes! One of them—the same one we kept chained up in a shed—saved our lives this morning. He warned us about the attack. They're not savages—they're confused and acting more out of fear than rational thought, just like us!"

"You're restricted to quarters!" ordered Oscaras, pointing to the door. "Soon we'll be rid of the *Enterprise,* and we can go back to solving our own problems. I do make mistakes, and calling on Starfleet was one of them. I should've known they were too buddy-buddy with the Klingon High Command to help us. By the time the *Enterprise* returns, this problem is going to be *over."*

Gregg Calvert pounded the desk with frustration one last time, then stalked out the door. Ensign Ro lingered for a moment in the doorway.

"You're wrong about Gregg and me," she told the president. "You're wrong about everything. And if you don't take that spy business seriously, it's going to come back to haunt you."

For a moment Raul Oscaras looked weary and uncertain. Then he pumped up his chest and bellowed, "Get out!"

Ro looked for Gregg Calvert upon leaving Oscaras's office, but he had evidently headed to his quarters in a great hurry. She didn't blame him for wanting to get away from her; she wasn't doing his case much good. She wandered aimlessly down a broad street with nothing left of the euphoric feeling she had had earlier in the day. All that remained was a hollow dread, a vague sense that matters were coming to a head—but not for the better. On this chilly gray day there was death in the air.

Thinking that she hadn't eaten since breakfast and that it was midafternoon, Ro made her way to the dining hall. She had no sooner selected a small salad and sat down to eat her meager repast than one of the researchers from the science lab passed her table.

"Oh, here you are," said the dark-skinned woman, who had scarcely spoken two words to Ro since her arrival. "I checked your seismograph a few minutes ago. You might want to take a look. There are some strange readings on the midzone chart."

The Bajoran bolted out of her chair. "Thank you," she muttered hastily, grabbing her salad and rushing toward the door.

With the day's many events she had not set foot in the lab nor checked her readings once. As she dashed along the wide street Ro bawled herself out for negligence. Monitoring seismic activity was her primary mission on Selva, she told herself angrily—not outings to the beach, acting like a social worker, or tagging along with Gregg Calvert.

She charged into the lab past several startled workers and went straightaway to the instrument array she had assembled for her task. Jagged lines were streaking up and down the midzone screen, and she held her breath as she punched up the commands to analyze the data. The tectonic plates were shifting, registering between four and five on the Richter scale, and volcanic activity was up twenty percent. Whether that would turn into a major underwater eruption or temblor was still unknown. Data scrawled across a second screen, and Ro held her breath, waiting to see if the activity would jump to a higher level. It didn't— the graphs went back to normal, and the temblors a thousand kilometers away gradually subsided.

Ro breathed again and slumped back in her chair. No one else in the room, or on the entire planet, knew how close they had been to cataclysm. Even now Ro wasn't certain, because there was no historical data to tell her what effect an undersea eruption would have on the land masses of Selva. Whatever it was, they had avoided it—for now.

* * *

Worf strolled through a gentler forest than the one on Selva. In this part of Ohio it was a bright day in early summer, and Klingon picnickers were spreading colorful tablecloths, throwing Frisbees, knocking around a softball, and performing other activities no real Klingon would ever do. Worf had to chuckle at the incongruity of the folksy Klingons, remembering how he had dropped them into the original holodeck simulation to make Turrok think that Klingons were ubiquitous. They were all over the Federation, it was true, but they would never be in this setting, doing these things.

He climbed the hill away from the picnic area toward the little dam overlooking the lake. Behind the dam, in the shallow pool, he saw a slim figure happily splashing away. Worf felt certain Turrok was catching and eating more than his share of crawdads. The boy didn't see him until he had reached the edge of the pool.

"Worf!" he cried joyously. "We are here! They let me come back!"

The lieutenant smiled and pulled off his boots. "That is good," he said. "I'm glad you got to see this place again."

"I want to live here forever and ever!" proclaimed Turrok, dancing around the rocks in the crystalline pool. "I not bother anyone. I will eat crawdads and whatever I find. I will make friends with the other Klingons. Please tell them it is okay, Worf."

Worf sat on the edge of the pool and dangled his feet in the water. "You must go back to your own forest," he said. "We must both go back."

Turrok pouted. "No! I won't go! For one thing, Balak will kill me."

"Balak is dead."

"Dead?" muttered the boy with disbelief. "The flat-heads?"

Worf shook his head. "We don't know how he died."

Turrok suddenly grinned. "I think Wolm killed him. She is very brave. She hate him because he only want to kill."

Worf replied, "Klingons have a proverb that says, 'A murder is not worthy unless it is earned.'"

"I see," said Turrok, sitting beside Worf on the concrete bank. "Tell me about other Klingons. Are they like these below? Eating and throwing things to each other?"

"No," said Worf. "That's the main reason you can't stay here. This isn't real. It's an illusion—something that looks real but isn't."

Turrok scoffed. "I not believe you. I *feel* this water! I taste the food and scrape my leg."

"All manipulation of forcefields, tractor beams, and replication technology," replied Worf. He got an uncomprehending stare in response. "Someday you'll understand how it works, but let me show you that it is an illusion.

"Computer," he intoned, "remove the Klingons from this program. No people at all."

The hordes of laughing and playing Klingons that dotted the hillside and the picnic grounds vanished. They weren't swallowed up in swirling columns of light—they just ceased to exist. Turrok stared in awe. Then he looked down at the water splashing over his feet and at the endless robin's-egg blue above his head.

"Is all life like this?" he asked numbly. "All . . . illusion?"

"The answer to that," said Worf, "is in the realm of philosophy and religion. Perhaps, with your experiences, you would make a good philosopher. In the days and weeks to come you will see many things that you may question. Always try to find what is real."

"O'Brien to Worf," came a voice over Worf's comm badge.

The Klingon tapped it to answer. "Worf here."

"All ashore that's going ashore," called the transporter chief. "We're pulling out of orbit in ten minutes."

"Aye, Chief," answered Worf. He patted the boy on the back and pulled his feet out of the water.

Turrok looked miserable. "I not want to go back."

"You have responsibilities," said Worf sternly as he grabbed his boots. "Someday, when the history of Selva is written, you will be one of the founders of a great civilization."

"How do I do that?" asked Turrok, amazed.

Worf smiled. "Just by making friends."

O'Brien transported them to the coordinates of the sacred mound, and Worf fingered his phaser weapon until he got a good look at the surrounding scene. Nineteen young Klingons were eagerly devouring as much food as Deanna had managed to secure, and they scarcely paid any attention to the two new arrivals. Turrok's eyes lit up, and he ran over to join the feast. Worf strode to the crest of the mound, where Data and Deanna stood watching their ravenous luncheon guests.

"The way to a Klingon's stomach is still working," said Deanna, smiling.

Worf shrugged. "Until the food runs out."

"There is another replicator in the village," said Data. "We could ask for their cooperation."

"With your permission, sir," answered Worf, "I intend to walk in there tomorrow with all of them in tow. And they'll have to feed us."

Deanna looked concerned when she said, "Balak may be gone, but they still aren't prep students. We haven't gotten the whole story, but apparently Wolm stabbed him to death as he lay wounded."

"He was a worthy opponent," said Worf, "but I didn't think Balak would live to an old age."

"Picard to away team," chirped a voice.

Data was the first to respond. "Data here. Counselor Troi and Lieutenant Worf are with me. The Klingons are occupied with eating."

"We're leaving now," said the captain. "We'll be six hours away, so the earliest we can return is in twelve hours. If you can, get into the village to report by subspace—I don't want to be out of contact for too long."

"We'll make it into the village," replied Worf. "The mission is proceeding as planned."

"Don't try to accomplish miracles," said Picard. "Just keep yourselves alive. *Enterprise* out."

Deanna and Worf looked instinctively at the sky, seeing nothing but glowering gray clouds and knowing the *Enterprise* would soon be far beyond them.

Ensign Ro had just returned to eating her salad, despite the stares of her colleagues, who apparently didn't eat at their posts in the lab. She didn't care—she had to eat, and she wouldn't leave the seismographs. So intent was her observation of the instruments that the voice on her communicator startled her.

"Picard to Ro."

"Ensign Ro here," she replied with a dry swallow. She knew perfectly well why he was calling.

"Is everything under control?" asked the captain.

Ro swallowed again. Was she going to mention the fluctuations? The records were so poor in the lab that minor temblors like that could have been occurring for months without meaning anything.

"Ensign?" said Picard with concern. "Is everything all right?"

"I don't trust those tectonic plates," answered Ro, "or Raul Oscraras."

"I share your concerns," Picard said gravely. "The ship is leaving orbit now, but we'll return as soon as possible, perhaps in as few as fourteen or fifteen hours. Look out for yourself and don't hesitate to use their radio."

"Understood, sir," answered Ro.

"Enterprise out."

Chapter Thirteen

THE FOOD WAS swiftly disappearing, and the young Klingons were glancing warily over their shoulders at Deanna, Worf, and Data, wondering what would happen next. So was Deanna. She was certain of only one thing—whatever happened, it would not involve the *Enterprise*. The ship was gone, and she wondered how much of the peacekeeping authority of the Federation was gone with it.

She glanced at the slim android and the brawny Klingon beside her. Data was watching the young Klingons with a studious detachment, as if they were specimens in a jar, and Worf seemed immersed in thought, his jaw working nervously, his fists clenching and unclenching.

"We made them wear comm badges inside their clothing as a condition of getting more food," she told Worf. "So we are ready to proceed to the next step—whatever that is."

Data replied, "I have the communicator given to us by Raul Oscaras—we could contact the settlement for more food."

"No," growled Worf, "their need is not more food for their stomachs, but food for their souls. They must be made to realize that they are Klingons, and Klingons do not hide in the woods or accept second-class citizenship. They are the original settlers of Selva, and it's time they claimed their rights."

"That is well to say," said Data, "but do you have a plan?"

"Only to turn them into *real* Klingons," answered Worf. "Do I have your permission to try, sir?"

Data nodded. "As long as we are not endangered, you may proceed."

Worf strode down the mound toward the diners, who were so sated by now that they were picking at their scraps. The roast turkey had proven to be very popular, and the biggest youth—now that Balak was gone—was gnawing on a bare carcass that had been picked as clean as a drum skin.

Maltz studied Worf from the corner of his eye as the uniformed adult sat cross-legged on the ground a few meters away from him. Deanna took that as a clue as to how she should behave, addressing the adolescents as equals rather than grownups who stood over them. She hurried down the hill and sat beside Worf. He nodded gratefully to her and just kept smiling benignly until he was sure he had the attention of each of them. Data, who could hear perfectly well from atop the mound, maintained his lookout post.

Deanna Troi glanced at Wolm, knowing the bruised girl had performed an act that was violent and reprehensible, yet nobody had seen fit to punish her for it. Perhaps, thought the Betazoid, she was punishing herself. Wolm sat apart from the others, and her head hung low; she seemed distracted and exhausted, as if the weight of her action had just hit home.

Turrok had been welcomed back and was sitting with a group of younger Klingons, but Wolm sat

alone, an instrument of change and an object of fear.
She had assassinated Balak, their first and so far only
leader, and she would always be known for that. Her
punishment or accolades would come later, when her
comrades knew what to think about these fast-moving
events.

"Did you like the food?" Worf asked them.

There were some grunts but no complaints, until
Maltz tossed the turkey carcass over his shoulder into
the woods. "You knew we would like the food," he
said with a scowl. "What do you want from us?
Friends? All right, we are friends." He sprang to his
feet. "Now we go home."

"Wait," said Worf. "There is plenty of light left in
the sky, and I thought we could sit and talk. I will tell
you exactly what we want."

The others looked expectantly from Maltz to Wolm,
then to one another, and there seemed to be a
consensus that they could sit a while longer. Deanna
was receiving so many conflicting emotions from this
troubled group that she didn't know how to interpret
them. Fear, curiousity, confusion, hope. Their in-
stincts told them to kill the strangers and run off to
their hutches, but their reason told them to listen.
Their faces reflected a childlike nativeté and a longing
to be nurtured, yet Deanna knew they practiced ritual
torture and slit throats without compunction. She
remembered the cold knife point at her own throat
and swallowed nervously.

Worf took a shaving mirror out of his pack and held
it up for all of them to see. "Do you know what this
is?" he asked. "It's called a mirror. You can use it to
see what you look like." He tossed the mirror to a
startled Maltz, who caught it in spite of the frown on
his face.

"If you look at yourselves," Worf continued, "you

will see that we are alike. We are of the same race—Klingon—with the same history and the same destiny. Even if you don't understand anything else that I tell you, you must admit that you are Klingon, like me."

Maltz scrutinized himself in the mirror, touching his cheekbones and rugged forehead. Then he handed it to a comrade, who twisted it, trying to find his best angle. Others peered over his shoulder at the glimmering object.

Worf pointed to Deanna and said, "Counselor Troi is not Klingon—she is half Betazoid and half human. You only know this one planet, this one place, but people from many different races live together peacefully on many other worlds."

He smiled. "You are not that much different from Klingons elsewhere. We are warriors!" he cried, pounding his chest. "We settle wars and disputes with blood, and the greatest joy for a Klingons is to die in battle!"

Now he had their attention, thought Deanna, but she hoped this wasn't giving in to their primitive tendencies. She caught herself biting her nail.

"But worlds are not founded on battle," said Worf, "they are founded on peace. War is destructive and tears things down. You need peace to build things."

He motioned to the sky and said, "I cannot teach you to be a citizen of the galaxy unless you first learn to be Klingon. In this life—the only life you remember—your allegiance has been only to one another. That is fine. You will always be brothers and sisters because of your experiences here. But you must bond with your people—the Klingons and the Klingon Empire."

He bowed his head and added, "I have also sworn my allegiance to the Federation, which is a group of races that share friendship. That is not a decision you have to make today. I made that decision because I was once like you—cut off from my family and heritage. Like you, I was not a Klingon, because I was not raised as one. But when I was old enough, as you are, my foster parents began to teach me what it was to be a Klingon." Worf smiled. "They are great believers in tradition."

He slapped his knee and added, "Later I went to live among my kinsmen, as you may choose to do. They taught me to be Klingon, as I will teach you. You will become one with me—and all other Klingons—and take me as your brother."

The young people looked at one another in confusion. "How will we do that?" asked one.

Worf smiled. "We have a ritual called the *R'uustai*. The Bonding. You will become part of my family and I of yours. We will be brothers and sisters forever, and you will *be* Klingons, not just look like Klingons."

Worf rose to his feet and added, "There is just one thing. You will have to bring back the lanterns you took from us. In fact, bring back all the lanterns, flashlights, and anything else that makes light before darkness. We will need them for the *R'uustai*."

Still looking shaggy and unfed despite their large meal, the young Klingons rose uncertainly to their feet and peered at one another. Deanna was waiting for one of them to object, to challenge the idea, but no one said anything. They were still in shock. She hoped they would be able to absorb what Worf was offering them, and she wondered if it was wise to let them go. But she knew that Worf was right in letting them discuss it in private—they had to accept change of their own free will.

Led by Maltz, they jogged off into the woods. Turrok grinned and waved, and Wolm hung back, looking like someone who wanted to talk. But her companions were racing away, and Wolm wanted to be with them. She managed a brief smile before dashing off into the forest.

Deanna said with all honesty and admiration, "That was very well done, Worf. I approve of this tack. It will increase their self-esteem."

Worf gazed after the fleeting figures and muttered, "Praise me later, Counselor—when they return."

Ensign Ro rubbed her bleary eyes and leaned back in her chair, which creaked in protest. She had fidgeted with her instruments for two hours, scouring the vast continent that sprawled along the ocean floor. Somewhere in that concave wilderness there was a temblor every second, but the trouble spot closest to them was quiet, having exhausted itself with those little shrugs a few hours earlier. With enough time, from a platform like the *Enterprise,* they could eventually map all the fault lines, volcanoes, and other forces at work, along with their interconnections down to the mantle and the core. But for now she could only watch and fine-tune the sensors, wondering what she would do if the planet suddenly erupted in a growing spurt. Crawling under the desk was about all she could think of.

The Bajoran's worried musings were interrupted by a small voice. "Ro?" it asked plaintively.

She turned to see a small girl with very large red eyes. Ro instinctively opened her arms and enveloped the child, and Myra responded with sobs hiccuping in her throat.

"They relieved him of duty," she murmured with incomprehension. "My dad. I feel awful for him, because he's done all he can, and they're stupid! But the kids in my class—they say *you* and *he* . . . I told them it wasn't true, and what difference would it make anyway?" Sobs overcame her, and her slight body trembled in Ro's grasp.

"Myra," said the ensign evenly, "it doesn't matter what they think. As for your father being relieved of his duties, I'm certain that is temporary. The one who should be relieved of his duties is Raul Oscaras. I've seen this my entire life, so perhaps I am cynical about it, but men such as he rule by force of personality, not aptitude. He'll be proved a fool eventually. And your father will be proved innocent of whatever accusations Oscaras has trumped up."

Myra stared at her, having never heard such frank criticism of authority before. She inhaled a great lungful of breath to make up for what she had lost crying. "I know you're right," she answered. "But my father takes great pride in his work. This is crushing to him."

"Someone had to break with Oscraras," answered Ro. "Your father was only the first. You have faith in him and in what you know is right, and people like Oscaras can't crush you."

"Thanks," said Myra, wiping her sleeve across her eyes. "But it's hard."

"Growing up *is* hard," the Bajoran agreed. "You discover that authority comes in all flavors—benign, cruel, gifted, and incompetent."

Ro glanced at her instruments. "Not to change the subject, but there was a series of temblors in the five range in that fissure a thousand kilometers from here. I just wonder if you've got any opinions about it."

"Well," answered Myra, looking professionally glum instead of personally glum, "I have an opinion on what happened to the forest, based on our trip to the seashore this morning. It definitely has something to do with what you're doing."

"What do you mean?" asked Ro, her heart beating unpleasantly faster.

"I mean," said the prodigy, "what happened ninety years ago that wiped out the forest. If you go outside our gate and dig in the topsoil, under the humus, you'll find a lot of those small black pebbles we saw on the beach today. There are also sulfuric acids and a number of trace elements in the topsoil that can only be explained if that weird creature that lives on top of the ocean was washed ashore here. It couldn't live, of course, and it just died away."

Ro experienced a queasy feeling in her stomach as she anticipated what was coming next from the mouth of this remarkable twelve-year-old.

Myra shrugged. "There really isn't enough of that animal to be dangerous, but it does prove that a giant tidal wave—a tsunami—rolled across here and wiped everything out. The trees grew back real fast, because there were plenty of seed cones in the muck that covered the area after the water ran off. Along with the pebbles and other stuff from the ocean."

"Could that happen again?" asked Ro.

"It *will* happen again," answered Myra. "In ten thousand years or ten years. Who knows?"

"It could happen anytime," said Ro absently, gazing at her instruments. "I've never lived on a watery planet, like Selva or Earth. What exactly causes a tsunami?"

"An earthquake or volcanic eruption in the ocean," answered Myra, pointing to the seismograph. "But it would have to be a big one that displaced a lot of water. The waves travel in concentric circles outward from the displacement, just like when you toss a rock into a pool. Sitting in a boat on the ocean, you could ride over a tsunami, but the shores can get hit with waves that are forty meters high. We're only twenty kilometers away, and these are lowlands—there are no mountains or hills between us and the ocean. To a tidal wave, we're part of the beach."

"Have you told this to any of the others?" asked Ro nervously. "They've got to be warned."

The girl shrugged. "They won't believe me. Oscaras and half the adults in the village were involved in the decision to settle here. This *is* the most stable place on the planet as far as being away from the main fault lines, but they didn't take the ocean into account. With everything else that's happened, who could tell them they put us in a tidal wave area? They wouldn't believe *me* at all—they don't accept my theory that the forest is only ninety years old. And where would they go? They're not gonna pick up and walk off into the forest while the Klingons are out there."

Ro rubbed her eyes, trying to expel the monstrous headache that was attacking her frontal lobe. "Myra," she said, "you've got to take me to the radio room. I have to call the *Enterprise*."

"Come on," chirped the girl, grabbing Ro's elbow.

The Bajoran tore herself away from the seismographic sensors and followed Myra Calvert through the laboratory. A handful of lab workers watched them suspiciously as they exited through the automatic door. They climbed the metal staircase on the outside wall of the two-story building and reached a landing on the second floor. Myra punched the large button that opened the door, and they entered a nondescript hallway with a number of open doorways beyond. Ro knew that the replicator, sickbay, radio, and other crucial systems were located there, but she was surprised at the number of people that seemed to be milling around. Immediately three brown-suited colonists converged on them.

A big-shouldered man stepped in front of Ro and blocked the hallway beyond. "What do you want?" he demanded.

"To use the transmitter," she said simply.

"You need permission from President Oscaras," the man replied.

Myra snapped in outrage, "Says who? This is Ensign Ro of the *Enterprise,* and she wants to contact her ship."

"I'm sorry," said the man, who clearly was not sorry, "but access to the subspace radio is restricted to authorized personnel."

Ensign Ro bristled. "The *Enterprise* will return even sooner if I don't contact them."

"I don't know anything about that," growled the man. "I only know you need the permission of President Oscaras to use the radio."

"My dad will vouch for her," proclaimed Myra.

The man stared down at the child and sneered. "Your dad has been restricted to quarters. Now get out of here, both of you."

This devastated the child, but she tightened her quivering lip and glared at the guard. The other two colonists also crossed their arms, looking like they meant business. Out of habit Ro lifted her hand to tap her communicator badge. But who was she going to call? The *Enterprise* was out of range by a couple dozen light-years, and what good could Worf and his party do in this predicament? They probably had their own hands full, and she didn't want to draw them into this maelstrom.

Down the hallway a man emerged from one of the adjoining rooms with four phaser rifles in his arms. He was besieged by a number of waiting colonists, who eagerly inspected the weapons.

"Very well," said Ro, "I'll get his permission. Will you alert me when the *Enterprise* calls and wishes to speak with me?"

"Uh," stammered the man, looking uncertain, "of course."

"Thank you," replied Ro. She put her arm around the girl's shoulder and steered the angry youngster out the door.

When the door slammed shut behind them Myra burst out, "My dad will kick their butts!"

For the girl's sake Ro tried to suppress the fear that was churning in her stomach. She turned blandly to Myra and asked, "Why don't we go talk to your dad? Is he at home?"

The girl averted her eyes. "Um, I don't know."

"I think you do know," said the Bajoran. "The three of us have to stick together until the *Enterprise* returns."

Myra bowed her head and plodded down the stairs. "He's home," she murmured, "but he's been drinking his allotment of mulled wine, and he hardly ever drinks."

"Come on," said Ro, charging down the stairs, "let's splash some water in his face."

Gregg Calvert was not falling-down drunk, but he was depressed and surly by the time his daughter and Ensign Ro reached the house. He poured the last of a bottle of amber wine into a glass and gulped it steadily while he listened to Myra's tale of their trip to the communications room.

"Those bastards," muttered Gregg, staring vacantly at Ensign Ro. "Oscaras has them all stirred up against you and me, and the *Enterprise*, too. I was such a damn fool to cast our lot with these idiots—now Myra and I are stranded here!" He shook his head, took a deep breath, and added, "I hate to judge them too harshly, though. They're just innocent dreamers whose dream has turned into a nightmare."

Ro responded, "It's a lot more complicated than that. Your daughter thinks we're in an area that's prone to tidal waves, and I have to agree. We just had a major earthquake in the ocean, and it might be only a foreshock. I wanted to call the *Enterprise* to tell them to evacuate this planet immediately."

Gregg snorted a laugh and tipped his glass toward her. "Good luck to you, Ensign. Raul Oscaras is not big on listening to reason, as you probably noticed. They won't be able to think about tidal waves until they do something about the Klingons. And the spy—he doesn't want to deal with that at all."

Ro paced the drab enclosure. "He must be planning to do something," she declared, "because he had your replicator busy making phaser rifles. Look, I don't have to convince Raul Oscaras he's wrong, but I do have to get access to that radio and contact the *Enterprise.*"

Gregg Calvert slapped his thighs and stood uneasily. "Okay," he muttered, "let's see what we can do." He turned to his daughter and smiled. "I'm sorry I got you into this, sweetheart. Stay here and try to keep out of everyone's way."

"But, Dad!" she protested. "I want to go with you and Ro!"

"No," he said sternly. "This may get ugly. Stay here and keep a low profile. Don't go to the lab or anywhere. We'll be back as soon as we can."

Myra flashed him a brave smile and nodded with a chin that quivered just a little.

When Ensign Ro and Gregg Calvert emerged from the tiny apartment, darkness was claiming the sky. The forest loomed behind the galvanized metal walls like a black velvet curtain, and lights flickered on in each guard tower and around the compound, giving the village an unreal look, like a stage awaiting actors to fill it. Nocturnal animals contributed their eerie howls to the setting, and Ro got a full dose of the dread that had dogged her all day. It had started, she recalled, upon her viewing the poisonous red sea—a sea that now appeared to be even more dangerous than the acidic animal that floated upon it.

"Come on," said Gregg, striding toward the two-story building that housed the lab, radio room, and replicator. "Let's see if I can talk some sense into those morons without going through Oscaras."

But there was no getting around Raul Oscaras. He stood just inside the second-story door, addressing a group of colonists who were armed with phaser rifles. Ro knew immediately they had made a terrible mistake, and she wanted to bolt for the door; but Gregg Calvert had a fiery look of determination in his normally placid blue eyes.

He charged up to Oscaras and demanded, "What do you mean by denying Ensign Ro access to the radio? She's entitled to contact her ship!"

For a moment fear and uncertainty flashed across the president's face, then he mustered his usual bravado. "You're supposed to be confined to quarters," he accused Calvert. "You've been relieved of duties."

"I don't care about me," explained the former security chief. "If I'm finished here, then that's the way it is. But this is a Starfleet officer and Starfleet business you're messing with!"

Several colonists glanced nervously from Raul Oscaras to Gregg Calvert to the bumpy-headed stranger in their midst. Ro could think of nothing to add to Gregg's argument except to cross her arms and look indignant at the treatment accorded her.

Oscaras smiled and tried his blustery charm. "It was never our intention to deny Ensign Ro access to the radio," he assured them. "I believe she was told that access required authorization, nothing more. As you said yourself, Gregg, we may have a traitor in our midst, and we can't be too careful."

"Then let me use the radio," demanded the Bajoran.

Oscraras smiled warily. "That would be difficult at the moment, Ensign. You see, we're on a security alert."

"For what?" asked Gregg Calvert.

"Klingon savages," sneered the president. "With the *Enterprise* gone for a few days we thought it best to be on alert."

"Could it be that you don't want the *Enterprise* to come back too quickly?" Gregg said accusingly.

Ro eyed the phaser rifles and the frightened colonists who held them, trying to decide what course of action would work with these misguided lunatics. Confrontation wasn't getting them very far. "I'll try again in the morning," she said, edging toward the door.

"Stop her!" screeched a voice that sliced across everyone's nerves.

They whirled to see the diminutive figure of Doctor Louise Drayton charging down the hallway. "Get her comm badge!" she shrieked, "before she calls the Klingons!"

Acting instinctively, Ro ducked under a beefy pair of arms and scrambled for the door. Just as it whooshed open another colonist lunged in front of her, and she careened into his chest, knocking them both outside onto the landing. When he groped for her she kicked him in the groin and heard him howl as he tumbled over the railing and fell two stories.

Ro heard shouts and saw a crush of bodies swarming out the door, Gregg in the lead. He tried to hold them off with a flurry of wild punches, but someone clubbed him with the butt of a phaser rifle. He dropped to his knees, blood smeared across his face. With no time to think Ro vaulted over the railing.

She landed off-stride and twisted her ankle, and she could only limp a few meters before she heard a shout.

"Stop!" ordered Oscaras from the top of the landing. He was holding a phaser rifle. "Let's be reasonable!"

Louise Drayton shouldered her way to his side and grabbed the weapon from him. "What are you waiting for?" she shrieked. She lifted the rifle to her shoulder and took aim.

"No!" shouted Ro, holding up her hands in a futile effort to ward off the blue beam. The pulse of energy ripped through her body like sparks through a Tesla coil until it reached her brain and exploded with white-hot intensity. Then all was darkness, and Ro crumpled to the ground in a senseless heap.

Chapter Fourteen

WITH THE RETURN of darkness came the return of the young Klingons, traipsing uncertainly out of the forest, dragging their musical instruments, flashlights, and lanterns with them. They wandered to the edge of the mound and stood expectantly. Deanna Troi saw Worf lift his huge shoulders and sigh with relief; he was beaming as he scampered down the hill to meet them.

Atop the mound Deanna smiled at Data. "I've never seen a *R'uustai* ceremony," she remarked.

"I believe this one may be atypical," answered the android. "I will remain here and observe."

"You keep your distance from them," observed Deanna. "Why?"

"Tactical reasons," answered Data. "This way it is not possible for all of us to be overpowered at once should the Klingons become violent. I will be able to stun a great many of them before they can reach me."

"I see," nodded Deanna, discomfited by the thought but unable to dispute the android's logic.

"I am also watching for a return of the goddess," added Data. "Do not let me stop you from assisting Worf. I will simply remain here and observe."

"Fine." Deanna nodded, wondering if everything was really fine. It had been less than four hours since the *Enterprise* had vacated this solar system for another, and they had no reason to complain. Worf's emphasis on Klingon tradition and values had apparently struck a nerve. The youths seemed ready—or at least resigned—to belonging to a community larger than their tiny lost tribe. So what was the problem? Why did she feel uneasy? In his own well-reasoned way, Data was also exhibiting anxiety, although he would never admit it. The drums were silent, but there was still violence lacing the air of Selva.

Deanna stepped cautiously down the slope because it was too dark to see well. Suddenly a light beamed on, and she saw Worf adjusting one of the lanterns that had vanished during their trip back to the *Enterprise* the night before. He dimmed the light to its lowest setting and handed it to Turrok.

"We always use five candles for the *R'uustai*," he explained to the young Klingons, "in honor of the five stages of birth. We have no candles, so we will use these lights."

He turned on a flashlight and handed it to Wolm with a smile. The teenager grinned back and pointed the beam toward the sky, where it was swallowed by the gathering clouds. Worf turned on the largest lantern and handed it to Maltz, who cracked a smile in spite of his dour expression. He rubbed Turrok's stringy hair and gave him the third lamp, then two more lights were lit and distributed to a pair of eager assistants.

"Now," said Worf, "we have our five lights. The other object that we use in the R'uustai but do not have with us is the sash with our family insignia. It is worn from shoulder to hip, much as you wear your chuck skins."

The Klingon smiled thoughtfully. "In many ways, the skin you wear now is your sash, because it represents your bond to the only family you know—each other. If you ever leave here, bring it with you, and you can sew it into a new sash, along with the insignia of your birth family."

As his audience looked on with rapt attention Worf continued. "Instead of lighting the candles and wearing the sash we will use another tradition—the handshake. You extend your hand, so, and clasp the other person's hand." He demonstrated on Turrok. "You look each other in the eyes and make a spiritual bond as well as a physical bond. To complete the *R'uustai* we say the words, '*SoS jIH batlh SoH.*'"

Several of the youngsters repeated the phrase and did much better than Deanna thought she could.

Worf nodded approvingly. "With those words we honor the memory of our mothers. It bonds us as one family that is stronger than two separate families."

"Will we ever see our mothers?" asked Maltz wistfully, as if dredging up a memory from a deep place.

Worf shook his head sadly. "No, we won't. That is another bond we share—our birth parents were killed by Romulans. But you have other family members—aunts, uncles, grandparents, perhaps brothers and sisters. You have each other, and after tonight you will also have me."

It was very dark now, yet the woods were strangely silent, as if the chucks, birds, sloths, and other families of Selva were listening to Worf with the same rapt attention. The Klingon motioned to the great mound that loomed behind them.

"With your permission," he said, "we will use your sacred mound." No one objected, and he nodded to the lantern bearers to lead the way.

Five pools of light silently ascended the dark hill, followed by a procession of Klingons. The two boys who always conducted the drumming could not resist beating their logs in a somber march as they followed the group. At the top of the hill the lantern bearers spread out in a semicircle, their lights wavering in their grasp as a strong wind buffeted the top of the mound. Worf stood in front of the lights and motioned the first youngster in line to come forward.

He warmly took her hand and looked into her eyes. *"SoS jlH batlh SoH,"* said the Klingon in a voice that was gripped with emotion.

"SoS jlH batlh SoH," the girl repeated.

One by one the young Klingons came forward under the mystical light of the five lanterns to exchange a vow that honored their mothers. One by one Worf welcomed them into his own family and the brotherhood of Klingons. When he finished with the larger group he exchanged the vow and handshake with each of the lantern bearers, ending with Turrok.

"You will always be my first brother," he told the youngster, and Turrok beamed.

When it was over they picked up both old and new instruments and beat them with joy. Worf danced with Wolm and Turrok, and Deanna clapped hands as the youngsters capered across the top of the mound. The Betazoid had all but forgotten her earlier dread until she saw Data watching them from a respectful distance. Silhouetted against the slate-gray clouds, the android nodded to her in acknowledgment, then turned his attention to the obscure forest beyond.

Ensign Ro woke up in a locked storage room, various aches and pains throbbing in her extremities. The worst pains were the headache at the base of her skull and her swollen ankle. She looked around and saw Gregg Calvert lying against a beige metal wall, still unconscious. There were no windows in the empty storeroom and nothing stored there except for a liter bottle of water, probably left as a humanitarian offering. She shook her head, thinking that it had to have been at least a level-three phaser blast she had absorbed—heavy stun. She groped for her communicator badge.

It was gone.

That was to be expected, she mumbled to herself, considering how badly Doctor Drayton had wanted it. Louise Drayton had just been taken off the list of reclamation projects and put back on the enemies list, along with several others. Ro checked her pocket and found her phaser gone, too, which compounded the feeling that she was in serious trouble. Far away she heard the ominous sound of drums, which didn't lift her spirits either.

She staggered to her feet and limped toward the door, assuming it was locked and wondering exactly how solid it was. It was a conventional door with a hand latch and a bolt lock, and she figured that she and Gregg, if he was feeling up to it, could probably get it open by brute force. That begged the question of whether there were guards outside.

"Hey!" she yelled, pounding on the door. "Let me out! Let me out this instant!"

"Pipe down!" called a voice that was muffled by both the wall and a distance of what sounded like several meters.

She didn't wish to give the guard any reason to come closer, so she hobbled away from the door and went to fetch the bottle of water. Ro found a pile of rags under Gregg's head, and she took the cleanest one and wet it. Kneeling down, she put too much weight on her bad ankle and yelped with pain. She grimaced as she painstakingly wiped the blood from his face. Gregg had a bad gash on his forehead and a lump that

made him look like a blond Klingon, but the caked
blood was hard and the wound didn't look infected.
After cleaning him up she sprinkled a few drops of
water on his eyelids.

His lips moved, and a groan issued from the back of
his throat. Disoriented, he flung his fists into the air.
Ro wrapped her arms around him and said soothing-
ly, "It's all right, Gregg. We're alive. Just relax. Lie
back and relax."

The big man's body went limp in her arms, and she
stroked back his hair. He blinked at her gratefully and
tried to smile.

"I take it we lost the fight," he croaked.

Ro nodded. "We're locked up in some kind of
storage room. No windows. One door."

"Oooh," moaned Gregg, "either I got pounded or I
have a helluva hangover." He started to touch his
wound, and Ro grasped his hand.

"It's healing," she said, "just leave it alone. You're
lucky we don't have a mirror in here."

Horror flashed over Gregg's blue eyes, and he
bolted upright. "Myra!" he gasped.

Ro gripped his shoulders. "Listen," she said, "we're
in no condition to help Myra or anyone else at the
moment. She's a resourceful girl, and, as she's always
telling me, the adults don't take her seriously. Do you
really think they would harm her?"

"No," muttered Gregg, lying back on the rags. "It's
her damn father who's the stupid one."

Ro scowled. "There's plenty of stupidity to go
around in New Reykjavik. The question is, how do we
get out of here? I don't think it's by asking or
demanding to be let out. There's at least one guard
beyond that door, but I don't think he's sitting right
on top of it."

Gregg sat up again, more slowly, and gazed around

their nondescript confines. "This looks like an interior room," he said. "That wall with the door adjoins a hallway, and the other three walls adjoin other rooms like this one. The quick way they construct these things, it would probably be easier to go through a wall than the door."

"Cut through it?" she asked. "Batter it down?"

"Bend it outward," answered Gregg, "from the bottom. They don't usually sink these walls into the ground, and the welding may be spotty. We'll use these rags to protect our hands, and we'll bend it up just enough to crawl out."

"Let's get started," said Ro, hobbling to her feet.

Gregg looked at her with concern. "You're hurt, too."

Ro muttered, "Don't worry about me—let's just get out of here and get to that radio."

Myra Calvert knew something was wrong when she heard the angry shouts from the direction of the lab. She never heard shouts like that unless the Klingons had attacked somebody, but then there would be searchlights sweeping the compound and a hue and cry that would last all night. She ran to the small window in her bedroom and looked out but didn't see any searchlights. There had been less than a minute of shouts and commotion, then silence again. She didn't like it.

She liked it even less when her dad and Ro didn't return for over an hour. At that point she was convinced something was desperately wrong. Her dad was a man of his word—when he told her he would be back quickly, he came back quickly. The shouts had come from the direction of the lab building, which she knew was their destination. She began to think—what could she do to help them?

Staying at liberty was her primary objective. If she ran into trouble with President Oscaras, as it seemed her dad and Ro had done, she wouldn't be able to help them at all. The departure of the *Enterprise* had started a chain reaction that was like an experiment out of control. The faraway chatter of drums just accentuated the feeling of chaos and runaway emotions. People she knew—her dad's so-called friends— had denied Ensign Ro access to the radio room; they had relieved her dad; and they were shouting in the middle of the night. She decided she had to do what Dad had told her and keep away from them.

Myra's heart pounded along with the distant drums as she wondered if President Oscaras would send people looking for *her*. She had to make a decision— should she stay there, where her dad and Ro expected to find her? Or should she hide somewhere else, in case President Oscaras sent someonelooking for her? Maybe there was a way to do both.

Myra ran into the living room and fired up the message center, which was part of a household computer system that controlled the climate and lights. She and her dad scarcely ever used it, because they both knew where to look for each other, and they seldom hung out at home. But the message system allowed the user to leave a blaring message on the screen that was impossible to miss in the tiny cubicle. She typed in:

"Dear Dad, I got scared being by myself and went over to Katie's house. If she's not home, I'll go to another friend's house. See you later. Love, Myra."

The girl smiled and sneaked back into her bedroom, where she scrunched down in the closet. And waited.

Worf bent over to catch his breath, exhausted from nonstop free-spirited dancing to impromptu riffs on drums, maracas, tambourines, and anything else the young Klingons could find that made noise. As the youths whirled around him he looked up at similar activity in the night sky. With the moon as a backlight, a swirling mass of charcoal and ivory clouds raced eastward, driven by the wind. That reminded him of what lay to the east of them—the settlement of New Reykjavik. The first step of his plan had succeeded, but the most important step lay unfulfilled, and he had no clear-cut idea how to broach the subject.

He caught movement to his left and looked over to find Data stopping at attention beside him. This was the closest the android had gotten to the festivities. Worf appreciated his vigilance, but the youths appeared more likely to drop from exhaustion than to attack them.

"I have a question for you, Lieutenant," the android projected over the music.

"Yes, Commander?" smiled Worf, unable to suppress his happy mood.

"Is the handshake a Klingon tradition?" asked Data. "I thought it was derived from terran customs, to show that neither person was carrying a weapon."

"It's not Klingon," admitted Worf, "but we didn't have candles to light. Besides, they'll be seeing more humans before they see more Klingons. They need to know the handshake."

"That is true," said Data. "How will we integrate them with the colonists?"

"I don't know," admitted Worf. "We must begin by making simple peaceterms. For Klingons, there must be equality and an understanding that this mound and their hutches are off limits to the colonists unless they're invited. In return, the castaways will use their knives to open shells from the river, nothing more.

When the *Enterprise* returns they may decide if they wish to remain on Selva or to be repatriated—probably in secret—to the homeworlds."

Data nodded curtly. "Then we must request that they return with us now to the settlement."

"That's right," said Worf. "Do you have any ideas how to accomplish that?"

"As you have begun," answered Data, "by asking them to express their demands. Focus their attention away from the initial act of walking into the settlement and onto the greater issues at stake."

"Excellent idea," said the big Klingon. He clapped his hands and barked in his loudest voice, "I must have your attention! Listen to me! Please stop for a moment!" He strode into the midst of throbbing instruments and whipping bodies and held up his hands. "We must talk of your demands!" he bellowed.

Finally the celebrations ceased. "Demands?" muttered Maltz. "What do you mean?"

Worf pointed to the east, along with the wind and swirling clouds. "When we march into their village tomorrow," he declared, "we must tell the colonists what we want from them. For example, we will insist that this mound and your hutches are forbidden to them, unless you wish it otherwise. Think—what else do you want from them?"

"Food!" screamed one youngster, and the others laughed.

All except for Maltz. "You want us to go into their hutch?" he asked incredulously.

"Yes," nodded Worf. "It is inevitable. If you wish to be Klingons and travel in the sky to your homeworlds, you must first make peace with the humans in the village. They must acknowledge your right to live here, if that is what you wish. You both have rights, but to live in peace without fearing for your life and liberty is the first of them."

Maltz looked confused and turned to his companions. "If Balak were here, he would say no," said the adolescent. "The goddess tells us to kill flat-heads, but Worf says we must go to their shining hutch and make peace. Who is right?"

"Worf!" insisted Wolm without hesitation. There was some muffled agreement, but the reality of what Worf was suggesting was just sinking in. The youngsters looked at one another as if Worf had asked them to walk off a cliff.

Their eyes shifted toward a slight figure, the only one among them who had been to the realm of the flat-heads and returned. Turrok fidgeted under their gaze, and Worf could imagine what he was thinking. He was as torn as the rest of them, because he had encountered both cruelty and compassion, wonders and horrors in his days of captivity.

"The ship," he began uncertainly. "I would go back there. They have a forest they make from the air, like their food. Can we go back there, Worf?"

"No," answered the big Klingon. "The *Enterprise* is away on another mission. *This* is your home, and you must make peace with the humans here first. Later, the *Enterprise* could take you to the homeworlds, where you could learn all the Klingon ways and met members of your family. Or you could stay here. If you stay here, it's even more important that you learn to share this world with the colonists."

Deanna Troi strode forward from the shadows. "You can never really go back to your previous existence," she explained. "Turrok knows—there are worlds and worlds beyond this mound, fantastic cities that float in the clouds and creatures with such intelligence they make *us* seem like insects. All the memories and dreams you have of other places and people are real. You can decide later if you want to see those other places, but you'll always know they're out there. And that knowledge has already changed you forever."

"Yes,"—Turrok nodded sadly—"she speaks the truth. I wanted to stay on the ship, though I would never see any of you again. I want to go back now—and fly!"

Maltz scowled. "But the flat-heads with their walls —that is what Worf wants! The ship is gone—he said so. Do you want them to beat you and chain you again?"

"No," answered Turrok, "but I trust Worf. All flat-heads are not like them. Look at Deanna and Data."

The attention turned to two beings who looked human but were really quite different. Data opened his mouth to correct the impression that he was human, but Worf shot him a glare that begged for his silence. The android simply strolled back to his observation post and watched the dark forest. It was Deanna Troi who made the final appeal:

"You are citizens of this planet with all rights," she said, "but those rights do not include killing the settlers. If you want our help and our friendship, you must make friends with the settlers. There is no other way."

"If we don't?" growled Maltz.

"Then we'll have to go away," she answered. "Perhaps we can persuade the colonists to settle elsewhere, and you can return to the way you lived before—with one difference: You will forever know there are other worlds out there and millions of Klingons like yourselves. But you will never know them. It is your decision—peace with *all* of us or *none* of us."

Maltz shifted under the gaze of his comrades, unaccustomed to the pressures of leadership. But he was the biggest and strongest now, and rightly or wrongly, the others were looking at him for his decision.

He nodded solemnly. "We go with you to the hutch of the flat-heads."

"Humans," Worf gently corrected him.

"Humans," muttered the youngster. "May the goddess protect us."

Wolm cheered loudly, grabbed a drum, and began beating it. The others grabbed their instruments and leapt for joy, and the celebrations began anew. Worf nodded to Deanna, and they slipped away to congregate at Data's side.

"We should contact Ensign Ro," said the Betazoid, "so she can inform the colonists."

"I do not believe we should travel during the night," observed Data. "Shall I inform her we will arrive tomorrow morning?"

Worf nodded. "Tomorrow morning. No later."

Data tapped his communicator badge, listened for the tone, then announced, "Data to Ensign Ro."

There was no answer. He tried again and received no answer. Worf also made an attempt to contact the ensign, with similar results.

"Could she be asleep?" asked Deanna.

"Her sleep period does not normally commence at twenty-one fifty-four hours," observed Data. "However, we have another means of communication." He took a hand-held communicator from his pocket and reminded them, "This was given to me by President Oscaras, and it will place us in contact with the colonists."

"Very well," said Worf. "We should tell them our plans."

Data twisted a tiny knob and spoke into the device. "Commander Data to New Reykjavik. Respond, please."

There was momentary static, then a voice boomed across the tiny device: "President Oscaras here. Is your party all right, Commander Data?"

"Perfectly all right," answered the android, "but we were unable to contact Ensign Ro on her communicator. Is she well?"

There was silence on the other end for a few seconds, then a feminine voice replied, "This is Doctor Louise Drayton. Ensign Ro is sedated, which is why she couldn't reply. She's still suffering from several aftereffects of the mantis bite, and we thought it best to restrict her to bed. She's a very active person, as you know, and the sedation was necessary. She should be able to resume her duties tomorrow."

"Please express our good wishes to her," said Data. "We want to inform you that we will be conducting the Klingons to the settlement sometime tomorrow morning."

"What?" bellowed Oscaras. "You're bringing them *here?*"

"They are coming peacefully," answered Data. "Can you make preparations to receive them? Their favorite activities are eating and using percussive instruments."

Oscaras chuckled. "We'll make all the preparations, don't you worry. We know how fond they are of food and drumming."

Worf added, "We will want to conduct negotiations. The castaways have certain demands they wish to make."

"Of course," said Oscaras magnanimously. "This is quite an occasion. Yes, indeed! We'll be ready for them. Bring them on in!"

Chapter Fifteen

HUNKERED DOWN in her closet on a pile of dirty clothes, Myra fought the temptation to drift off to sleep. She knew somebody would be arriving in the tiny apartment eventually, but she didn't know whether it would be her father, Ensign Ro, or people sent by President Oscaras to fetch her. Whoever they were, if she fell asleep, they would see the message on the computer and go to Katie's house without her even knowing they were there. So she had to stay awake.

Just as she was actually prying her eyes open with her fingers she heard the latch turning. Then the door banged open in a clumsy way that didn't sound like her father's. She held her breath, awaiting his loving call, but it never came. Instead she could barely make out the muffled voices of at least two men:

"Is she here?"

"Look at the screen."

Myra's heart counted off the milliseconds.

"Damn!" muttered one of them. "Oscaras didn't want to alert anyone. He wanted to keep it quiet."

"Well, what harm can a little girl cause? In a few hours it'll all be over."

"I hope so."

"Let's report back."

She heard the men tromp out and the door slam shut behind them. Myra had inhaled several times, but her chest was too constricted with fear to exhale fully. When she finally let out a long sigh it brought no relief. The girl crawled out of the closet and stood stiffly, feeling as though she had been kicked in the stomach by a steel-toed boot.

Her dad and Ro were not coming back tonight. They were in real trouble, and there was no one she could turn to for help. The feeling of betrayal by her friends and neighbors was almost worse than the fear for her father. She didn't feel she had broken with President Oscaras; she felt he had broken with her and let her down.

Where could she go? Sooner or later they would actually check her friends' homes and maybe search this one. She couldn't run off into the woods with the Klingons out there, even if she knew a way to get past the guards and the wall. That would be suicide. Myra knew the village as well as anyone, and she could envision several possible hiding places; but how could she get there without being seen? There might be a guard posted right out front, for all she knew, and ten o'clock was too late at night for a twelve-year-old to be walking around the compound by herself.

She sank onto her bed, exhausted by worry, indecision, and lack of sleep. What would her dad do in this situation? Answering that question wasn't much help —he'd walk up to President Oscaras and punch him in the nose, which was probably what he had done to get himself into so much trouble.

From what she could tell, Ro had a similiar

temperment. Great. That left her as the only sensible one. But the two of them were preferable to most of the adults in the village, who just kept quiet, kept going along, even though they knew it was wrong for Oscaras to make himself a dictator. Ever since the attacks by the Klingons had begun the community had turned more inward, more fearful, replacing idealism with security.

The night remained eerily silent for all that had to be taking place, thought Myra, and even the drums sounded different. She had stretched out on her bed for a temporary respite, but the comfortable old mattress claimed the girl and stole her away from the fear and chaos into the peaceful realm of sleep.

Squatting upon the floor, with their backs against the wall for maximum leverage, Ensign Ro and Gregg Calvert gripped the bottom of the beige sheet metal. Their hands were wrapped in rags, but the sharp edge of the wall still cut painfully into their flesh. Gregg had pried it up enough to make this hand-hold, and now it was a matter of brute strength. They would pull it inward, ripping up the sloppy welding as they went.

Gregg breathed hard, and sweat was already dribbling off his ruddy face. "Ready?" he grunted. "One, two, three—go!"

Groaning and grimacing with the effort, Ro and Calvert pulled with all their might, trying to use their legs for as much lifting power as they could get. The metal groaned in harmony with them and lifted off the floor a few centimeters.

"Stop," panted Gregg. "I want to see what we're breaking into."

Ro hardly complained about the rest, and she could feel the muscles in her shoulders and thighs screaming from the effort. She was dismayed when she saw how little they had lifted the sheet-metal wall, but it was enough for Gregg to get down on his stomach and peer into the darkness beyond.

"Good," he breathed. "Another storeroom, filled with stuff but no people."

They had chosen the wall opposite the door of their cell, figuring that the room beyond would have a door that opened into another corridor, giving them a better chance to escape undetected. Gregg stood and tightened the rags around his hands.

"Are you all right?" he asked Ro. "How's your ankle?"

"Great," she gulped. "Now the pain in my back and my hands is making me forget all about it."

Gregg nodded sympathetically. "We shouldn't have to pull it up much more to get *you* out."

"No, you're coming with me," Ro insisted. "You know your way around here, and I don't."

"Then let's put our backs into it," muttered Gregg.

They resumed their positions, which was an easier matter with the wall having been raised a few centimeters. They grunted, grimaced, and sweated their way through five more tugging contests against the welded metal. Finally the gap was big enough for Ro to fit her head and half her torso inside the adjoining storeroom. With her long reach she grabbed a metal broom, which they used as a lever to pry the metal up enough to let Gregg pass under. Scraping along on their bellies, they crawled out.

More accurately, they crawled into another storeroom, which contained cleaning supplies and linen and smelled strongly of various disinfectants. In the darkness they stumbled to the doorway, and Gregg tried the latch. It wasn't locked and opened easily, but he kept the door closed for the moment.

"Grab some sheets, buckets, or mops," he said, pointing to the stuff that surrounded them, "so we look like we came in here to get supplies. If we see anyone out there, just turn and walk in the opposite direction."

"Okay," nodded Ro, glad she was still wearing the plain clothing of the colonists. She grabbed a bucket and a mop and tried to find something that might actually make a useful weapon. Her hand landed upon a spray bottle filled with what smelled like ammonia. She grabbed it.

Gregg took a stack of towels and a bucket. He carefully opened the door and stepped out. The immediate area was deserted, but to their right figures rushed past in a corridor that intersected theirs. Ro and Gregg immediately turned to the left and walked briskly until they found a door that led to the outside.

The cool night air was like a welcome splash of water after rolling in the dirt, but there was no time to dally. Gregg motioned with his head toward a side street, and Ro quickly followed. They left their towels and cleaning materials in a dark corner, although Ro held on to her spray bottle of ammonia. They moved between rows of nondescript one-story buildings until they reached an intersection with a brightly lit street beyond. Gregg motioned Ro to stay in the shadows while he edged around the corner into the light. A second or two later he had seen all he needed to see, and he ducked back into the alley and flattened himself against the wall.

"No way to get to the radio," he whispered. "The building must be surrounded by a dozen armed men. I don't know what's going on, but it looks like the whole place is getting ready for a war."

"Then," said Ro, "we should try to find the rest of the away team."

"In the forest?" asked Gregg in shock.

"That's where they are," said Ro. "They're probably safer than we are right now."

The former security chief couldn't argue with that. "Can we stop to get Myra?" he asked.

Ro couldn't argue with that, so they scurried off into the darkness. Thanks to Gregg's extensive knowledge of the compound, they were able to maneuver in the shadows and stay out of sight of the bands of colonists that rushed importantly from one place to another.

Gregg Calvert fought the pangs of being left out of whatever big thing was happening, because it was evident that a volunteer force of the most able men and women was being assembled. He could only imagine it had something to do with the Klingons. He shook off the feeling of having wasted a year's worth of sweat and blood and tried to concentrate on his own survival, and that of his beloved daughter.

Ensign Ro could take care of herself, he figured, and he glanced admiringly at the lithe woman creeping along beside him. He could tell from her agonized gait that her ankle must be bothering her, but she had said nothing more about it. She was a fighter, as evidenced by the spray bottle she gripped like a phaser pistol. He wouldn't want to cross her. In fact, Ro was exactly the kind of no-nonsense, straightforward role model he wanted for his daughter. A woman like . . . He brushed aside thoughts of his dead wife, because they were far more painful than thoughts of President Oscaras's treachery. Besides, if Janna hadn't plowed into that asteroid, he wouldn't be in this rotten predicament.

They were nearing his street, and Gregg reached out to keep Ensign Ro from stepping into the light. For a moment her body crushed back against his, and he held her longer than he needed to. She looked up at him with dark eyes that seemed to say: This isn't the time or place, but if we're smart and resourceful, maybe there will be another time and place.

He let her go and whispered, "The door to our apartment is about twenty meters away. Give me about thirty seconds, and if you don't hear anything that sounds like trouble, come after me."

Ro smiled fondly. "I may come after you anyway."

Gregg straightened his broad shoulders and strode into the street as if there wasn't a thing wrong in the world. It was fortunate he was armed with his cocky attitude, because there was a guard with a phaser rifle lurking in the shadows of his front door. It was too late to turn back, so he strode up to the man, smiling.

"Hi, Bill," he said cheerfully.

"Gregg!" said the man, blinking with surprise, "I thought you—"

"Oscaras let me go." Gregg shrugged. "We need every person we've got for what's coming up."

"No kidding," sighed Bill, obviously relieved that Gregg Calvert was back in the fold. "Your daughter's not home—I was supposed to wait for her."

"Well, she's not going to be coming home this time of night," Gregg replied, suppressing the seething anger inside of him. "I'm going to try to get a couple hours of sleep, and I suggest you do the same."

"Okay," said Bill, uncertain whether to accept this good fortune and return to his bed or to obey his orders to the letter.

"I'll see you later," concluded Gregg, opening the door to his home and stepping inside.

"Yeah, see ya," said the man. He looked at his watch and the night sky and figured yes, maybe there was time for a couple hours of sleep.

Ro heard the man's footsteps coming closer, and she pressed against the wall as he ambled past. When the man was out of sight she straightened her shoulders as Gregg had done and strolled into the street. Luckily, it was empty, and she saw Gregg motioning to her from a nearby doorway. She rushed inside as quickly as her swollen ankle would let her, and Gregg shut the door behind her.

"Bastards!" he seethed. "They're not only after me, they're after Myra. I'll strangle Oscaras by his fat red neck!"

"Daddy," said a small voice. They turned to see Myra in the doorway, rubbing the sleep from her eyes.

"Honey!" said Gregg, beaming. He swept the girl up in his muscular arms. She wrapped her scrawny arms around his neck, and they hugged each other as if to make sure that they would never be separated again.

"They came to get me," she said breathlessly, "but I hid and left a phony message. Daddy, what happened to your head? What's going on?"

"I can't explain now, sweetheart," answered Gregg. "We can't stay here any longer."

"We've got to get out of the compound," Ro reminded him, "and find the away team."

"Right," sighed the blond man. "There's only one person who knows how to get out of the compound, past the guards and the wall."

"Who?" asked Myra.

"Whoever our spy is."

"Do you know who it is?" asked Ro.

Gregg nodded. "I have a hunch. Even if I'm wrong, it'll be a good hiding place, because it's the last place they would look for us. And it's close by."

He reached into a drawer and pulled out a key chain. "Master keys," he said with a smile. "One of the advantages of being the ex-security chief. Come on."

Once again they tried to look as natural as possible as they stepped into the eerie salmon-colored lights of the compound. People were running to and fro, and three more people in a hurry didn't raise much suspicion. They walked briskly down an adjoining street and followed Gregg as he dashed toward a doorway that was bathed in shadows. He tried the door, found it locked, and fumbled with his key chain for the magic key. As he did, Ro read the nameplate on the door.

Doctor Louise Drayton, the sign said.

Gregg cursed under his breath as he fumbled with the keys, but he finally got the door open, and they slipped inside. As Gregg had suspected, Louise Drayton was not at home. Too busy playing the new security chief, thought Ro.

Gregg brushed his hand over a panel on the wall and turned on a few lights, then rushed to the only window in the small cubicle and closed the curtains tight. At once, he began moving the bed, couch, and other furniture, searching for something on the floor.

"How do you know Drayton is the spy?" asked Ro. The nasty entomologist would certainly be her first choice, but she had seen no evidence.

"I had my first suspicions when we were aboard your ship," answered Gregg. "When we questioned that Klingon who saved our lives on the beach he said something about Balak. I asked who Balak was, and Drayton immediately answered that he was their leader. How did she know that?"

Myra suggested, "Maybe the boy said that when he was our captive."

Gregg shook head. "I was present every time we questioned him, and he never told us anything that useful. My suspicions were confirmed when Drayton turned on us outside the radio room and ordered that Ro's communicator be confiscated." He sank down to his knees and ran his hands over the floor. "Now where is that damn thing? It's gotta be here."

"What are you looking for?" asked Myra.

The only other room in the tiny studio apartment was the bathroom, and Gregg Calvert jumped to his feet and ducked into it. Myra and Ro ran to the doorway and peered curiously over his broad shoulders. The bathroom had an ugly brown carpet on the floor that wasn't fastened down, because Gregg grabbed a corner and easily peeled it off. Under the carpet, resting on the cement floor, was a metal plate about a meter square.

"Bingo!" exclaimed Gregg Calvert. He grabbed the chunk of sheet metal and threw it off. There was a gaping black hole underneath.

"Wow!" gasped Myra. "A tunnel!"

"Yeah," said Gregg, "I couldn't figure out any other way she could get past the guards and the wall." He got down on his hands and knees and peered into the narrow abyss. "There's a ladder," he said, "and what looks like a lantern and some other stuff at the bottom."

"How did she dig it?" asked Myra.

Ro answered, "It wouldn't be much problem with a phaser. She could carve it out in a couple of nights if she knew what she was doing."

"She knows what she's doing all right," muttered Gregg. "She's destroying New Reykjavik by pitting the Klingons and the colonists against each other. But why?"

Ro frowned. "So the Federation and the Klingons will both clear out and leave Selva to the Romulans."

They stood in silence for a few seconds, mulling over the ramifications of their discovery. They were so silent they could hear the latch turning on the outside door. Ro motioned them back into the bathroom, and they stepped gingerly around the exposed hole. They barely got the bathroom door shut before the small dark woman entered her quarters.

"What's this?" Louise Drayton muttered to herself. "What happened to my furniture?"

Ro decided not to let her make any more discoveries. She stepped boldly out of the bathroom, one hand behind her back.

"Hi!" said the Bajoran cheerfully.

Drayton gasped with surprise, then a smile crept across her ageless face. Ageless, thought Ro, thanks to a substantial amount of plastic surgery that had turned her from a Romulan into a human.

"Aren't you the cheeky one," said Drayton with a begrudging admiration.

"Where's the *real* Louise Drayton?" asked Ensign Ro. "Is her body buried on some far-off planet?"

The scientist smiled. "I think I'll go tell President Oscaras you're here."

"Please do," replied Ro. "I've got something to show him in the bathroom."

That wiped the smile off the woman's face. She started to reach into her jacket pocket, but Ro was prepared. She whipped the spray bottle from behind her back and shot a burning stream of ammonia into the spy's face.

"Aaagh!" shrieked Drayton, staggering backward, ripping at her eyes. Despite her bad ankle, Ro charged across the room and smashed her fist into Drayton's face, sending the woman sprawling to the floor. Ro quickly grabbed the phaser from the woman's jacket pocket and leveled it at her. Her hand hurt from the blow she had delivered, but she felt awfully good otherwise.

"Where's my comm badge?" Ro demanded.

"I don't have it," Drayton muttered. "Oscaras has it." She started to get up on one elbow.

"Don't move," cautioned Ro. "I haven't checked this phaser, but knowing you, it's probably set to kill." She checked it and saw that it was, in fact, set to kill. She changed the setting to heavy stun.

Gregg and Myra stepped out of the bathroom, and Gregg's balled fists made it obvious that he wouldn't mind punching the doctor, too. "What's going on out there?" he demanded.

Drayton blinked. "You don't know?"

"They haven't exactly kept us informed," said Gregg. "What's going on?"

The doctor leapt to her feet and made a dash for the door, but Gregg stretched out a long leg and tripped her. That gave Ro time to paralyze her with a blue phaser beam. Louise Drayton lay crumpled on the floor.

Ro slumped into Drayton's couch and muttered, "She'll be out at least an hour."

Gregg shrugged. "I doubt she would've told us anything, anyway." He pointed to the bathroom. "There's our way out of here. Do you still want to take it?"

"We have to," said the ensign. "When she doesn't return they'll come looking for her. And sometime they'll figure out we escaped, if they haven't already. But let's take her with us."

Gregg Calvert was the first to lower himself into the tunnel, and he made a couple of interesting discoveries. "This halogen lantern will be useful," he said. "And here's the costume she used to seduce the Klingons. There's also some kind of whip."

"Let me see the whip," said Ro. Gregg handed it up, and the Bajoran admired the peculiar device. "This is no ordinary whip. I'm not sure how it works, but we need every weapon we can find." She curled it up and stuck it into her belt, not far from Drayton's phaser. "Are you ready for me to send down the doctor?"

"Sure," answered Gregg, turning on the lantern and filling the hole with an eerie green-tinged light.

Ro smiled at Myra. "Come on, you can help me."

Fortunately, the diminutive doctor didn't weigh very much, even as a limp body, and Ro and Myra were able to carry her to the hole and lower her into

Gregg's sturdy arms. He had to duck to enter the tunnel with her, but he and the doctor were soon out of sight.

He returned a moment later and called up, "Let's go! You first, Myra. Ro, will you turn off the lights and see if you can cover the hole?"

"Right," she answered. The ensign quickly shoved the furniture back into some semblance of order, locked the door, and turned off the lights. She lowered herself into the tunnel, feeling for the ladder with her feet. There was no way she could pull both the metal plate and the carpet over her head, so she opted to cover the hole with only the carpet. If somebody walked in to use the bathroom, they would get a rude surprise, but that couldn't be helped.

Once she had pulled the carpet over the hole and climbed down the rest of the way she felt like a mole in its burrow, despite the green light that emanated from the lantern only a few meters away. She could see Gregg and Myra silhouetted in its strange glow, plus the limp body of Doctor Drayton in Gregg's arms.

The tunnel had not been dug but rather vaporized with a phaser, leaving smooth walls that would have been the envy of ancient tunnel diggers. Nevertheless, a few roots and furry lichens poked their way through the soil, and the smell of damp earth was overpowering. Drayton had made the tunnel for herself, and Ro had to duck to keep from touching the wet things growing over her head.

Gregg spoke in the darkness. "Myra, can you pick up the lantern and lead the way?"

"Sure, Dad!" said the girl excitedly. "Gee, this is cool!"

Cool it was, literally, and Ro shivered as they walked along. The light bobbed ahead of her in Myra's hands, but Gregg's hulking body cut off most of it. He warned them to keep their voices down, because they would be passing under the wall soon, and he had no idea how close the tunnel passed to a guard tower. Ro thought it was doubtful anybody could hear them down here. Her main concern was that Selva would pick this moment to have a major earthquake, and they'd be buried alive. She tried to tell herself that the earthquake faults were a thousand kilometers away and posed no danger, except for the resultant tidal waves, but the dank earth all around whispered to her of an early grave.

She walked bent over in the darkness for what seemed like a dozen kilometers but was probably less than one. No question about it, thought Ro, Louise Drayton—or whoever she was—had had guts to come down into the blackness and carve out this tunnel, even if she had a phaser to do the hard work. It was also quite an assignment for one woman to rid an entire planet of a Federation colony, but Louise Drayton had nearly succeeded. In fact, she might yet. The primitive planet would be a perfect place for a hidden Romulan base, especially after a Federation colony had failed there. Its location would allow them to monitor both Federation and Klingon space.

Finally Myra stopped and pointed the beam upward. "There's a ladder here," she called. "It goes straight up."

"Let me go first," said Ro, shouldering her way past the Calverts.

Maybe she was just eager to get out of that pit, but Ro climbed the ladder as quickly as she could and pushed back a flap covered with leaves that hid the opening. Without much regard to what she would find she poked her head out.

She found only darkness and rows of black tree trunks reaching upward to black boughs, where not the slightest speck of light penetrated. The forest reminded her uncomfortably of the tunnel she had just come from. They might as well have been a million kilometers away from New Reykjavik, because there was absolutely no sign of it.

"It's okay," she called down to Myra and Gregg, hoping that was really true. They were no longer in the realm of frightened and deceitful colonists but in the realm of murderous Klingons raised in the wilderness. She shivered at the cold and climbed out of the hole.

She helped Myra up first, then the two of them reached down and pulled the unconscious form of Doctor Drayton to the surface. Gregg Calvert climbed out, looking more frightened than either of the two females. He flinched at a rustling sound overhead, even though it was obviously just some nocturnal animal on the prowl. He turned off the halogen lantern.

"Well," said Gregg, "any idea how to find your friends?"

"No," answered Ro glumly. Wandering around in the unfamiliar woods at nights would be the height of lunacy.

Once again, there was nothing to do but wait.

Chapter Sixteen

BY THE TIME the first rays of dawn seeped through the canopy of leaves that spanned the forest, the party of twenty-one Klingons, a Betazoid, and an android was already on the march. It was a surly group, thought Deanna Troi, made more so by the fact that they had been celebrating much of the night and hadn't eaten anything since the day before. Worf had promised them food upon reaching the settlement, and that was enough to get them going. Although they would never admit it, Deanna suspected the Klingons had already been spoiled by the meals furnished by the *Enterprise;* they had little stomach for their usual fare of grubs, dried chuck meat, mussels, and whatever greens they could dig up.

The young Klingons gripped the knives in their belts nervously as they trudged through the forest, looking like people headed to their own funerals. On another occasion, thought Deanna, they might have been leaping through the trees, but now they were walking like the clumsy flat-heads. At first she had tried to assure them they would be welcomed by the colonists, but she soon gave up that approach. The Klingons were going in, and perhaps their gloomy air of resignation was based more on the fact that they were giving up their way of life than that they were giving in to the colonists. This was a walk into the unknown, a journey into a new life, and there was no way she could make predictions about their future.

So they walked in silence, listening to the twitterings of birds and the chattering of animals, which sounded more cheerful this morning than ever before. Perhaps they sensed that sole possession of the forest was returning to them. Deanna had some vague feelings of unease, but she attributed them to the fact that the *Enterprise* and Captain Picard were light-years away and they had to complete this mission on their own. Without Worf's determination they would never have been able to do so. If there was ever a right man for the job, he was it.

In short order they saw the glimmer of metal through the stark tree trunks, and Deanna was surprised that they had reached the village in what seemed like only an hour. Of course, they had never walked directly between the mound and the village before, and the youths' hutches were spread out all over the forest. Such a short distance, she thought, separated these two groups, yet what chasms of experience and expectations separated them. It was indeed time to close those gaps and heal the wounds.

As they drew closer they saw the sun glinting off the high metal walls, making the structure appear totally alien next to the earthy black and greens of the forest. The Klingons stopped and began to fade back, murmuring in the guttural tones they had used before remembering their language.

"Be brave," Worf encouraged them. "A Klingon holds up his head and does not look afraid."

They didn't exactly hold up their heads and look

unafraid, but they did continue onward, and a man waved to them from the guard tower beside the gate. "I'm opening the gate!" he called cheerfully. "Just step forward, single file."

Worf took the lead to set an example, and Wolm and Turrok fell into step behind him. The others followed in a more or less orderly fashion, and Deanna found herself drifting back to the rear of the column, where Data had stationed himself. A plethora of emotions was assaulting her, ranging from fear and anxiety to unrepentent hatred. She tried to tell herself that such feelings were normal—on both sides—but it was still difficult to confront so many raw emotions at one time.

Noticing her discomfort, Data asked, "Are you all right, Counselor?"

"I . . . I think so," she mumbled. "There's so much fear, from both sides. It's a little overwhelming."

"If all goes well," answered Data, "it will subside gradually, will it not?"

"If all goes well," she repeated numbly. Why was she beginning to think that all was not going to go well? It wasn't so much the youngsters' fear that was disturbing as it was the waves of hatred emanating from within those steel walls. Worf had already passed through the fortified door, and the young Klingons were dutifully following. It was too late to turn back. Nevertheless, Deanna told herself she was going to get to the radio as soon as possible and ask Captain Picard to return.

She and Data were the last to pass through the metal walls, and she heard the door clanging shut behind her. It was an ominous sound. Also ominous was the deserted appearance of the courtyard, as if all the colonists had been told to remain safely in their homes. Finally a small welcoming party led by President Oscaras approached them from the far end of the square and stopped a considerable distance away. Broad smiles graced their faces, and Deanna felt a little bit better.

"Welcome!" said the beaming Oscaras, although he made no movement to come closer. "Is this all of them?"

"Yes," answered Worf, standing before a group of scrawny, unkempt youngsters who huddled meekly together. They hardly looked like the fearsome savages who had kept two-hundred colonists terrified for months. "I promised them food," said Worf. "Could that be arranged?"

"Of course!" said Oscaras. "Thank you for bringing them here, Lieutenant. You saved us a lot of trouble." He raised his arm over his head and shouted, *"Fire!"*

At once a handful of colonists sprang up from each guard tower, and dozens more fanned out from behind each building. As soon as they aimed their phaser rifles they fired, and blinding beams streaked across the courtyard. Some of the haphazard beams crossed each other and scorched the air with blistering explosions.

"You betrayed us!" screamed Maltz, drawing his knife and lunging for Worf. But a blue beam cut him down before he had taken a single step, and he crumpled at Worf's feet. The lieutenant snarled and started to draw his own phaser. But to the colonists, a Klingon was a Klingon, and he was blasted in the crossfire. He staggered a few steps, then slumped lifelessly to the ground.

Standing at the rear, Deanna was frozen in horror. The youngsters ran in circles, shrieking and trying to escape, but the gate was shut and the walls were too high to vault. Now she knew what the Earth saying "shooting fish in a barrel" meant. One by one the young Klingons were felled, and their bodies littered the courtyard.

Only Data remained calm. He drew his hand phaser and meticulously picked off every settler in the guard tower that overlooked the gate. Then he made a superhuman leap into the tower itself and threw the latch that opened the gate. But it was too late. No Klingons were left standing to escape. Deanna made a dash for the open door but was cut down herself. Her last memory before blackness was the grimy dirt that struck her face when she hit the ground.

Data could do nothing more than he had already done, and he knew it. He didn't fear the stun blasts that were felling the others, but one of the colonists might crank up his phaser rifle to full and vaporize his circuitry. So Data picked up a phaser rifle in each hand and leapt over the wall. Beams blasted the dirt at his heels, but he reached the cover of the forest without harm.

"Data!" called a voice among the trees.

He whirled around, expecting he would have to defend himself. Instead he saw the concerned face of Ensign Ro.

"We must remove ourselves from this place," said the android.

Ro motioned him to follow her. "What's going on in there?" she asked as they moved through the trees. "We heard the explosions and shouting, and I ran over to investigate."

"Without knowing the colonists' intentions," answered Data, "I would say they have taken the Klingons, Counselor Troi, and Lieutenant Worf prisoner."

"So that's what they were up to," muttered Ro. "You convinced the Klingons to turn themselves in, and that's what you got in return. Oscaras is as treacherous as a pit mantis."

"I would agree with that assessment," answered

Data. "He told us you were sedated in sickbay when you failed to answer my hail."

"Bastards!" snarled Ro. "At least we're not totally alone."

They reached a small clearing where Data was moderately surprised to find three humans—a tall blond man, a female child, and a dark-haired woman who was bound and gagged and propped against a tree. Ro made quick introductions, and they exchanged stories of their separate ambushes and escapes.

Data considered the dark-haired woman. "So you are the goddess," he remarked. "I observed you engaging in sex with Balak. You are the cause of much of the enmity on Selva."

"No kidding," grumbled Gregg Calvert. "We know she's a spy, but is there any way to find out if she's a Romulan who's had plastic surgery?"

Data cocked his head and answered, "Yes. Plastic surgery is seldom performed on the hands, and Romulans have a tiny bone spur at the base of their palms that is missing in humans. May I examine her?"

Drayton struggled when he bent down to inspect her hands, but it took him only a moment to locate the telltale bone spur. "She is a Romulan," he declared. "Do you have her displacer?"

"This?" asked Ro, reaching under some leaves and drawing out the high-tech whip.

"Precisely," replied the android, taking the weapon from her. "It is a fascinating device, but I am unfamiliar with its operation."

"Perhaps," Gregg Calvert suggested, "we could try it out on Doctor Drayton."

Even bound and gagged, the doctor squirmed fiercely.

Suddenly a beep sounded in Data's pocket. He made a quizzical expression and reached in to remove the hand-held communicator given to him by President Oscaras. He opened it and answered, "Data here."

"This is President Oscaras," bellowed an arrogant voice. "We are completely in charge of the planet, and we ask you to turn yourself in. Also, do you know the whereabouts of Ensign Ro, Gregg and Myra Calvert, and Doctor Drayton?"

"Yes," answered Data honestly. But that was all the information he furnished.

"We won't harm you," said Oscaras, "if you turn yourselves in."

The android replied, "That promise does not correspond with the events I just witnessed. What was the purpose of attacking our party and the Klingons?"

"That's simple," answered Oscaras. "To put the Klingons on trial."

"For what crime?"

"Murder."

Data asked, "If you found them guilty of murder, what would be their punishment?"

"We expect to hang them."

"Are you aware," the android replied, "that capital punishment is forbidden in the Federation, according to the second directive?"

"Yes," answered Oscaras, "and we expect to withdraw from the Federation now that we have stabilized Selva."

"I see," said Data. "If you are going to withdraw from the Federation, then you have no reason to detain Counselor Troi and Lieutenant Worf. I request that you release them immediately."

"As soon as the trial is over," Oscaras agreed. "We'll release you, too."

"I am not in custody," answered Data, "and I do not intend to be."

"Can I talk to him?" asked Gregg Calvert.

226

Data nodded and handed the communicator to the former security chief of New Reykjavik. He took a deep breath, trying to control his anger. "This is Calvert," he said.

"Gregg!" thundered Oscaras. "Come back to us. Our dream has been fulfilled—we finally captured the savages! You should be here with us, not against us."

"Oscaras," muttered the blond man, "I used to respect you, but now I realize you're an idiot. I'm begging you—let them all go and call back the *Enterprise*. If you act now, there may be time to save New Reykjavik. The way you're going, you'll just destroy it."

"You can't defy me!" bellowed the president. "I'm completely in charge of Selva. Turn yourself in, and we can make this planet the paradise we set out to make it."

"By hanging a bunch of children and defying the Federation?" Gregg shook his head. "That's no way to found a civilization. When the *Enterprise* doesn't hear from its away team they'll come back, and Data still has his communicator. You can't keep this a secret."

Ensign Ro could almost envision the apoplectic expression on Raul Oscaras's face as he shouted, "If you don't stand with us, you stand against us! I'll come out there myself and get you!"

"Yeah, come and get us, you fat windbag. You couldn't find your nose with your finger!" He snapped the communicator shut.

Myra chuckled, but Data asked, "Was that wise, antagonizing him?"

"Yes, it was, if you want to free your friends. If we can get him to lead a large party out to find us, we can go back in there and free your people and the Klingons."

"How will we do that?" asked Data.

"The same way we escaped," answered Calvert. He

took a couple steps and threw open the trapdoor that led to Drayton's tunnel. "We have a private entrance."

Worf awoke in an angry mood, made angrier by the fact that his hands were tied behind his back and his ankles were bound by tough polymer cord. He struggled for almost a minute before he realized it was futile; only then did he take time to study his surroundings. He was lying on the floor in somebody's private quarters, and Counselor Troi was lying on the bed, bound in a similar fashion. She appeared to be still unconscious.

"Counselor!" he called. "Counselor Troi!" he barked hoarsely.

She moaned, then began to stir. Gradually she came to, only to make her own disheartening discovery of their predicament. She rolled over to face him, her black hair matted against a grimy cheek.

"Worf," she groaned. "We made a terrible mistake. We led them into an ambush."

"They call *us* savages," he spat. "The settlers never intended to make peace—only to betray us."

"Have you talked to any of them?" she asked. "Where are we?"

"Somebody's quarters. I haven't seen anybody but you. They took our comm badges, and I don't know where Turrok and the others are. For all I know, they may be dead."

"We have to talk to them," Deanna insisted. "We have to make them see reason."

"Reason," he scoffed. "Revenge is all they want." With all the volume he could muster, Worf yelled, "Release us! Release us now! *I demand it!*"

The door opened, and President Oscaras entered, accompanied by a man who kept a phaser rifle trained on them. Worf did nothing to hide his hateful glare.

"I hear you, Mister Worf," said Oscaras, "there's no

reason to shout. I apologize for the precautions we have to take, but this is a moment we've been planning for ten months. We don't want anything to go wrong."

"I'm the one tied up," seethed the Klingon, "but you're the one who's in trouble. Release us now. I demand it!"

Oscaras scowled. "You're in no position to demand anything, do you understand me?" He turned to Deanna and said with more sympathy, "I do apologize for this treatment, Counselor Troi, but we allowed Ensign Ro and a traitor to be untied, and they escaped. If I have your assurance you won't try to escape, I will arrange for *you* to be untied."

"I would keep my word," she replied, "but I don't believe a promise means anything to you."

Oscaras's lips thinned under his salt-and-pepper beard. "You've never understood the hell we've gone through here. If I took a knife and slit Lieutenant Worf's throat, do you think I should escape punishment? If I attacked peaceful people for no reason, should I escape punishment?"

"You *did* attack us for no reason," barked Worf, "and you won't escape punishment!"

"Lieutenant Worf, I tire of you." Oscaras frowned. "I fear you have more in common with those murderous savages than with the people you claim to serve." He motioned to his henchman. "If he talks again, stun him."

Deanna had seen the big Klingon angry before, but never quite like this. He looked as if he could bite through the cords that tied his legs and wrists, if only he could only get his teeth on them.

"You have us at your mercy," she said calmly, "and there's no reason to torment us. What are your intentions?"

"There will be a trial," answered the president. "A murder trial. We wish to hold it as quickly as possible and to resolve everything before the *Enterprise* returns. But first we have to find Ensign Ro, Commander Data, and one or two traitors who escaped. I'm afraid you will both have to remain bound until we return."

"You're going to kill them, aren't you?" asked Worf.

The guard aimed his phaser rifle at Worf, but Oscaras lowered the barrel with his hand. "That's all right, Edward, I'll answer his question. Yes, Mister Worf, we intend to hang them. It's more humane than what they've done to so many of our people."

"Two wrongs don't make a right," protested Deanna. "They were turning themselves in to make peace!"

"That will be the end result," said Oscaras. "Come, Edward, let's find the rest of them."

The two men left the quarters, and Deanna heard the door being locked behind them.

"Do'Ha!" cursed Worf, struggling in vain against his bindings. "If they kill them, do you know what that means?"

"What?" asked the Betazoid, unable to hide the fear in her voice.

"It means they'll have to kill us, too. There's only one way they can get away with this—by making sure we're not around to tell Captain Picard what happened."

Deanna Troi joined Lieutenant Worf in a desperate effort to lossen the ropes that bound her arms and legs.

Data crouched behind a fallen log, watching the main gate of the compound from a safe distance. With his acute hearing he heard the voices and footsteps even before the fortified door opened and at least fifty armed colonists filed out. Raul Oscaras took the lead, dividing his force into smaller groups and pointing them in various directions. That was as much as the android needed to see, and he ran swiftly through the trees toward the tunnel entrance.

Only Ensign Ro remained above ground, waiting for him. "Have they come out?" she asked.

"Yes," replied the android. "We must be quick and efficient."

Ro lowered herself into the hole first, and Data followed, pulling the camouflaged flap over his head. The halogen lantern illuminated the musty darkness of the tunnel and revealed Gregg Calvert, impatiently gripping one of the phaser rifles stolen by Data during his escape. Louise Drayton remained bound and gagged, leaning against a muddy wall. Myra Calvert stood a few meters away from her, nearly obscured by the darkness. The girl nervously gripped a hand phaser.

"They have left the compound," Data told Gregg. "There are approximately fifty of them."

"Good," said the man. He turned to his young daughter. "Myra, I've shown you how to use the phaser. Don't hesitate to stun Doctor Drayton if she tries to escape or does anything to alert Oscaras. And stay down here, out of sight."

"Yes, Daddy." She nodded grimly.

"We must go now," said Data. "I will lead, because my vision allows me to see in the darkness."

Ensign Ro grabbed the second phaser rifle and followed the android. Several hours of inactivity had done a great deal to relieve the pain and swelling in her ankle, and she walked with barely a limp. Gregg followed her, gripping his phaser rifle. The tunnel grew darker as they walked, because they had left the lantern behind with Myra and her prisoner. Their voices echoed in the dank chamber.

"Let's go over our plan," said Ro. "I'll attack the guard tower by the front gate and keep it closed, in case Oscaras and his people come back early."

"Right," answered Gregg. "Data and I will find the prisoners. We'll release them, and all of us will meet back at the tunnel."

Data added, "If possible, I would like to go to the communications room and alert the *Enterprise* to our situation."

"But that's secondary," said Calvert. "If I know Oscaras, that place is still well guarded."

"Agreed," answered Data. "If necessary, I believe we can elude the colonists in the forest until the *Enterprise* returns."

Ro sighed. "The only problem is, will the Klingons stay peaceful after what's happened to them?"

"That is unknown," answered Data.

They walked the rest of the way in silence, and Ro fingered her new comm badge. Data still had a supply of them, after equipping the Klingons. Finally the android stopped, and Ro and Gregg nearly ran up his back. "I see an opening above us," he reported. His companions saw only darkness.

"There should be a ladder there, too," answered Ro, "and there's only a piece of carpet over the opening."

"Affirmative," answered Data. He began to climb. After a few seconds welcome rays of light streaked down the opening, and Ro was relieved to be able to see again. "You may ascend," Data called down.

Ro and Gregg strapped their phaser rifles to their backs and climbed the ladder. A moment later they were standing in Louise Drayton's small apartment. Data drew his hand phaser, and the two humanoids leveled their rifles.

"Phasers on stun," ordered Data. His companions checked their weapons and nodded. Data put his hand on the door latch. "Ready?"

"Ready," replied his companions.

The android opened the door, and they stepped into one of the nondescript streets of New Reykjavik. A woman was walking past with two small children, and she immediately shrank back upon seeing the unfamiliar faces and the weapons. She wrapped her arms protectively around her children.

"Valerie," said Gregg, "we don't want to hurt you. Where are they keeping the prisoners?"

Ro could see the indecision on the woman's face, but she could also see the determination on Calvert's face. "All right," he said, "let's take the children hostage until they release the prisoners."

"No!" shrieked the woman.

"Then tell us!"

She pointed a quivering hand toward the second largest building in the compound. "They converted the dining hall into a holding cell. That's where the Klingons are. The crew people are in Tony and Jan's quarters."

Gregg ordered, "Get to your house and stay there." The woman didn't have to be told twice, and she quickly shepherded her children down the narrow street.

"Signal me when you're ready to leave," said Ro. "I'll meet you back here."

The Bajoran jogged in the direction of the gate and emerged in the broad courtyard with its three forlorn trees. Once again she was glad she was wearing the brown uniform of the colonists, because a number of people had congregated around the open gate and its guard tower. Fortunately, their attention was directed toward the forest. She lowered both her head and her rifle and was able to cover two dozen meters before someone spotted her. A man looked curiously at her.

"Hey," he said, "who are—"

The blue beam caught him in the midsection, and

he collapsed into the dust. She took aim at the three colonists in the guard tower and stunned them all with one sweeping blast. The colonists on the ground whirled around, only to be zapped by another sweeping arc of blue light. They had barely struck the ground before Ro was climbing the ladder into the guard tower. She grabbed the lever and slammed the gate shut.

The shouts from the main gate had alerted the guards in the dining hall, and two of them ran out, only to be cut down by Data and Gregg Calvert.

"The Klingons know me," said Data. "You go release Worf and Troi."

"Right," said Gregg, dashing off in another direction.

Data strode to the door and smashed it open with one kick. He was instantly hit by a blue beam, but the stun setting had no effect upon him. Before the two guards inside realized they were dealing with an android, Data dropped them into a deep sleep with his own phaser.

Data saw that several of the larger tables had been overturned, and the young Klingons were tied to the table legs, bound hand and foot. They gaped in awe at their rescuer.

"Data!" screamed Wolm.

"Silence is advisable," said the android. "Please obey my instructions, and we will escape unharmed."

Everyone, including Maltz, nodded in agreement. Data used his hands to snap the tough polymer cords that bound each youngster's hands and feet. When Maltz was freed he ran to one of the fallen colonists and gripped the woman by her throat.

"Stop that," ordered Data. "Do not sink to their level."

There was a tense moment as the youths looked

from Data to their nominal leader, wondering whose philosophy would triumph. Finally Maltz dropped the stunned colonist back to the floor and picked up her phaser weapon. "We follow you," he muttered.

A hundred meters away Gregg Calvert rounded a corner and saw two guards crouching inside the entryway of a typical residence. He immediately ducked out of sight. The guards had evidently heard the shouting and weren't sure if it was good news or bad news, but their crouching position made them difficult targets.

Gregg leapt into their view, waving and yelling, "Hey! Oscaras needs help!"

No sooner had the men risen to their feet and taken a few steps into the open than Gregg leveled his rifle and fired. They crumpled where they stood. Gregg ran to the door, found it was locked, and rifled through the bodies to find the key. When he opened the door he found Worf and Troi lying back to back on the floor, trying valiantly to untie each other's hands.

"We demand to be released!" yelled Worf.

"No problem," said Gregg. "That's what I'm here for. Data is releasing the Klingons, and Ro is guarding the gate."

Deanna blinked. "You're here to *rescue* us?"

Gregg bent down and started to untie her ankles. "That is, unless you'd rather stay here."

"No!" growled Worf, struggling impatiently against his bindings. "Use the phaser to cut the ropes. Try setting four, narrow beam."

The ex-security officer did as he was told and soon had them released. Worf and Deanna rose stiffly to their feet. "Here," said Gregg, handing each of them a comm badge, "you'll need these."

Worf affixed the insignia to his chest and tapped it. "Worf to Data!" he called.

"Data here," came the response. "I assume you have been rescued. Follow Mister Calvert to the tunnel and obey his instructions. He planned this escape."

Worf looked with some amazement at the tall blond man. "Thank you," he murmured.

"Time for that later," said Gregg, moving to the doorway. "There are two stunned colonists outside in the street. Get their phaser rifles."

Worf grinned. "With pleasure."

Chapter Seventeen

IN THE TOWER by the main gate Ensign Ro remained in a watchful crouch, but she didn't see the phaser beam until it ripped the roof off the tiny structure, showering her with sparks and drops of molten steel. She sprawled on her back as more blasts converged on the tower, and she realized the shots were coming from the forest. Oscaras and his force were back, and they weren't shooting to stun. Somebody inside the compound must have alerted them about what was happening.

Ro barely had time to crawl to the rope ladder and drop to the ground before another salvo of phasers sent the entire structure toppling over. It crashed only a meter away from her, spewing dirt and singed metal into the air. Ro screamed as a piece of flying metal cut deeply into her shoulder. She heard more crackling noises and whirled around to see the gate itself evaporating in smoke and sparks. A glowing hole was getting bigger and bigger.

She knew that in a matter of seconds fifty armed colonists would be pouring through that hole.

Gripping her bleeding shoulder, Ro dashed toward Louise Drayton's apartment. She was extremely relieved to see Data and the band of bedraggled Klingons waiting outside the door.

"You've got to get out of here!" she shouted. "They're blasting through the gate!"

"I will conduct the Klingons to safety," said Data. "Please remain here and tell the others we are safe."

"You're not safe yet," she replied. "You'd better get going!"

As Data ushered the Klingons into Drayton's cramped quarters Ro lifted the rifle to her blood-covered shoulder and waited. Two armed colonists rushed around the corner of a building, and Ro cut them down. Tensely she awaited the onslaught of Oscaras's entire force, and she nearly shot Gregg Calvert when he came charging between two buildings across the street. Fortunately, she saw a large Klingon and a slim Betazoid following him, and she held her fire.

"Get going!" she called to them. "Oscaras is breaking through the gate!"

"Aren't you coming?" asked Worf.

Ro shook her head. "No. I'm wounded, and somebody's got to stay and try to contact the *Enterprise.*"

The Klingon muttered, "Then we will all stay."

"No, Worf," said Deanna Troi. "I'll stay with her, but it's far too dangerous for you. Go protect the children."

Gregg protested, "This is crazy. Both of you come with us right now!"

"Go, Gregg," Ro told him, managing a smile. "We'll put down our weapons—they won't hurt us. Go on, you'll be safe with Worf and Data."

An explosion sounded somewhere within the compound, followed by a number of shouts. Reluctantly Worf and Gregg left the women and disappeared into

Drayton's quarters. When the door was shut behind them and the tunnel safely hidden once again, Ro tossed her phaser rifle to the ground. Deanna did likewise.

"Lie down," ordered Deanna, "I want to stop that bleeding."

The Bajoran did as she was told, thinking a wounded person lying on the ground wouldn't look very threatening. With both hands Deanna applied pressure to the wound. She heard more shouting and footsteps, but Ro blacked out before Oscaras and his people reached them.

"Where did they go?" bellowed Raul Oscaras.

Deanna Troi shrugged. "I told you—back to the forest."

"But how did they get in? How did they escape?"

Deanna shook her head wearily. "I don't know." That was practically the truth, because she hadn't seen the secret escape route.

Oscaras towered over her. "Could you lead us to their hideout?"

"Maybe I could lead you to one of their hutches," she said, "but there's no guarantee they would be there. I wouldn't do it anyway."

Oscaras snarled and raised a beefy hand over his head as if to slap her, but Deanna glared defiantly at him. "I wouldn't," she warned. "We came here for only one purpose—to save lives. And if you don't like that, call the *Enterprise* back, and we'll leave."

"You ruined it!" he wailed. "We finally had a solution for the Klingon problem!"

"So did we," muttered Deanna. "Face it: You failed to kill them, and they failed to kill you. So the only alternative is to learn to live with one another."

Raul Oscaras growled like the Klingons he hated, slammed his fist into his palm, and began to pace. He knew he was defeated, thought the Betazoid. As they had led her to his office she had heard several of the colonists beginning to question his recent decisions, especially the one that alienated the away team from the *Enterprise.* When he had marched off into the forest and allowed the Klingons to be rescued by three people, the deficiencies of his leadership had become even more apparent.

"Can I go see how Ensign Ro is?" she asked.

The president fumed, "Do you think I should just let you walk out of here?"

"Put me on trial if you like," Deanna scoffed. "Let me see, what is my crime?" Bringing the Klingons to turn themselves in? That was stupid, I admit, and I won't do it again."

President Oscaras motioned angrily toward the door. "Get out. Sickbay is to the right, at the end of the hall."

He followed her out the door and made sure she didn't linger too long outside the radio room. There were two guards armed with phaser rifles standing in the doorway of the radio room, and Deanna decided not to press that issue for the moment. The immediate danger was over, the Klingons were safe, and President Oscaras was losing his stranglehold on New Reykjavik. She proceeded to sickbay at the end of the hall.

Ensign Ro was lying on an examination table, and a young male doctor was ministering to her injury. Her shoulder was wrapped in bandages, and the doctor was fixing a sling under her arm. Despite her recent heroics, Ensign Ro didn't look particularly relieved to be out of action.

"I've got to check the seismograph," Ro insisted.

Deanna smiled reassuringly, but it was the doctor to whom she spoke: "How is she?"

"We stopped the bleeding," said Doctor Freleng,

"but I want her to take it easy. By the way, I want you to know how sick I am about all of this. I'm tired of patching people up—I want to deliver babies again."

"I can imagine," said the Betazoid sympathetically. "Can she move around?"

"She can walk, but that's all," warned the doctor. He looked pointedly at Ro. "Nothing strenuous."

"I'll take responsibility for her," said Deanna, helping the ensign to her feet.

Ro leaned against the table for a moment, summoning what strength she had left. "Thanks again," she told the doctor.

"Doctor, do you have any influence with those men guarding the radio room?" Deanna asked.

"I'm afraid not," said Freleng. "Oscaras handpicked them. But I'm on my way to see our president now, and I have a lot of questions for him. I don't think I'm the only one."

Ro gripped Deanna's arm. "Let's get to the seismograph," she insisted. "I've got to see if there have been any changes."

Captain Picard fidgeted in his seat and felt like loosening the stiff collar of his dress uniform, but he maintained his polite smile and kept his hands folded properly in his lap. For days, it seemed, he had been listening to speeches. Apparently scores of important personages had to speak at great length on this grand occasion of the peaceful division of the Aretian solar system.

Picard had requested a chance to speak but wasn't scheduled to do so until the next day. He merely wanted to tell the parties what was already taking place—namely that Commander Riker, Lieutenant Commander La Forge, and six shuttlecraft were already busy charting their mutual solar system. He intended to inform the Aretians and Pargites of the success of the ongoing mission, then excuse the *Enterprise* to return to Selva.

"And so," a rotund politician concluded for the tenth time, "it was our steadfast determination to seek equitable solutions to the disagreements that have plagued our solar system for fifty years that resulted in this historical agreement. Over twenty years ago we proposed the establishment of enterprise zones in the undeveloped areas, in order to better facilitate our plans for a solar system–wide monetary unit. Our unwavering belief in free trade has accounted for the tremendous leap in the standard of living of our people, and we wish to impart this benefit to all citizens of the solar system. Only through a determined application of the Fairness Doctrine can we hope to allay the distrust that . . ."

The captain tuned out. He was beginning to realize why this agreement had taken months to conclude, and he had the deepest sympathy for the female Vulcan mediator who sat beside him. But worry kept intruding on his mind—worry about the lack of contact with the away team on Selva. He knew it was a delicate mission, and he didn't want to appear to be pressuring them by demanding reports. Picard imagined the team was still winning converts one by one, working toward a peaceful resolution. He certainly hoped they weren't making speeches like this deadly dull one from the minister of commerce.

"Excuse me," he whispered to the Vulcan mediator. "I have to contact my ship."

The Vulcan requested, "Please do not be gone long. Your presence is very reassuring."

Everyone in the vast auditorium looked as though they were about to fall asleep, thought Picard, and his presence hadn't accomplished anything so far. But he said nothing and simply rose from his chair and walked to the back of the room.

He tapped his communicator badge. "Picard to *Enterprise.*"

"Enterprise," responded an efficient female voice. "Lieutenant Wallins reporting."

"Lieutenant, any word from the away team on Selva?"

"No, sir, I'm afraid not. Commander La Forge just reported in, and he says the survey should be done in approximately sixty hours. The computer is processing the information concurrently, and we should have our first recommendations shortly."

The captain pursed his lips. "Thank you," he said. "Picard out."

For the first time he was beginning to get angry and impatient. This was drudge work—a first-year cadet could command this mission. Normally he was quite proud of the renown of the *Enterprise,* but it was working against him in this instance. He heard the voice droning behind him, and he knew there was nothing he could do but wait.

Doctor Drayton stared wild-eyed at the ragtag collection of Klingons that confronted her, and she struggled to mouth something through her gag. Her frightened eyes turned beseechingly to the tall blond man and the tall dark android beside him. Data found her plight unfortunate but acceptable, considering the language she had been using when they had found her and Myra in the tunnel. Doctor Drayton knew how to swear expertly in at least three languages.

They were ensconced in a nearby hutch—one that was stocked with stolen goods—and their perimeter was well guarded by Worf and ten of the castaways, who communicated by drum. Data would have preferred to take some action, but the irrational behavior of the colonists offered them no course of action except to await the *Enterprise*'s return. Counselor Troi and Ensign Ro were a persuasive pair, and they would gain access to the colonists' subspace radio if it was possible to do so. Meanwhile, it was advisable to keep the Klingons and colonists separated.

Data wasn't programmed for surprise, but he never ceased to be intrigued by the diverse behavior practiced by humans. He wished to debate the failings of capital punishment with the colonists, because he knew most of the history and pertinent statistics; but that debate would have to wait for another day.

For the moment, they had to be prepared to move quickly, and having a prisoner was a detriment. Carrying the entomologist to this hutch, with her kicking and attempting to scream, had been a chore in itself. Data didn't think that President Oscaras would be able to mount another maneuver outside the compound for some time, but they had to be prepared to move quickly. Mobility, concluded Data, had been the Klingons' strongest advantage during this entire conflict.

"I believe we must return Doctor Drayton to New Reykjavik," the android told Gregg Calvert.

"What?" barked the ex-security chief. "She's a spy—a Romulan."

"Knowing she is a spy," said Data, "effectively removes the threat she poses. We cannot keep her bound and gagged indefinitely, and she is an impediment to quick movement."

"Besides," said Myra Calvert, taking her daddy's hand and looking up at him, "it sets a bad example."

"All right," muttered Gregg. "But Data, tell Oscaras what he's getting. Tell them about the tunnel, too. We're done with it."

"I agree," said Data. He reached into his pocket and opened up the hand-held communicator. "Commander Data to New Reykjavik."

A nervous female voice answered, "Yes?"

"Please inform Raul Oscaras and the other colonists that we are returning Doctor Louise Drayton. She is a Romulan spy, and the proof is the tunnel she dug in the lavatory of her quarters."

Data felt a disturbance in the region of his ankle, and he looked down to see Doctor Drayton kicking him with her bound legs.

"Check her quarters!" shouted Gregg Calvert into the communicator. "And keep her locked up."

"That is all," said Data. He looked down at the floor and requested, "Doctor, will you please stop kicking me?"

She shook her head furiously, as if she wanted to talk.

Data remarked, "I will remove your gag if you promise not to shout and curse."

She nodded furiously, and Data untied the gag. Drayton sputtered as the cloth fell out, "I—I can get you off this planet!"

Gregg sneered. "By calling a Romulan vessel?"

Drayton nodded. "Yes. But you've got to call that girl back and tell her you're wrong! I need access to the subspace radio room."

"A common need," answered Data. "It is my belief that having a Romulan ship in orbit would be a needless complication under the circumstances." He pressed his comm badge. "Data to Worf."

"Worf here," barked a deep voice. "The forest is quiet, and it should be dark soon."

"That is well," answered the android. "Lieutenant, I have decided to release Doctor Drayton into the hands of the colonists. Her presence serves no useful purpose. I have informed the colonists that she is a spy, and I have given them the location of the tunnel. We need to appoint a detail to conduct her to the compound."

"Maltz and I can do that," answered Worf. "I was

concerned about how long we could hold her. Put a blindfold on her, and I'll meet you at the top of the hutch."

Worf gripped Louise Drayton's slim shoulder in a massive palm and steered her through the forest while Maltz strolled ahead of them, ever watchful. Both Klingons were armed with captured phaser rifles, but Worf sincerely intended not to use his. There had been entirely too much shooting lately, even for a Klingon. Darkness was oozing down the stark tree trunks like the sap, and the forest would soon be bathed in it. The night brought a peace and security that Worf was beginning to appreciate. The only predators on the planet were human, he decided, and humans were notoriously scared of darkness.

"Lieutenant," whispered Drayton suddenly, "I must speak with you."

Worf snarled under his breath, "You were told to be quiet."

"I want to be with you," said the small brunette coquettishly. "Don't turn me over to the settlers—I'll be the best ally you've ever had. I'll help you defeat them."

The Klingon scowled. "You sound more like a Romulan all the time. Be quiet, or I'll drop you down that pit you dug in the forest."

Drayton gulped, put her head down, and concentrated on walking blindfolded.

Ahead of them Maltz sank into a crouch and crept cautiously toward the last row of trees. Beyond the clearing the sun was deserting the shiny metal wall, turning it a dull gray. Maltz motioned to Worf to come forward, and the big Klingon wrapped his hand around Drayton's mouth and hauled her roughly through the underbrush. They were close to the main gate, and he could see half a dozen nervous colonists congregated in front of it. The hole blasted through the door by Oscaras had yet to be repaired, and the guards didn't appear to want to get far away from the jagged entrance.

Roughly, Worf pushed Louise Drayton to her knees and warned her, "If you call out, you'll get what a Romulan deserves. When I release your bindings I expect you to walk directly toward those guards. Speak only to identify yourself."

She batted her dark eyes helplessly at him. "You're making a mistake, Lieutenant. I've been trying to help the Klingons."

"Get going," hissed Worf, lifting Drayton to her feet and shoving her into the clearing.

For ten meters or so Louise Drayton did exactly as she had been ordered to do. The guards didn't notice her until she dropped to her knees, pointed frantically behind her, and shouted, *"Klingons!* A hundred of them! They're going to attack!"

The colonists whirled around and pranced nervously, phasers leveled for business. Led by one hothead, they began to fire indiscriminately into the forest, forcing Worf and Maltz to drop to their bellies.

Worf scrambled forward to see what the spy was up to, but all he caught was a glimpse of the dark woman running past the gate toward another section of the forest. One of the guards had the presence of mind to shoot at her, but he didn't have the skill to hit a moving target. Doctor Drayton sprang into the woods and was gone.

Cutting loose with several colorful Klingon phrases, Worf grabbed Maltz by the shoulder and motioned him to retreat. On their bellies the two Klingons crawled out of the range of fire. Worf decided he would not go after Louise Drayton—in the pitch blackness of the Selvan woods, pursuit was pointless. Drayton had escaped, but at least she wouldn't be a burden to them anymore.

Deanna Troi looked out the barred window in the science lab at the profound darkness that had swallowed that part of the planet. Even the salmon-colored lights of the compound could barely make a dent in it. Ro lay asleep on her cot in front of her instrument panels. The Bajoran had spent several hours calibrating a sonar device and training it on the midzone she kept talking about. Deanna had tried to listen to Ro's explanation of tectonic plates and tsunamis, but her attention kept drifting to the searing memory of the ambush early that morning. After that, everything had seemed an incredible blur, a surrealistic trip to the holodeck. But it was all real—from the mass hangings threatened by Raul Oscaras to the blood oozing from Ro's shoulder.

She was trying to decide who was to blame, but she finally decided it was everyone. Despite decades of rhetoric about peace between humans and Klingons, the fact remained that the two races were still mostly segregated. The crew of the *Enterprise* took Worf for granted, forgetting that few other humans ever came into direct contact with Klingons.

Captain Picard had turned into one of the foremost experts on Klingon affairs, but that was due entirely to his involvement with Worf. How many humans ever had face-to-face contact with Klingons, let alone spent extended time with them? A handful of ambassadors perhaps. Given the right circumstances, thought Deanna, Selva could have been a marvelous proving ground for interspecies relationships. Now it was just a battleground.

She sighed and looked back at the sleeping figure of

Ensign Ro. Half her body was wrapped in bandages, it seemed, but she appeared to be sleeping comfortably. Except for her insistence on staying close to her instruments, the Bajoran had been content to follow doctor's orders and exert herself very little. Deanna had brought her dinner, and they had done nothing more strenuous than talk.

The Betazoid wondered if it was worth the effort to try to get into the radio room that night. Oscaras had stationed himself there, surrounded by a number of loyal if misguided associates who vowed to protect him as long as he was president. There seemed to be no way to remove him except by force. An emergency election was being called for by several of the colonists, and there was considerable doubt about how much longer Raul Oscaras would be president of New Reykjavik.

Politics mattered little at the moment, thought Deanna. They were still out of contact with the *Enterprise,* and there was nothing to do but wait. The counselor rubbed her eyes and wondered how much longer she could stay awake. In a dark corner of the deserted laboratory she had set up her own cot, and it was beckoning her. What was the point of staying awake, she wondered, except to feed her fears and dread? She tried to tell herself the worst was over. Raul Oscaras was on his way out, and now they were all safe, weren't they? This unnamed dread was the worst kind of all, and she resolved to put it out of her mind with sleep. Or at least to try.

The morning was inordinately peaceful, even sunny, and a solid shaft of light stretched through the narrow windows on the east side of the lab building. Ensign Ro pushed herself away from her array of instruments, stood, and stretched her sinewy limbs.

Her shoulder responded with a dull throb that brought barely a grimace. That was good, she thought —it was healing.

Ro looked around the vast laboratory and saw that it was still mostly deserted. Either the workers were at home, cowering in fear and expecting more trouble, or they were ashamed to face her. She hoped it was the latter. A few showed up to check briefly on their experiments, cultures, simulations, or whatever was worrying them; they ignored her and left quickly. That was fine with Ro. All she wanted for the present was to be left alone to do her work.

She could see Counselor Troi in a far corner, still asleep, and the ensign had made sure no one bothered her. If anyone deserved some rest, it was Deanna Troi. Ro's admiration for the Betazoid was boundless, although they were of much different temperments and had never become close friends.

Ro knew she wasn't great on interpersonal skills and was very impressed to see someone who had mastered them much as Deanna Troi. For one thing, her team had been totally successful with the supposed savages, inducing them give themselves up and to seek peace. In contrast, Ro had been a miserable failure in her relationship with the colonists, excepting Myra and Gregg Calvert. She took no comfort from the fact that Louise Drayton and Raul Oscaras had hidden agendas that made them impossible to deal with. She should have foreseen what would happen and found a way to warn the rest of the away team. Ro slumped back in her chair, gloomy despite the unaccustomed sunshine streaming through the windows.

What brought Ro out of her chair was a very slight vibration, like somebody running past her desk. The ground under her feet seemed to rise slightly, then the alarm on the seismograph blasted in her ears, as if she needed such a warning. In New Reykjavik the temblor was barely enough to rattle the windows, but crazy zigzags were streaking across her instrument panels, warning her that the eggshell was breaking apart a thousand kilometers out in the ocean.

If she stayed perfectly still, Ro could feel the slight temblor under the balls of her feet, but she couldn't hold still. She had a dozen instruments to check at once. Despite the zigzag patterns on the seismographs and a Richter scale reading approaching ten, Ro's eyes were drawn to the newest instrument, the sonar detector she had installed the night before. Its readings were not zigzagging but were growing steadily. She watched in horror as a mere blip on the screen widened into a ball, then blossomed outward in a concentric circle from the gigantic displacement in the ocean.

She looked up to see Deanna Troi, obviously horrified by Ro's own expression. "What's the matter?" breathed Deanna.

"It's happened," Ro rasped. "The tsunami."

Chapter Eighteen

CAPTAIN PICARD stood patiently in the wings of the Polar Auditorium, awaiting his turn at the podium. The slim Vulcan mediator stood beside him, as if making sure he wouldn't escape. She hadn't been enthusiastic about his plan to take the *Enterprise* out of the Aretian system, leaving shuttlecraft to continue the survey, but the disputed moons and asteroids had already been charted. A preliminary plan was on her desk. Now it was a matter of being thorough by including established settlements in the survey. Riker and La Forge were over qualified to complete the task.

Calmly, the Vulcan asked, "Captain Picard, if there is considerable opposition to your plan to leave, will you insist?"

Picard whispered, "I was told by Admiral Bryant that I have complete autonomy in this mission, and I intend to exercise it. I don't foresee any problems. We are certainly proceeding more efficiently than this conference—I was due to speak two hours ago."

A voice sounded on his comm badge: *"Enterprise* to Captain Picard."

"Picard here," said the captain. He had left word not to be interrupted unless it was urgent, so there was concern in his voice.

"Captain," said Lieutenant Wallins, "I have a subspace transmission from Ensign Ro. She insists upon speaking directly to you."

"By all means," replied Picard, "patch her through."

"Captain Picard?" asked a voice that was normally businesslike but sounded stressed on this occasion.

"Picard here," he confirmed. "What is it, Ensign?"

"I have very bad news," she began. "They're only letting me use the transmitter for a moment, so I haven't got time to go into detail. There's been a major earthquake in the ocean, and a tsunami is headed our way. This is a tidal wave that is forty meters high and is traveling at four hundred kilometers per hour. At that rate we have approximately two and a half hours to . . . well, probably, to live."

"A tsunami," muttered Picard. He shook off the shock. "You must take cover—you must get out of there!"

Ro sighed. "We have no transporter, and it's unlikely we could walk far enough in the short time we have. There's no high ground, but we'll try something, I'm sure. I am extremely sorry to bring you this news so abruptly, but I must end this transmission now."

Picard wiped his dry lips and tried to think of something to say. "We are on our way," he promised. "I'll see if any other ships are closer. Out."

He tapped his comm badge again. "Picard to *Enterprise*. There's an emergency on Selva. Notify Starfleet and see what ships are in the area. Prepare to leave orbit immediately."

"Yes, sir," came the reply. "Shall I recall the shuttlecraft?"

253

"There's no time," said Picard. "I'll notify them. Out."

He looked around and tried to compose himself. The female Vulcan looked dispassionately at him. "If you could give them a few words," she said, "I shall handle the rest."

Picard nodded and strode toward the podium. Gently he shoved an elderly politician out of the way and commandeered the microphone. "Pardon me," he told the gentleman, "I must speak now."

As the man sputtered something the captain turned to a crowd that had suddenly grown interested. He spoke loudly to quiet their murmuring: "I am Captain Picard, and I'm sorry to say that the *Enterprise* must leave immediately. Rest assured, the division of your solar system will continue. I only ask that you stop making speeches, appointing committees, and writing doctrines—and start taking responsibility."

He tapped his comm badge. "Transporter room, beam me up."

"Locking on, sir," answered O'Brien.

As a stunned crowd looked on Captain Picard vanished in a swirling column of molecules.

Striding off the transporter platform toward the corridor, he slapped his comm badge again. "Picard to Riker."

"Riker here," answered a cheerful voice. "We were just about ready to head back."

Picard stopped in his tracks, trying to phrase the impossible. "Will," he said finally, "the away team called from Selva, and they're threatened by a tidal wave that's going to hit them in two and a half hours. I gather there's a good chance no one will survive."

All he heard was a sharp intake of breath. "No survivors?" croaked the first officer.

"The *Enterprise* is going back immediately," Picard

declared. "You must notify Geordi and the other shuttlecraft and continue the mission."

Riker protested, "I have to come with you, sir!"

"There's no time for discussion," said the captain. "We'll do what we can, and let's hope for the best. Picard out."

Will Riker sat back in his chair and took his hand off the shuttlecraft controls. "Take over," he told his copilot. He stood and wandered to the back of the shuttlecraft, ducking as he passed through a bulkhead. What was he looking for back there? A drink of water? A time machine? It wasn't possible that Deanna, Worf, Data, and Ro were going to be killed. He would just tell himself they would be rescued. The captain would find a way. To die like that, in a tidal wave on a godforsaken planet—it was preposterous! They would find a way to escape.

Will Riker sank onto a storage cabinet and rubbed his eyes, thinking about what it would be like if they didn't.

Raul Oscaras just glared at Ensign Ro. "You're sure about this?" he muttered.

"Go check my instruments yourself," she snapped. "We're all done playing games. You and the Klingons couldn't live together, but you're going to die together."

That stunned the colonists in the radio room into a nervous silence. Two of them were already on their way to check Ro's instruments, but it didn't matter, she thought. They were probably going to die no matter what action they took. Running from a tsunami was useless. If it could devastate a forest, it would devastate them.

"These buildings won't stand up," said Ro. "If we only had some high ground—"

"I don't know if it's high enough," interjected Deanna Troi, "but I know the highest ground in the forest. It's a mound built by the Klingons. When the water recedes it will be the highest spot for a wide area, and it's only about an hour's walk from here."

"I know it!" barked Oscaras. "I saw it quite a long time ago but never had a chance to go back. Can you guide us there?"

The Betazoid glanced out the window. "Yes"—she nodded—"I think so. Data certainly could."

"First," said Ro, "give me back my comm badge." The Bajoran put her hand under Oscaras's nose, and he sheepily handed over the tiny communication device. Ro stuck it on her settler's shirt and was about to use it when one of the scientists rushed into the radio room and blurted:

"She's telling the truth! That earthquake set loose a tidal wave you wouldn't believe. It's coming right for us!"

When Oscaras did an openmouthed fish imitation, Ro tapped her badge and said, "Ro to Data."

"Data here."

The Bajoran tried not to rush in her anxiety. "Commander," she began, "the *Enterprise* is on its way back, but we have a serious problem. In about two and a half hours we're going to be hit by a tsunami that's forty meters high and doing four hundred kilometers an hour. Counselor Troi says you know of a mound that's the highest point in the vicinity, and she says she can guide us there. We expect to reach there in slightly over one hour. Sir, if you have a better suggestion, I would certainly be willing to listen to it."

"I felt the temblor," said the android matter-of-factly. "Richter scale nine point eight was my estimate. I believe your course of action is prudent until a better course presents itself. Although there is room for everyone to stand atop the mound, I believe it unlikely that many will survive a wave such as you describe."

"We can try to lash ourselves down, use tent stakes," Ro said determinedly. "We'll just try to survive it any way we can."

"Affirmative," answered the android. "We will meet you there. We will also beat drums to guide you."

"Thank you. Ro out."

Raul Oscaras mustered some of his old bravado and clapped his hands together. "Listen, everyone!" he bellowed. "We have to vacate the village and go to this Klingon high ground. We have no choice. Gather everyone at the main gate in ten minutes. Bring only the clothes on your back and ropes, stakes, welding equipment—anything we can use to secure ourselves to the ground and one another."

"*No* phasers!" warned Ensign Ro. "I don't want any misunderstandings."

"All right," muttered Oscaras, "no phasers. Now get going. I'll make a broadcast on the audio system." When his underlings didn't move fast enough the president clapped his hands together again and roared, "Get going!"

Several of the Klingons looked suspiciously at Data, and Worf couldn't blame them. The android's dispassionate account of the tidal wave that was about to sweep over them sounded like the hallucination from a mantis bite. The fact that Worf had lived on Earth and was familiar with tsunamis didn't help him believe it either. Denial was a much easier response under the circumstances.

"Is this another trick," asked Maltz, "to deliver us to the flat-heads?"

"If we were going to deceive you," answered Data, "we would not have taken the risks necessary to free you. This time the settlers are coming to *you* for help. We must leave immediately for the mound—there is no time for discussion."

Myra Calvert took a deep breath and pulled away from her father. She stepped into the center of the unruly band of Klingons and said, "Data speaks the truth. And so does Ensign Ro. This giant wave has happened before, as I tried to tell them. We're living in a lowland water plain. Please, even if you don't understand what I'm saying, do what Data says. Go with Data."

No one moved. Worf knew he had to break the impasse, and he bent down and picked up a phaser rifle and several musical instruments. "If you stay here," he declared, "you will die. Forget the past—come with me, and let's do what we can to save lives."

Wolm ran to Worf's side, and Turrok limped there. The youngest Klingon turned to his fellows and pointed to Myra and Gregg Calvert. "They helped us escape," he said. "The flat-heads are like us—they do not agree with their leaders. If the flat-heads come to us, let us greet them. Let us show them we are *Klingons!*"

Maltz took out his knife, and several of the others shrank away from him. He leveled the blade at Worf and snarled, "This is for you if you betray us again."

"If I betray you," pledged the big Klingon, "I will use it on myself. But nobody will be alive if we wait. Bring the lanterns and anything else you can carry." He took a step between dark tree trunks that were shot with flecks of sunlight, and Wolm and Turrok scampered after him.

About half an hour into their trek through the forest Deanna Troi could hear the murmurings of discontent behind her. They were the only sounds in a forest that had grown strangely quiet. She didn't blame the colonists—they were running from something un-seen, a threat that sounded nebulous and unreal. A wall of water ten stories high? It wasn't something a rational mind could conceive. Yet here they were, rushing into the jaws of the enemy for refuge. The forest was fearsome enough, but to know they were headed toward a Klingon stronghold—it was more than some colonists could handle, and eight of them had refused to come.

Except for that handful, even the loudest complain-ers remained part of the straggling exodus from New Reykjavik. If their lives hadn't already been turned upside down, thought Deanna, they might never have accepted such a drastic turnabout. But endemic de-pression had given way to fatalism, and most of the colonists were numbly accepting of whatever came next. Considering all that they had been through, they weren't surprised that natural forces had turned against them, too. Several colonists were certain of destruction and talked like they deserved it.

After the underhanded capture of the Klingons and the failed attempt to hold them, most of the colonists had lost faith in Raul Oscaras. They obeyed him more out of habit than out of conviction, but it helped that Oscaras and Ro were circulating among the colonists, painstakingly explaining what was happening.

Apparently one scientist in the village had found evidence of a past tsunami, but no one had listened to her. They were willing to listen now, thought Deanna, because most of them had felt the earthquake. Some colonists complained, some talked of a new begin-ning, some stoically carried their children, and others wept as they trudged through the forest toward their destiny.

Suddenly the drums began beating. The counselor recognized the steady homing rhythm she had heard her first day in the forest. That day it had been to welcome Turrok home; now it was to welcome all of them. Before she could ascertain the exact direction, the counselor heard frightened voices, and she whirled around to see several colonists preparing to bolt.

"Don't fear the drums!" she called. "They are welcoming us. I've heard this rhythm before, and they are trying to lead us!"

"To what?" growled a colonist. "An ambush?"

"You ambushed *them!"* shouted Ensign Ro above the voices. "All that hatred doesn't matter now! The question is, will you be alive in two hours? That's the only thing that matters."

"Move on!" ordered Oscaras. He pointed in the direction Deanna had been leading the snakelike column. "The drumming is due west. Let's move out!"

Like an especially lugubrious reptile the line of about two hundred colonists staggered onward. For half an hour they marched to the beat of drums that sounded far away, then seemed to be coming from the branches over their heads. Perhaps they were, thought Deanna. The marchers finally entered the clearing that surrounded the great oval mound. Colonists set down their children and welding equipment and stared at the strange pile of dirt and the scrawny saplings that graced it. The mound had looked immense only a few days ago, she thought, but now it looked woefully inadequate to protect them from a wave forty meters high.

Worf and Data were striding toward her, leaving the motley collection of Klingons to stake out their own territory atop the mound. To Deanna's right Ensign Ro was having a reunion with a young girl and the handsome blond man who had rescued them. Everyone seemed relieved to have reached their destination, but no one was sure what to do next. Between the small band of Klingons on top of the mound and a clearing that was filling up with settlers, the crew from the *Enterprise* conferred.

"Is everyone present?" asked Data.

"All except for eight settlers who refused to come," answered Deanna, "and Doctor Drayton." She lowered her voice to ask, "What are we going to do? That mound doesn't look like it can protect all of us."

Adjusting the sling on her arm, Ensign Ro joined the group, and the attention turned toward her.

"How serious is this threat?" asked Worf. "If it's flooding—"

"It's more than flooding," answered Ro. "We are on a very volatile planet, which we knew when we came down here." She pointed toward Myra Calvert. "That young lady has been trying to tell everybody that something wiped out this forest ninety years ago. Well, now we know exactly what it was, and another one is headed our way. In approximately one hour and fifteen minutes a wave as tall as these trees is going to come crashing through here at four hundred kilometers per hour. It's going to turn this forest into a beach."

"How can we withstand that," Worf whispered, "out here in the open?"

"We cannot," answered Data. "I think it unlikely that many humanoids will survive. I estimate my own chances of survival at less than thirty percent."

Raul Oscaras swaggered up to them. "What's going on here? I demand to know what you're talking about!"

"We're talking about how to survive," snarled Worf. "For that, we don't need *your* help."

Deanna noticed that one of the Klingons had rushed down the hill to Worf's side just as Oscaras joined the conference. It was the gangly female, Wolm, and she yanked urgently on Worf's jacket.

"I must talk to you," she insisted.

"Not now, Wolm," muttered the big Klingon. "We must develop a plan." He turned his attention to Data. "Perhaps, Commander, if we dug trenches or sank pylons—"

"Quiet, all of you!" Deanna found herself shouting. Her unexpected outburst halted the discussion in midsentence, and she pointed to Wolm. "This young lady has something to tell us. I don't know what it is, but she believes it's important. Let's listen to her."

"By all means," agreed Data. "What do you wish to tell us, Wolm?"

The girl glanced behind her, and Maltz and some of the others were glaring at her. "It's a trick!" shouted Maltz. "Don't tell them!"

"I must," countered the girl. "A giant wave cannot wash us away if we are inside."

"Inside what?" asked Deanna.

The girl licked her lips and pointed at the mound. "Inside . . . inside the mound. The old place."

"No!" shrieked Maltz, charging down the hill. He was about to leap on Wolm when Worf grabbed him and wrestled him to the ground. "They will take it from us!" screamed the boy. "The flat-heads will take it!"

"They won't take anything," countered Deanna. She turned to Raul Oscaras and said forcefully, "Tell them you won't take it. Tell them whatever is theirs is theirs forever."

"I swear it!" shouted the bearded human. "Whatever belongs to the Klingons belongs to them forever."

Maltz stopped struggling in Worf's grip and looked plaintively at Wolm. "The dead," he said sadly. "You defile the dead."

"They not mind," answered Wolm, "if the rest of us live." She turned to Deanna and Data and said, "Follow me."

Over two hundred people watched with rapt attention as the gangly young female led the away team and President Oscaras to a clump of dirt that protruded slightly from one end of the oval mound. Now that she had pointed it out, thought Deanna, the clump did look as if it had recently been disturbed.

Wolm knelt down and began to scoop away the dirt with her hands. "We had to hide it," she explained, "long ago, when the flat-heads first came to look. So we covered it with dirt. It's the old place . . . home for our dead."

At once Worf dropped to his knees and began to dig frantically. Oscaras yelled for a shovel, and one of the colonists came forward and started to scoop away huge shovelfuls of dirt. Soon the colonists were eagerly pressing forward to see what the scrawny Klingon was going to unearth. They gasped when the shovel struck something metallic and dirt fell away from a dull metal surface.

"My God," muttered Oscaras, "it's their ship!"

A dozen hands and shovels fell upon the mound, and Deanna climbed higher to avoid the crush of people wanting to help. She looked back at Maltz and the other Klingons, most of whom looked saddened and stunned. Their ultimate secret was no longer— the flat-heads knew all there was to know about them.

"It's a hatch!" called a voice. "Open it up!"

"Let them open it!" responded Deanna. "It's their ship."

Data, Worf, and Oscaras motioned the colonists back while Wolm gripped the pressure wheel and tried to turn it. Turrok came stumbling down the hill to help her, and between the two of them they got the hatch open. A belch of putrid air rushed out, sending most of the colonists stumbling farther back. The only one unaffected by the foul air was Data, who entered the old Klingon freighter and emerged carrying the putrefying body of Balak. He made several more trips and came out each time carrying smaller and smaller bodies, many of which had become mummified in the airtight chamber.

The android efficiently set the bodies in the clearing beside the mound, and the colonists watched in hushed silence as the graves were exhumed. Or, thought Deanna, maybe it was the size of the wizened bodies that hushed them, because these were clearly children. For the first time the colonists seemed to realize what these hearty youngsters had gone through in the past ten years, burying more than half their number in the ship that had marooned them. Then Data emerged with a full-grown Klingon skeleton, and Deanna knew that must have been the pilot of the ill-fated vessel.

The android turned to his comrades and reported, "That is the last of the bodies. The ship is trapezohedral in shape with three decks: the bridge, crew quarters/life support, and a large cargo bay. The cargo bay is below ground in a crater caused by the impact. We must examine the hull and make repairs, but I believe it unlikely that we can guarantee the integrity of the cargo bay, where the impact occurred. If we can only use the bridge, it will be close quarters, but I believe the vessel is large enough to accommodate all of us."

"I'm not dying in that Klingon contraption," muttered the older settler, Edward.

"What about the transporter?" asked Ro. "Can we get it working?"

"Highly unlikely," answered Data. "After ten years the reactor and fuel cells would be depleted. Using generators and phasers, we may be able to get some life support systems working, but that is the best we can reasonably expect."

Suddenly the initial euphoria of the colonists had

vanished as they realized they would be risking their lives in a rusted hulk that probably had a thousand leaks. Deanna knew humans hated to die in cramped, enclosed places. A splash of rain hit her in the face. It was followed by a blast of wind that made her stagger backward and grip her collar tightly around her throat. Everyone looked nervously toward the ocean. How much warning would they get? She could almost envision it—a forest of trees borne along like toothpicks on a red wave.

Then Raul Oscaras waded into their midst, waving his arms like a maniac. "What are we waiting for?" he yelled. "Let's get some teams down there! Clemons, Arden, Monroe—start inspecting that hull. Everyone with generators—get the life support going. You welders—get down in that hold and get it patched up. Let's make some safety straps for the children. It doesn't have to fly—it just has to keep water out. Let's move it!"

His roaring voice galvanized them, and several of the colonists grabbed lanterns and welding kits and started into the wrecked freighter. When the colonists struggled with the heavy generators Maltz and some other Klingons rushed to help them. Soon there was a strange procession of humans and Klingons carrying equipment into the buried freighter.

Deanna felt more icy rain on her face, and she looked up at the darkening sky. There was a stampede of ominous-looking clouds, and she didn't want to think about what was chasing them.

Jean-Luc Picard fidgeted impatiently in his captain's chair, as if nervous energy could make them go faster. He worried about whether they might be able to get more speed if Geordi was on board, but they were already on the wrong side of warp nine. No matter what he tried, five hours was the best he could do in getting back to Selva, and that was at least two hours too late.

"Klingon subspace transmission," announced the tactical officer at Worf's usual station. "Message only. They regret to inform us that they have no starships in the immediate vicinity. They are dispatching the *BaHchu,* which will reach Selva in nine hours."

Picard pounded the arm of his chair. That was his last hope, because Starfleet didn't have any ships closer than the *Enterprise,* and there were no spacefaring worlds near the solar system. The away team was on its own, left to its own devices. He had radioed New Reykjavik and found the radio switched over to a repeater signal. That had told him the colonists were making some sort of run for it.

If only some of them could survive, he told himself, it would make this mad dash worthwhile. The alternative was to retrieve hundreds of bodies, bloated and mangled by rushing water, and Picard fought to keep that image out of his mind.

Sparks crackled over the heads of two Klingons as they pushed a metal plate against a cracked porthole and a female colonist welded it in place. Deanna nodded with satisfaction and moved to the other side of the bridge, where Klingons and colonists were pounding together makeshift seats out of packing crates and rope. In the sickly glow of a green lantern a group of small children stood shivering—the seats were for them. Deanna knelt near the children and zipped tight the jacket of the six-year-old girl who had greeted them their first day on Selva.

"Are we going home?" she asked Deanna.

Deanna swallowed dryly and mustered a smile. "I'm not sure where we're going, but it's probably going to be a bumpy ride. Can all of you be brave?"

The children nodded, and Deanna was relieved

when Wolm knelt beside them. "I watch them," promised the young Klingon.

"You were about their age when you came here," said Deanna.

Wolm nodded. "I know. They my brothers and sisters now."

The wind howled in Lieutenant Worf's ears, and he squinted against raindrops that stung his face like a swarm of insects. He was herding the last of the colonists inside the Klingon freighter, but he couldn't see more than two meters in front of him. Maybe he didn't want to see. They were still working inside, although Ro had told him they were out of time—the tsunami could hit any minute. At this point they just assumed there would be leaks in the hull, even if the obvious damage had been hastily repaired. It didn't have to fly, he reminded himself.

Already it smelled like a Klingon zoo in the tight confines of the old freighter, and he had about twenty more colonists to get inside. All of them were volunteers who had let everyone else—including the Klingons—board ahead of them. In fact, all of the colonists had insisted that the Klingons enter first. They might regret that now, he thought, with people pressed together shoulder to shoulder on the bridge, in the corridors, wherever there was a spot on the first deck. They weren't using the cargo hold in the belly of the ship, because Data was concerned about hidden leaks near the impact area. Data and Ro were trying to get life support systems going with converted energy from a phaser rifle, but Worf doubted they could do much more than recirculate the stale air. Children got the seats and restraints, and the rest of them were packed in like that terran delicacy, sardines.

Worf pushed two more people through the hatch and got a whiff of sheer sweat, terror, and anxiety. He would have to try to keep the door open as long as possible, he decided, considering himself lucky that he was still outside. He wasn't looking forward to going back inside—until he heard the noise.

The noise was the sound of hundreds of tree trunks snapping at once, a mountain of debris clattering along at four hundred kilometers per hour, and the elemental wave crashing to shore. It was a dull, horrifying roar, and Worf found himself tossing the colonists into the tiny hatch.

"Get in there! Move it!" he yelled.

Worf could barely hear his own words as the roar filled his senses and the ground vibrated with impending doom. He peered desperately into the thick rain for more colonists but saw none. The Klingon had never moved faster or more efficiently, and he leapt through the hatch and spun the wheel shut behind him. He braced himself on the wheel, daring the wave to rip the hatch open. He felt another big body nearby, and he looked to see Gregg Calvert ease into position on the other side of the wheel.

Louise Drayton, as she was known on this planet, came running out of the forest, screaming at the top of her lungs. She had waited too long! When she had found the colonists gathered there she wasn't sure what they were doing. But now she was sure! Something god-awful was ripping its way through the forest, and they were saving themselves.

"Help! Help!" the Romulan screamed into a murderous wind that only devoured her words. "Let me in!" she shrieked. She tried to pound on the hatch door, but she slipped in the mud and stumbled.

The hideous roar got so loud, the dark-haired woman had to cover her ears to keep her sanity. She forced herself to look up to find the hatch. It was then she saw it—an immense blood-red wave, tall as the skyline of Romulus, juggling the trees in front of it like a pile of twigs. The sound was monstrous, crushing her eardrums, but she couldn't look away. For one thing, she knew it was the last thing she would ever see. The Romulan saw the wave loom over her like a blanket over a sleeping child, and she saw the jagged tree trunks come hurtling down.

Chapter Nineteen

THE MONSTROUS WAVE crashed over the ship, uprooting it from the mound and pitching it forward. Screaming colonists and Klingons were hurled on top of one another, and the ship shuddered and groaned like a beast that had been harpooned. Tree trunks beat on the hull like giant drumsticks wielded by Titans, and leaks showered the horrified passengers. Awful creaking noises nearly drowned out their terrified shrieks.

Wolm tried to cover the young children who had been strapped into makeshift seats, but she was slammed against the dark instrument panel. She shook her head and felt hands trying to lift her up. The ship rocked again, and Myra Calvert tumbled into her lap. Together the girls staggered to their knees and crawled back to the terrified children. They wrapped their thin arms around the little ones and held them as the ship continued to buck out of control and water sprayed them from overhead.

From a life support duct over the main bridge Data and Ensign Ro had just managed to make some lights flicker on when the tsunami hit. Ro lurched onto her stomach, gripped a bar with her good hand, and held on. The screaming below her was almost the worst sensation, and she dreaded the possibility that the ship might flip over. Back and forth they rocked with each succeeding wave, and it was like a terrible carnival ride she had once experienced.

"Troi to Data!" shouted Deanna over the android's comm badge. "I'm at the lower bulkhead. Water has breached the cargo bay, and we can't get the hatch shut!"

"On my way," Data replied calmly. He turned back to Ro. "We can access the turbolift shaft from this duct and avoid the passengers below us."

Ro followed the android, crawling on all fours down the filthy duct. Brackish water spewed into her hair from the darkness. She ignored the pain in her shoulder and the possibility that she would reopen her wound. If they all drowned inside this old can, a little blood wouldn't matter much. She saw Data jump onto a cable that ran down the center of the turbolift and ride it to the bottom. Ro gritted her teeth and made the same leap. The pain of the thick cable hitting her chest was worse than the throb in her shoulder, but she held on, climbing down the cable toward the bottom deck of the old freighter.

She landed seconds after Data but found that he was gone. She saw where he had kicked out a grille to gain access to the lower corridor. Ro slipped through the grille and landed painfully on her still-tender ankle. Damn, she muttered to herself, she was a wreck. The ensign could hear voices ahead of her, and she skittered around a bend in the corridor to see a sight that chilled her: Deanna Troi and Raul Oscaras were pulling desperately on a bulkhead door, trying to close it, but filthy water was shooting from the edges. Judging by the pressure of the water they were fighting against, the entire cargo bay was already full.

271

Oscaras's grimy face was puffed and reddened, and he looked about to pass out. "The pressure seals have rotted!" he panted. "The door won't stay shut!"

Data made no move to help them. "Please stand back," he said.

"If we let go," gasped Deanna, "it'll flood in seconds!"

"Perhaps not," answered Data. He reached to his belt and came away holding a long black whip. He adjusted his grip slightly, and the greenish tip of the whip began to glow and tremble.

"What the hell's that?" growled Oscaras.

"A displacer," answered Data. "It combines artificial intelligence with air pressure manipulation. Please observe."

When Data stepped back and uncoiled the strange weapon Oscaras and Deanna got out of the way in a hurry. Water shot around the edges of the door as if shot from a fire hose, but Data snapped the displacer several times and drove the water back.

"Adjusting the air pressure is temporary," he added.

In movements almost too rapid to see Data used both hands to twist the handle and enter a stream of commands to the weapon. Then he cracked the glowing whip over his head, and it glowed like live neon as it rippled across the corridor toward the door. He let go of the handle, and the glowing coil wrapped around the edge of the door. Data took two steps and, with his enormous strength, gripped the center wheel and yanked the door shut. The displacer pulsated for a moment as it settled into place where the rotted seal should have been. The flow of water had stopped completely.

The android stepped back, nonchalantly wiping the slime from his face. "It should hold for perhaps three hours," he remarked. "We should fall back to the next bulkhead and secure it in a more conventional manner."

"I bet you were practicing with that thing," Deanna said hoarsely.

"For almost an entire hour," admitted Data.

The vessel bucked again, throwing Ro off her feet. She groaned as her injured shoulder crashed into the deck. Then a hand reached under her arm and lifted her up like a rag doll.

"The bridge is flooding," said Data. "We must return there."

Captain Picard jumped to his feet as soon as they dropped out of warp and the gray planet came into view. "Helm," he said, "standard orbit, bearing one twenty-eight Mach-two."

"Aye, sir," answered a young female ensign, playing the control panel in front of her. "Orbit in twenty-two seconds."

Picard was glad to see that the mostly young and untried bridge crew was snapping to—in place of all the people who were missing. Of course, they were trained to do their duty, and a rescue was the most fundamental of all missions. In fact, thought Picard, they were probably calmer than he, because they didn't work closely with the people who were in danger. The replacement crew had certainly gotten him to Selva in less time than he had reason to expect.

"Try to raise New Reykjavik," he ordered.

"I'm sorry, sir," answered the tactical officer, "sensors show that area is underwater. Even the repeater is inoperable."

"How soon before communicator range?"

"Ten seconds."

Picard stood tensely in front of a viewscreen that

was filling with a cloudy sphere. It looked as unfriendly now as the day he had first seen it. He paced for a second, then finally hit his comm badge.

"Picard to away team. Come in. Picard to away team." He waited, scarcely drawing a breath.

"Data here," answered the nonplussed android. "We are glad you have returned. In all, two hundred and twenty-eight are accounted for, although there are several injuries."

"Where are you? How did you—" stammered Picard. "Never mind. Should we beam you aboard?"

"The sooner the better," answered Data. "We are up to our knees in water."

"All transporter rooms stand by," barked Captain Picard. "Hold for coordinates."

A cheer went up from all those standing around Commander Data, and word quickly spread to everyone crammed shoulder to shoulder on the bridge. Deanna could see humans and Klingons warmly shaking hands and slapping one another on the back. The scene was even stranger once they started to disappear—Klingons and humans dissolving together into beams of light. Wolm squealed with delight when the transporter scrambled her molecules, but Turrok was an old hand and barely raised a shaggy eyebrow.

A hoarse voice said, "I'm sorry." She turned to see a tearful Raul Oscaras. "I've been wrong. I'm resigning. But I still have a strong back to devote to this planet. I thank you for saving it."

The counselor nodded, but before she could say anything Raul Oscaras started to break up and turn into shimmering light. The hatred was breaking up and floating away just as surely, thought Deanna, and she smiled with satisfaction as the old freighter faded from view.

* * *

Twenty-four hours later Ensign Ro and Myra Calvert were sharing a root beer float with two straws in the Ten-Forward lounge. They were taking time out to sip their confection, which was making the flamboyant dark-skinned woman seated across from them extremely impatient.

"What happened next?" asked Guinan. "Don't stop now."

Ro shrugged. "We never found the body of Louise Drayton, or whoever she was. Or the eight colonists who stayed in the village. If the Klingons hadn't kept that old ship intact, you'd still be looking for all of us."

"Wow," breathed Guinan. "And we think *space* is dangerous. I saw some of the colonists in here last night, and they said they were going back."

"They're rebuilding," affirmed Myra. "Now that they know exactly how far inland a tsunami can reach, they know exactly where to build. There's plenty of free lumber lying around, too."

"But you're not staying?" asked Guinan.

The red-haired twelve-year-old shook her head and smiled. "My dad and I have had enough adventure for a while. It's back to Earth . . . and maybe Starfleet Academy in a few years." She glanced with frank admiration at Ensign Ro.

"What about the Klingons?" asked Guinan. "How many of them decided to stay?"

"Almost all of them," answered Myra. "They're going to rebuild together. They have a lot they can show one another."

Ro added, "A couple of the younger ones, Wolm and Turrok, decided to go with the Klingon vessel. They want to learn what they can from the empire and return home to Selva."

The attractive Bajoran shook her head and admitted, "I've never felt like that about a place. But the colonists want to build something, and the Klingons have invested their entire lives in a battle to survive there. They have a lot in common, and both of them want to make amends."

"Hmm," said Guinan thoughtfully. "I'd better re-stock the synthehol. When Commander Riker gets back on board tomorrow he's going to be hosting a celebration. I'm glad you're back, Ro."

"You were right," remarked the Bajoran, "they needed me down there."

"That's all anyone wants," said Guinan, "to feel needed."

The bartender smiled and bustled off. As Myra slurped the last of the root beer float Ro gazed out the window at the blur of stars that rushed by at warp speed. All her life, it seemed, she had felt inadequate —unable to prevent her father's death or ease her people's suffering, unable to get along and go along. Always the Other, the outcast. But that self-hate was just as destructive as the overt bigotry she had witnessed on Selva. If the settlers and Klingons could make peace with each other, she thought, perhaps she could make peace with herself. It was worth a try.